SPIES NEVER SWOON

BANANA GIRLS
BOOK 2

SPIES NEVER SWOON

M. TAYLOR CHRISTENSEN

MOON ZOOM PRESS

Paperback ISBN: 978-1-951454-07-4
Hardback ISBN: 978-1-951454-08-1

Moon Zoom Press
Orem, Utah
www.moonzoompress.com

Cover Layout by Myles Christensen
Copy Edit by Courtney Larkin Editing

Printed in the United States of America

For James and Matthew:
"Someday you may not mind so much."

Chapter 1

Sitting in the glittering four-story atrium of the most luxurious hotel in downtown Atlanta wasn't exactly how Anna Rivers had planned to spend her Friday evening. She had nearly been sitting in the back of a movie theater with the tall hunk from her chemical engineering class. It had taken her weeks of encouraging his confidence to finally get him to ask her out. She had only needed to mention the new James Bond movie about five times before he got the hint.

And then an hour before the movie, this mission assignment came in. That meant no sitting close to a hot guy in a dark theater. No casually brushing hands on the armrest. No nuzzling into his muscular shoulder. No stroll through Midtown looking for a nice place to have ice cream.

Anna shook her head. Now her imagination was getting carried away. After all, sitting awkwardly next to each other in the theater was probably the best she could have hoped for on a first date.

She'd have to make it up to him later.

On the other hand, as far as missions went, sitting in a posh hotel lobby wasn't too bad. She'd definitely had worse.

Anna glanced up from the random sales brochure in her hand—it was important to look busy or interested in something—and checked her reflection in a nearby window. She'd had worse mission outfits, too. Anna smoothed the edge of her dark burgundy suit jacket and picked a piece of lint from the matching dress pants. She had actually preferred the royal blue outfit with the bright gold buttons, but Katie—her friend and fellow Banana Girl—had insisted that the darker suit was smarter, considering the mission requirement that she not be noticed. Katie had also declared that the burgundy complimented Anna's brown skin to perfection. So there was that.

As a concession, Anna had been allowed to wear one of her favorite tracking devices, the gold filigree stick barrette. Not only did the pin double as a stiletto dagger, but the barrette's intricate swoops also reminded her of the beautiful shapes the syrup drizzles formed when she made candy with her mother.

The hardest part of missions like this was forcing herself to stay focused and not get too comfortable, especially in such a beautiful place. Anna straightened and glanced out the front door, watching for her target.

Ten boring minutes later, she saw a handsome young man—flanked by two beefy bodyguards in black suits and trailed by a harried assistant or staff member of some kind—walk in through the large front doors. They perfectly matched the description she'd been given.

Anna watched as the young man strode confidently across the atrium, moving well thanks to his athletic build. The mission write-up had included the detail that he was handsome, and from what Anna could see, that was definitely true. In fact, that particular description didn't do him justice. Katie would have called him *hot*. Of course, Katie said that about any guy with strong arms and a cute face. However, in this case, *hot* wasn't quite enough to capture the man's poise and self-assurance.

He had strong, broad shoulders that fit perfectly in his tailored gray suit and a clean-shaven, well-defined jaw. His skin was just sun-touched enough to not be called pale, but not quite bronzed. His brown hair appeared to have been professionally styled to look messy.

Without any other information about him in the mission dossier, Anna was left to make her best guess. He looked about twenty-five, maybe thirty, years old. Based on his clothing, he was rich. Either that, or he wanted to look like he was rich. She assumed that he must be some sort of important businessman, maybe an up-and-coming startup founder. Judging by his strut, he likely had an ego to match. Based on previous experience with guys like that, Anna doubted she could stand to be around him for more than two minutes at a time.

Discarding the brochure on the seat beside her, Anna stood and pulled out her phone. "Hi, Bianca," she said to the imaginary caller. "Yeah, I'm down in the lobby. Okay." She walked casually past the handsome businessman and his entourage as they informed the concierge of their arrival. "Right. I'll meet you up there. Bye."

She ended her pretend conversation just in time to overhear the hotel employee inform the businessman's group that their meeting was to take place in the boardroom on the second floor. That would have been Anna's guess anyway, but it made her job that much easier.

Bypassing the bank of elevators, Anna mounted the grand staircase casually, one step at a time. Anyone watching would think she was in no hurry to meet her friend for dinner. At the top of the stairs and out of sight of the atrium, she turned the corner and hustled forward, ducking into an alcove across the hall from the boardroom. A few minutes later, the young businessman's group finally found their way to the correct door. Anna pressed herself into the shadows as they entered the conference room.

Now all she had to do was wait. Again.

The clink of plates and the tinkling of silverware echoed down the hall from the restaurant on the other side of the mezzanine. The drone of distant conversations hummed in the background.

A few minutes later, footsteps echoed down the hall from the direction of the grand staircase. Anna risked a quick peek around the corner and saw Atlanta's mayor coming up the stairs with several staff members. The group reached the boardroom door and was ushered quickly inside.

This guy must be important if he was meeting with the mayor.

Her primary objective for this mission—now that all of the parties were presumably assembled—was to keep anyone from interrupting the meeting. It was a strange assignment considering that just about any agent on the federal payroll, not to mention several municipal police departments, would have been better suited for what was essentially a security posting. But after two years as a special task force agent, Anna was used to missions that didn't always make sense.

From her position in the small alcove, Anna could see the rest of the hall beyond the boardroom. If anyone tried to approach the meeting from the back of the hotel, she would easily see them coming. The grand staircase and landing were out of view behind her, but the polished wood made so much noise that she would easily hear anyone approaching from that direction. A girl had to get creative when she was forced to cover two directions by herself.

Not knowing how long the meeting would go, Anna settled

herself softly against the wall, fully intending to make sure it was an uneventful night.

After about ten minutes, when Anna had pretty much made up her mind to insist on being told all the details of any future mission, the softest whisper of a footstep reached her hiding place from the direction of the grand staircase.

Anna's body tensed. The footsteps were close. Either the person routinely tiptoed around the halls of a hotel, or they were intentionally trying to sneak around. Her money was on the second one.

Slowly inching herself backward, deeper into the shadow, she kept her eyes riveted on the door of the boardroom and the large space of hall between her and the meeting she was meant to secretly guard.

A figure dressed as a bellhop stepped slowly and deliberately toward the boardroom door. The guy looked to be in his early twenties, skinny, with a lightly tanned face and sparse goatee. There was no logical reason for his behavior. No one would need to sneak up on a meeting, especially walking like that. And if that was the way he normally walked, the guy must freak out guests all the time.

He didn't really look like much of an assassin, and Anna was tempted to let him continue, just to see what he was going to attempt.

Ten feet from the boardroom door, the bellhop happened to glance to the side, straight at the alcove where Anna was hiding. Now with a good view of the guy, she saw how young and inexperienced he looked. Their eyes locked. His expression morphed from wariness to surprise to resignation.

Now that he knew he was caught, hopefully getting rid of him would be easy.

A split second later, his expression shifted again, hardening in grim determination.

Was he really going to make a try for the door with her standing right there? The fact that she had been waiting for him should have clued the guy in to the fact that she had the upper hand. Did he not comprehend the very real likelihood that she would completely embarrass him in the middle of a fancy hotel hallway?

He leaned away from Anna, his muscles tensed.

Apparently not.

The bellhop guy bolted for the door, and Anna sprang from the shadows like an incredibly well-dressed jungle cat. He nearly made it there, his finger mere inches from the handle, when Anna grabbed his shoulder and jerked him backward.

He grunted and spun away from her grip.

Anna moved to stand in front of the door, lowering into her fighting stance. "I think we both know you shouldn't be here. The only question now is whether you're going to leave with your dignity intact." She didn't know who this guy was, but her only instructions were to guard the door and not be seen— presumably by the meeting attendees. Given that her orders didn't say anything about apprehending meddlers, all she really needed to do was get rid of him.

The fake bellhop glared at her but didn't speak. He paced back and forth a few times, obviously looking for a way around her. Finally, he stopped and faced her, holding up his fists in a classic boxing pose.

Was this guy for real?

He lunged forward and jabbed for her head. Anna easily deflected his punch and—while he was off balance—landed a blow to his ribs.

"Ow," he said under his breath before swinging another poorly aimed fist in her direction.

Once again, Anna deflected his attack. She almost felt bad for the guy. He was clearly out of his depth. She kicked him gently in the midsection, just enough to push him away.

Bellhop-boy staggered backward, panting and holding his stomach.

After considering him for several seconds, Anna moved toward him—her muscles relaxing slightly—hoping she could talk some sense into the young guy. Either that or finish him off. "Listen, I don't know what you're trying to do, but you're not getting into that room."

He glanced up at her and shook his head. Apparently he wasn't done. After a quick feint to her left, he juked, attempting to go around her the other way.

As he went by, Anna caught his wrist and wrenched it behind his back. With her other hand, she pinched his shoulder muscle hard. She didn't normally get this close to an adversary unless it was to deliver a blow, but she hoped—with the coaxing of a little more discomfort—she might convince him to give it up and leave.

"Let go of me!" he yelled.

A flailing elbow caught Anna square in the nose. The sudden pain, especially when her defenses were down, caught her off guard. She released him and took a step back, hand to her face.

In a flash, his tough-guy exterior slipped. "I'm so sorry," he said quickly, looking back at her in concern.

She noticed that he had a unique accent. Something European, but she'd have to hear more to know for sure. They stared at each other in bewilderment for several seconds, neither quite sure how to react to the situation.

The guy realized that he was now between Anna and the boardroom just a split-second before she did. His eyes went wide with the dawning information, and he twisted and dove for the door. Anna might have been off her normal game, but she was still fast enough to stop him.

Almost.

With a diving tackle that would have made a linebacker coach proud, Anna caught him by the ankle and pulled hard. Unfortunately, his lunge had gotten him close enough to grab the handle, and as she dragged him back, the boardroom door creaked open.

In the two seconds before the bellboy lost his grip and face-planted onto the hard floor, Anna caught a glimpse of the handsome businessman seated at the end of the conference table. His head snapped her direction—as did the heads of his two bulky bodyguards—right as the door clicked closed again.

Her brain processed two things in the next second. First, the businessman was more handsome than she had initially given him credit for, and second, the massive bodyguards were definitely coming out into the hall in a matter of moments.

Now that she had pretty much failed both of her mission objectives, she figured she'd better not make either of them any worse.

The bellboy had gotten to his knees and was checking his face for damage. Anna jerked him up to a standing position and pushed him hard in the direction of the grand staircase. "Get out of here," she hissed. Whether he decided to leave or not, Anna was sure the two bodybuilders in suits that were about to burst out into the hall would be able to take care of him. Now all she had to do was not get caught herself.

She bolted down the hall, heading away from the grand staircase, and had almost made it to the first side corridor when the boardroom doors crashed open. Anna glanced over her shoulder as she rounded the corner. Even though the fake bellboy stood not ten feet from them, half-heartedly moping away, the two bodyguards only gave him a passing glance before turning her way in hot pursuit.

So much for seeming to be less of a threat.

The hallway opened up into the mezzanine balcony

overlooking the atrium. She had hoped for more cover, not less. The last thing she needed was to have a lobby full of guests and staff see her fleeing two bodyguards. She swerved away from the mezzanine at the next side hall, the sound of the mean-looking bodyguards echoing behind her.

"Hey, stop!" one of them called out.

Luckily, a few feet down the hall, Anna came to a set of stairs. She pulled the door open and rushed into the stairwell. Glancing at the landings above and below her, Anna considered her options. She couldn't outrun the bodyguards indefinitely. She had to get out of the hotel, but sprinting back through the lobby was sure to draw attention. She needed to lose them first.

Fishing in her jacket pocket, Anna pulled out a small, marble-sized plastic ball. With a quick squeeze, she broke the internal seal between the two chemicals, shook vigorously, and tossed it down the stairwell. As the ball bounced down the stairs and ricocheted off the lower landing, Anna took the stairs in the opposite direction, two at a time, toward the next floor up.

At the exit door to the third floor, she paused and listened, mentally counting down the seconds and hoping she had timed it right.

Three. Two. One.

The door below her banged open right as the little ball, by now expanded to more than ten times its original size, exploded in a series of pitiful pops. For a little kid hoping for an explosive fireworks display, it would have been the most disappointing moment ever. But the getaway bomb wasn't designed to sound like a firecracker; it was designed to sound like the clatter of distant footsteps.

With her hand on the door, Anna held her breath. Hopefully, the big guards would fall for the little trick. A second later, loud footsteps tumbled down the stairs, growing softer and softer until she heard the door at the bottom of the stairwell open and slam shut.

Anna let herself out onto the third floor and walked toward the very back of the hotel. There she found another set of stairs and cautiously made her way down to the first floor and out the exit into a back street.

Rather than head straight for Hot Banana—her favorite Banana Girls' car, which at the moment was colored candy-apple red—Anna took a long, circuitous route past several popular downtown restaurants and bars, weaving in and out of the evening crowds.

Ten minutes later, she was behind the steering wheel of Hot Banana, halfway back home.

And she wanted some answers.

Chapter 2

Anna waved her chip-embedded bracelet in front of the control panel, and the gleaming silver elevator car shot up toward the top floor. When the doors opened, she marched down the hall to the door of Club Banana.

As Anna opened the front door and stepped through the entryway toward the living area, she waved at Mari, the newest Banana Girl, sitting on a nearby sofa. Mari was a brand-new freshman in college, which explained the heavy physics textbook propped on the yellow decorative pillow in her lap.

Mari waved back. "Back already? How was the mission?"

"A moderately successful disaster." Anna said as she plopped down on one of the wide couches facing the full-wall video display, currently showing an image to match the rest of the living room—brilliant white walls with yellow banana decorations. She kicked off her dress shoes and collapsed backward into the soft white leather with a sigh.

"Why? What happened?" Mari's big brown eyes went wide. She had only ever been on one mission—to rescue her mother— and that was before she had technically joined the Banana Girls.

Her normally dark brown hair still had the blonde highlights from the mission's makeover.

"It was weird, the attack seemed a little too . . ."

An alert sounded from the video wall, accompanied by a flashing icon in the center—a spinning gold ninja star.

Mari looked at Anna. "Uh oh. How did Stacia know you were back already?"

Anna held up her arm and shook the bracelet on her wrist. Turning to Hannah, her Banana Girls co-founder who was sitting in her favorite yellow lounge chair in the corner, Anna said, "You don't think we could get anonymous access to Club Banana, do you?"

"Doubtful," Anna's sullen blonde friend muttered without looking up from her tablet. "That sort of defeats the purpose of all the security measures."

With a sigh, Anna touched the control pad on the table, and the wall flashed to life. A video feed of their boss, Stacia, sitting in her normal spot behind a wide cherry-wood desk in an office somewhere at some government headquarters, filled the wall. Her mouth spread in a thin, but sympathetic, smile.

Though she had never dared ask Stacia's age, Anna knew from her nearly two years as a Banana Girl, interacting with Stacia, and receiving mission assignments and training from her, that their boss had worked missions as a field agent at least twenty years ago. Stacia barely looked forty. She wore her light brown hair pulled back, and her hazel eyes seemed to catch everything, even the small knowing looks the Banana Girls gave each other. Stacia always pretended not to notice, but Anna was pretty sure she knew everything the girls whispered and giggled about during mission briefings.

"Hello, Anna. How was the mission?" Stacia asked.

"A success, I think," Anna answered with a note of

uncertainty in her voice. "But there was something strange about it."

Stacia said nothing, but the small uptick of her eyebrow was an invitation for Anna to continue.

Anna took a deep breath, attempting to collect her scattered thoughts. "For starters, the mission details were incredibly sparse, even for a sensitive mission."

"Sometimes that's all an agent gets," Stacia said matter-of-factly.

"Also, if it had been a really important meeting, the security was too lax. The two bodyguards inside the conference room didn't even make it out into the hall until at least eight seconds after the door opened. One should have been standing next to the entrance the entire time."

"An interesting choice by the security team, but not indicative of a conspiracy." Stacia's tone was one of reluctant devil's advocate. Anna's confidence in her gut-feel about the mission grew.

"And the assailant was pathetic. I mean, truly pitiful. I could have taken him down even before I became a Banana Girl."

A soft giggle came from Mari's direction.

The corner of Stacia's mouth lifted in a half smile. "I would ask you to elaborate, but I've already received a brief from the security team."

Anna frowned. "What security team?"

"The two bodyguards who chased you through the hotel," Stacia replied drily.

That was a red flag. Sparse mission briefing, Stacia's uncharacteristic demeanor, reports from another security team. It all added up to something very odd about the mission. "Why would the bodyguards report to you? Unless . . ." Anna's mouth nearly fell open. "This was a setup, wasn't it?"

Stacia stared at Anna—or more likely, Anna's picture on her

video screen—for several moments. Anna stared back, almost daring Stacia to contradict her assertions.

"Bravo, Miss Rivers." Stacia sounded like a pleased instructor. "It was indeed a test—an audition of sorts—to see if you would be a good fit."

Anna frowned. "You've never given us a secret test before."

"It was not by choice, but sometimes these things are out of my control," Stacia said. "The VIP you'll be protecting insisted on it."

"Well, it feels like a very unprofessional way to start a mission. I mean, think about that poor bellboy. I could have annihilated him," Anna said.

Stacia's brows went up in surprise. "You'll have to tell me more about that later. But on that subject, the prince did add a line to the security report, asking me to thank you for not . . . what were his words?" Stacia checked her nearby computer "Grinding his newest security guard to a pulp."

Anna was still fuming over the fake mission, to the point that she wasn't really listening. "To tell you the truth, I'm not really sure I would want to work with someone who . . . wait a second, did you say 'prince'?"

A broad smile spread across Stacia's face. "I thought that might get your attention. He is a European prince that has been living here in the states since his graduation from college several years ago." There was a laugh behind her eyes. And something else. Was that envy? "I've been told he's quite handsome, and—assuming you agree to take the mission—you'll need to work closely with him."

Mari and Anna glanced at each other with matching expressions of curiosity.

Loud footsteps pounded from the bedroom hallway. A second later, Katie burst into the living room. "Did you say 'handsome prince'? I'd be happy to volunteer, Stacia." Katie wore frayed jean shorts and a light pink cami. Her lightly-tanned skin was still flushed from the sprint down the hall. Her hair, skin, and eye color were actually similar to Mari's except, of course, that Katie, who was from Hawaii, had mostly Japanese ancestors, and Mari, who grew up in Atlanta, was mostly of Mexican heritage.

Anna and Mari laughed at Katie's antics. Stacia smiled patiently. Hannah rolled her eyes, never even looking up from her tablet.

"Sorry, Katie," Stacia said. "This particular prince would be a little too charming for you. I need someone with a cooler head."

"I can have a cool head," Katie said as she twirled a lock of long black hair with her finger.

Stacia shook her head. "Nope. This one's for Anna."

Katie plopped down on the sofa with an exaggerated huff. When she turned toward Anna, her pout instantly dissolved into a resigned grin. "It was worth a shot," she said with a shrug.

Anna shook her head and turned back to Stacia. "I'm not saying yes, but who's the prince?"

Stacia glanced at a file on her desk. "His Royal Highness, Prince Léopold Jean Adolphe Guillaume of Luxembourg."

"Easy for you to say," Mari quipped.

"And what does a prince from Luxembourg need a Banana Girl for?" Anna asked.

"I could come up with a few things," Katie said under her breath.

"There was an attack on the prince at a party last week," Stacia said. "The prince escaped unharmed, but one of his security agents was injured. She'll be out of commission for a while."

"And what? Does he think we're a bodyguard temp agency?" Anna said with a laugh.

Stacia didn't smile or even blink. One eyebrow went up as if waiting for Anna to get it.

Anna's eyes went wide. "Seriously?"

Apparently satisfied that Anna was on the same page, Stacia pressed forward. "Temporarily filling in as a member of the prince's security team would be the perfect opportunity to investigate the attack. It will cause minimal disruption to the prince's routine and won't draw any additional attention to the investigation."

"Wait, I think I heard about this," Katie said. "It was at one of those sandbar parties down in Miami, right?"

"What's a sandbar party?" Mari asked.

"It's where a few hundred boats anchor in shallow water over the sandbars and everyone wades around partying. I think the prince was there with his whole entourage of friends, wasn't he?"

Stacia rifled through her papers. "I don't have information about any sandbar party." Stacia gave Katie a blank look.

"We're talking about the Party Prince, right?" Katie asked.

"I don't understand what you mean," Stacie replied.

"This Léopold Jean . . . whatever, he's the one they call the Prince of Party." Katie glanced around at the other Banana Girls, who only looked confused. Katie slapped her legs in frustration. "Don't you guys keep up with the gossip?"

"No," the other girls answered in unison.

"Don't read those gossip magazines, Katie. They're just a waste of time." Stacia sounded like a mother now.

"Apparently not in this case," Katie muttered away from the video screen.

Mari covered a giggle with her hand.

"And the investigation gets federal agency attention?" Anna tried to pull the conversation back to the mission briefing.

"This was an attack on foreign royalty on US soil—or rather, water," Stacia said with a smirk. "Our government needs it taken care of quickly and quietly."

"Why a Banana Girl?" Hannah asked from her corner. "Why not use a local Miami agent?"

Stacia didn't miss a beat. "Good question, Hannah. There are certain . . . shall we say . . . requirements for this particular agent. Requirements that your run-of-the-mill field office wouldn't have the agents to fill. But it's the perfect assignment for a Banana Girl."

"What type of requirements?" Anna asked.

"For the last few years, the prince's closest security agents have been female, highly trained, and beautiful," Stacia said.

Anna glanced around at the other girls, whose expressions matched her own look of surprise.

"They are some of the best. You should consider it a compliment."

"Hang on a minute. The prince only hires attractive, female bodyguards?" Anna said. "Doesn't that seem weird?"

"He's a prince!" Katie said. "He can do whatever he wants."

"I admit, it does seem strange," Stacia continued. "Perhaps you'll get a chance to ask him about it. He has set up an interview with you over breakfast tomorrow morning."

Anna's brows shot up. "You mean like a job interview? Wasn't the audition enough? Can't you just wave your hands and tell him I've got the assignment?"

Stacia gave her a patient smile. "Foreign prince, remember?"

This mission was definitely going to be out of the ordinary. "Fine. I can do breakfast with the prince," Anna said.

"Yeah, he'll love you," Mari said with a nod of encouragement.

"Though the prince is insisting on the interview," Stacia continued. "It's really more of a formality. The Grand Ducal

Family is anxious to have the matter investigated and resolved. The prince was obviously impressed with your performance tonight. I think he just wants to make sure you'll get along."

"Why would we need to get along?" Anna asked.

Stacia pressed forward without answering her question. "Your job is to join his team, look into the details of the attack, and figure out who is trying to kill the prince."

"And don't completely destroy international relations," Hannah added with a smirk.

Anna stuck out her tongue at Hannah.

With a knowing smile, Stacia continued, "On that subject, I don't know about him being called the Party Prince, but according to the information I have, he's supposedly an incorrigible flirt, not to mention being very attractive. What was that rule you and Hannah came up with? The one where you're not supposed to get romantically involved with a guy on a mission?"

Anna opened her mouth to reply, but Katie and Mari—in unison—beat her to it, "Rule Number One."

"That's the one." Stacia's friendly smile turned mischievous. "It sounds like you might need it."

The next morning, Anna walked into the small burger joint southwest of campus at fifteen minutes till eight. Trailing behind a middle-aged couple, she slipped past the hostess and took a seat at the far end of the counter. She ordered an almond vanilla tea and scanned the rest of the dining room out of the corner of her eye. Unless the prince was undercover dressed like a college student, a truck driver, or a pharmaceutical salesman, she had succeeded in beating him there.

She watched as people entered, were seated, and ordered their food. There were lone diners, couples, and small groups of friends out for a casual breakfast. She assumed that a prince of Luxembourg would arrive early to an appointment and stick out like a sore thumb.

Five minutes later, her intuition proved correct when one of the bodyguards from the night before—still in a dark suit but with sunglasses this time—walked into the diner. He made a cursory comment to the hostess and marched straight to the back of the restaurant. He found the rear exit, next to the restroom, and did his best to fade into the shadows. She was pleased to see that the prince's security team did actually take his safety seriously when it wasn't just a secret audition.

The next moment, the handsome young businessman—correction: prince—ambled into the diner wearing golf shorts, leather loafers, and a light blue polo shirt. He paused and looked around, most likely searching for her. Anna ducked her head slightly and sipped her tea. She used the mirror behind the counter to scan out front. The other bodyguard stood outside facing the street, his back to the entrance.

After a few moments of unsuccessful searching, the prince asked the hostess for a booth halfway back, telling her he was expecting a guest to join him soon.

Anna watched as he walked confidently to the small table. Her assessment of the previous night still held true. He was quite handsome, there was no doubt about that. Good thing she had Rule Number One.

The prince sat up straight in his seat, exuding confidence as he surveyed the diner. Several times, Anna was forced to duck behind the large truck driver next to her to avoid being spotted.

Anna debated slipping out and entering the restaurant again as he would expect. But she didn't see any reason not to just walk right up to his table. Sliding off the bar stool, she maneuvered herself past the serving counter toward the rear of the dining area.

She caught the eye of the large bodyguard in the back of the room. It would be closer to the truth to say that he had already been watching her as she circled around the tables towards the prince. Hoping he would know who she was, Anna communicated her intentions with a quick tilt of her head toward the prince. It was never a good idea to surprise someone of this bodyguard's size. He nodded his acknowledgment.

She doubled back down the main aisle toward the prince. As she passed his table, she quickly slid onto the seat across from him. His eyes had been fixed on the entrance watching intently for her, so he jumped when someone suddenly appeared across from him. "I'm sorry, but that seat is . . ."

Anna cocked her head to the side.

He recovered quickly from his shock. "Oh, my goodness, it's you! How did you . . . I mean, where did you . . ."

She smiled at the prince's befuddlement. He had an adorable European accent that Anna would have thought was either French or Dutch if she hadn't already known better. Up close, she could see that his eyes weren't brown, as they had initially seemed, but a very dark blue.

"You are good," he said with a look of admiration. "See, I knew we would get the best if we called the CIA."

Anna's brows went up a fraction of an inch, but she didn't feel the need to immediately correct him on which spy branch she was from. "So, Your Highness, why don't you tell me about—"

The prince glanced at the nearby diners and lowered his voice. "Actually, given that we're in America, you can dispense with the 'Your Highness' and 'Prince Léopold'." He leaned back in his seat, trying to affect an air of casualness, but like his hair and his shirt, even his relaxed posture came across as refined. "My friends call me Leo. It sort of started in college."

Anna nodded. "Okay, Leo, where did you go to college?"

Leo's face lit up. "University of Miami."

"I guess that explains the Party Prince thing," she said.

Leo laughed. Anna had to begrudgingly admit that he had an okay laugh.

He leaned toward her. "Don't believe everything you hear. I don't even party that much. Let me buy you breakfast," he said with a wave to the waiter.

After they put in their orders, Anna returned her attention to the prince. "So, there is something about this assignment that has me puzzled . . ."

Leo lifted his brows and gave a regal wave for her to continue.

"Why do you specifically need female security agents? It seems like the bulky guys are doing a pretty good job keeping you safe."

"Bulky guys?" Leo asked innocently.

"The two body guards you brought along."

Leo's face fell. "They are very obvious, aren't they?"

Anna smiled and nodded.

Leaning forward, Leo's eyes flashed with annoyance. "You see, that's really the problem. My family requires that I have protection at all times. So I can't go anywhere without causing a scene with my security incursion. I can't be just a normal guy."

"You're not really a normal guy, though, are you? Your safety is important."

"Now you sound like my mother," Leo said, rolling his eyes and slumping back in his seat. Even while slumping, he still had good posture.

Anna shrugged. "So your family wants you to have security with you. What's wrong with that?"

"You think it's noticeable here. Imagine having to take Thing One and Thing Two to frat parties or nightclubs. It's intolerable. After all," his hands spread wide, "I'm just a young bachelor prince trying to have a little fun living the American Dream."

"You know, that's not really what the American Dream means." Anna sighed and pinched the bridge of her nose. Best not to get into an argument with him right off the bat. "So you need young agents who can party with you?"

"Exactly!" Leo said a little too loudly. Several diners looked their way. He lowered his voice and continued, "Exactly. If I'm forced to have bodyguards at my side any time I'm out in public, at least I can have ones who will blend in with my friends."

"Why not young, male security agents then? Why do they need to be female?"

One of Leo's brows went up. He stared at her for a long moment then pointed at himself with obvious pride. "Young bachelor prince. Remember?"

"I'm sure it wouldn't hurt if these young female agents were beautiful, too, would it?" Anna said, glaring at him.

Leo smiled. "I do have an image to maintain."

With great effort, Anna didn't roll her eyes. With this kind of ego, even Katie could have made it through the mission without breaking Rule Number One. She glanced at a passing waitress before returning her attention to the confident prince. "Listen, Your Highness—" He shot her a dirty look. "—Leo, ultimately, my assignment is to investigate the recent attack on you and your security agent. I've been chosen because my superiors think I can blend in with this strange arrangement you have."

The prince scowled, but Anna wasn't willing to recant her assessment.

His expression turned playful, a sly grin spreading across his face. "Well, do you think you fit the requirements?"

Anna lifted her chin and stared at Leo. "All I've heard so far is that she needs to be trained in security and be beautiful. Oh, and know how to party."

He gazed back at her with those dark blue eyes. "Given your agency credentials, all that's left is to determine whether you know how to party."

Anna felt heat creeping up her neck at the obvious compliment, but she didn't avert her eyes. The prince was evidently all too aware of how handsome and charming he was. Anna didn't want to give him the satisfaction of thinking she was some demure little girl who could be swayed by his flattery. At least no more than the average girl who had always wanted to meet a handsome prince.

The staring contest ended a moment later with the welcome arrival of their breakfast plates. She tried the waffles, and they weren't bad. Not as good as her mother's recipe, of course, but still delicious.

Between bites, Anna glanced up at Leo and saw him studying her. She stared back a moment before speaking. "So how is your agent doing? The one who was injured?"

He arched a brow at her. "Investigating the crime already?"

"You may not have decided whether you want me in your entourage, but I've been given an assignment to find out who attacked you. I plan to do my job."

He nodded his acknowledgment. "Makenna was released from the hospital a few days ago. I spoke to her this morning, and she's recovering well."

"What was her injury?"

"She was shot in the leg with a speargun," Leo said.

Anna's eyes went wide. "A speargun?"

Leo nodded, taking his last bite of waffle.

"Spearguns don't have a very long range, do they? Five or so feet, max. You must have seen who tried to shoot you."

Leo shook his head and swallowed. "The party was winding down, and we were wading through the water back toward the boat. The water was about four feet deep, so we had to haul ourselves up onto the boat's swim platform. The shooter must have been beneath the boat, because just as I was about to help Makenna up, she was shot in the leg."

"You didn't see anyone come out from under the boat?" Anna pressed.

Leo paused to signal the waiter to bring another plate. "Unfortunately, no. With the confusion and the blood and the screaming—from my guests, not Makenna—we didn't really think to look for who had done it until it was too late."

As Leo worked on his second plate of waffles, Anna peppered him with more questions about the sandbar party and the guests and how many people he had been around. She also asked him about his friends in the states, and whether he might have any enemies with a reason to hurt him.

Leo shrugged. "If I have enemies, I don't know about them. I'm not important enough to have influenced any public policies, either at home in Luxembourg or here. And I always try to be nice to everyone."

Given her brief interaction with him so far, Anna decided he was probably right. Unless people got upset with princes for being overly-confident or polite, he didn't seem like the type of guy who would go around making enemies. "What about former business partners?"

"I don't own any businesses, though I do participate in events like ribbon cuttings and grand openings for friends' businesses."

Anna frowned. Not much there.

"I am part of a charitable foundation to feed the less fortunate. But I hope most of my fellow board members and associates are pleased with my help."

Charity work. Not many enemies to be had there either. "What about ex-girlfriends?" Anna asked. "A handsome guy like you must have plenty of those."

Prince Leo's expression clouded briefly. "I do have two ex-girlfriends here in America." He paused as if considering them. Finally, he shook his head. "In both cases, we parted amicably. In fact, they broke up with me," he said with a wry grin. "Don't tell anyone."

A smile tugged at Anna's lips, but she did her best to fight it.

When the waiter brought Leo his third plate of peach waffles, Anna was forced to admit that she might have finally met her match in waffle eating.

"Your American cuisine is incredibly rich." Leo smiled as he precisely sliced the last chunk of waffle in half.

"What do you normally eat for breakfast in Luxembourg?" Anna asked.

"Bread and cheese with jam. Sometimes a piece of chocolate," he said as he considered the final bite of waffle hanging from the end of his fork, dripping with peach syrup and melted whipped cream.

Anna drank the last of her juice as she watched a twenty-something guy in ripped jeans and a T-shirt get up from his booth in the back of the restaurant. He brushed near a recently vacated table and very deftly swiped the five-dollar tip that had been left for the waitress.

Without even thinking, Anna snagged him by the arm as he walked by. "Not cool," she said in a low tone, barely bothering to look up at him. Anna didn't want to make a scene, but she wasn't about to let him steal from the hardworking waitress.

The punk tried to pull his arm free. "Why don't you mind your own business, you crazy—" Anna dug her fingernails deeper into his wrist. "Argh!" He continued to wrestle against her grip.

She stood and jerked downward on his arm. "Are you going to put it back, or do I have to make you?"

The muscle in his arm twitched. As he swung his free hand

at her, Anna released his other arm and caught his fist with both hands. She twisted hard, spinning his body away from her. He grunted in pain and released his grip on the money.

She plucked the bill from his hand. "Thank you," she said brightly, pushing him away from her.

He reeled around, his face twisted in anger. He stepped forward and swung at her again. She ducked below his punch and moved closer. In one well-practiced motion, she jammed him in the chest with both palms and hooked his leg as he teetered backward. Legs flailing helplessly through the air, the punk landed hard on the tile floor.

Nearby customers had already noticed the scuffle, but his impact caught the attention of the entire diner. The room went completely silent as he staggered back to his feet.

The jerk scowled, shooting daggers her way. The silence must have caught his attention because he looked around at his new audience.

Anna saw the moment when his face changed, the instant he realized that he would rather walk away than get beaten to a pulp by a girl.

She loved that moment.

Every. Time.

Anna let out a breath as the guy sulked out the door. Once he had gone, she gently returned the money to the nearby table. As she walked back to Leo, she became aware that several of the other patrons were watching her. Some of them smiled and nodded, others offered soft claps.

Leo beamed at her. "That . . . was amazing," he said breathlessly.

Anna's cheeks flushed at the sudden attention, and she smiled back at him.

"You're hired," he said simply. "I mean, I know you already

have the investigation assignment, but I'd give you the security job even if you didn't."

Anna dipped her head. "Thanks. That's nice of you to say."

Leo continued to smile at her across the small table like he'd found a buried treasure. "Will you come to dinner with me this evening? I need to introduce you to some of the members of my staff."

Anna sighed. Another outing with the prince. She supposed the mission would have plenty of those. She nodded reluctantly. "If I have to."

Leo grinned. He probably thought she was being sarcastic.

Chapter 3

"The prince's security agent was skewered in the leg with a harpoon?" Katie's voice squeaked in surprise.

"That's what he said." Anna handed Katie the slacks she had just tried on.

"I didn't know whaling activity was still one of the occupational hazards of being a prince," Katie said as she rehung the pants in the middle of the long clothing rack.

Anna laughed. She stood in front of the full-length mirror in the wardrobe room as Katie scoured the racks of clothing for something appropriate for her meeting with the prince. Anna glanced down and tugged at the tan, faux-leather pencil skirt. It didn't feel as comfortable as the slacks she'd just tried on, but definitely looked the best, hugging her waist and hips perfectly while opening up nicely below her knees. She turned around. "How does the back look?"

Katie peeked from behind a rack of blouses. "Amazing. As always," she said.

Hannah walked into the dressing room holding several gadgets. "You ready for your gear?"

Anna gave herself one last look in the mirror before nodding to her friend.

"Okay. Here's your purse." She passed the small clutch to Anna. "It has all your standard stuff: perfume bottle with mace in the second compartment, mascara with blow dart tranquilizer pins in the cap, and floss."

Anna waited for additional explanation. "Just . . . floss?"

"Well, it's really fifty feet of graphene wire, but I'm sure you could use it as floss in a pinch," Hannah said.

Anna shook her head and laughed. "What will you come up with next?"

Susan—the fiery red-haired Banana Girl with a knack for software bugs and five-star Sudokus—hobbled in with a tablet in her hand. The gunshot wound she received during their mission to rescue Mari's mother had nearly healed, but she wasn't one hundred percent yet. "Don't laugh," she said. "I could have really used some of that on my date last weekend. The guy cooked us corn on the cob." She chomped her teeth and mimicked eating a cob of corn.

Anna considered the weapons and gear in her hands. "I'm only going out to dinner. Do I really need all this?"

As Anna fiddled with her earrings, Susan reached up and teased a dark curl from Anna's swept-back hair. Anna batted her hand away. "Susan, leave it alone. I'm sure it looks good enough for dinner."

"You're going out with a prince—to the fanciest restaurant in the city. It's okay to look a little gorgeous for something like that," Susan said.

"Do we have the profile on Leo yet?" Anna asked, hoping to distract Susan from doing anything else with her hair.

"Yep. See?" Susan held out the tablet then quickly pulled it back. "Actually, I can't show you while Katie's around. She'll start drooling."

Katie frowned. "I won't drool."

Hannah plopped herself onto a yellow pouf by a rack of dresses. "Katie not drooling over an attractive guy—this I have to see."

At that moment, Mari walked into the room. "Is Katie drooling over a hottie again?"

Hannah held a hand out in Mari's direction. "See, even Mari knows about it, and she's only been here for a few weeks."

Susan made a surprised O shape with her mouth and looked with big eyes back and forth between Katie and Hannah. Finally, with a few swipes on her tablet, the large mirrors went blank, replaced by the prince's official profile. A large professional headshot of Leo filled half the screen next to several paragraphs of description.

"His Royal Highness Prince Léopold Jean Adolphe Guillaume of Luxembourg," Susan read. "Age twenty-four. Recently graduated in marine biology from the University of Miami."

"What would Luxembourg need a marine biologist prince for?" Hannah asked. "Aren't they landlocked?"

"Maybe that's why he came to school in the states," Susan offered.

"Well, he's certainly nice to look at," Mari said.

All eyes turned to Anna. She shrugged and nodded. "Sure, he's cute."

"Don't mind me. I'll just be over here in the corner not drooling," Katie said with a wistful note in her voice.

The Banana Girls laughed.

"And he's got blue eyes and brown hair. Isn't that your favorite combo, Anna?" Susan said with a grin.

Anna felt her face heat up. "I like guys with all sorts of hair and eye colors."

"Hmph." Hannah didn't sound convinced.

"Besides . . ." Anna felt the need to get this conversation back under control. "It doesn't matter if he's handsome or not. The assignment is to investigate the attack. I would be happy to do it regardless of what he looked like. And remember," She wagged a finger in Katie's direction. "We don't get emotionally involved with guys on missions."

"Hey, I haven't fallen for a guy on a mission in at least two months," Katie said.

"Wasn't your last mission about two months ago?" Susan asked innocently.

Katie tried to scowl at her, but it turned into a sheepish grin.

"What's your favorite type of guy, Katie?" Mari asked.

"Hot ones," Hannah and Susan said together.

Katie lifted her chin in mock disdain. "I have more discerning taste than that!" She looked at Mari with a mischievous gleam in her eye. "They have to be good kissers, too."

The girls laughed.

Anna shook her head and looked at the ceiling. "Katie, you should be smarter about the guys you date," she chided.

Katie plunked herself down next to Hannah on the pouf. "I'm smart all the time in class. I need a break from being so smart sometimes."

"Good thing you don't date guys from your engineering classes," Hannah said with a smirk.

"Why do you think I always park next to the athletics building?" Katie whispered back.

Hannah rolled her eyes, and Mari giggled.

Anna tried to focus on the profile page up on the screen. Somewhere out there, someone was trying to hurt this attractive and incredibly over-confident prince.

It was her job to find out who.

———

The limousine was waiting on the street outside when Anna exited the elevator and stepped confidently across the lobby's white marble floor.

"Go easy on 'em," Thomas, the front desk attendant, said.

"I'll do my best," Anna replied.

"Unless they mess with you," Thomas' grin turned mischievous. "Then go ahead and kick their butts."

Anna smiled back. Thomas probably knew more than he should about the fighting skills of the girls on the top floor.

The ride from the Banana Girls' Midtown high-rise to the tower restaurant downtown was uneventful. Anna had ridden in limos before, but usually she was with another agent or undercover with a date. Riding alone was a new—and luxurious—experience.

And it was over all too soon. A valet opened the limo door for her and pointed toward the entrance. Two attendants stood waiting to usher her inside.

Prince Leo met her at the door and, taking her hand through his arm, escorted her across the lobby. "I'm glad you could come. I know it was a last minute arrangement."

Anna smiled. "It's fine. Fancy dinners are always welcome."

When they stepped into the elevator, Anna saw they weren't alone. The large bodyguard from the diner was already inside, one hand on the elevator controls. Leo nodded to him and he pushed the button for the top floor restaurant.

The prince turned to Anna. "You'll likely be working together, so it seems introductions are in order. Miss Rivers, this is Andre, a member of my security detail."

Andre dipped his head. "How d'you do, Miss Rivers." He extended a meaty hand, and Anna grasped it firmly.

"Please, call me Anna." She turned to Leo as well. "Both of you."

Andre nodded again and tried unsuccessfully to shrink into the corner.

Leo took Anna's arm and pulled her toward the tall glass windows of the elevator. "What do you think of this view?"

Anna stifled a gasp as she watched the city receding below her. Pedestrians shrank to the size of little multicolored dots, buses and cars contracted to the size of toys, and garish retail displays faded into cheerful, twinkling lights in the distance.

It was breathtaking.

So much beauty and commotion growing smaller beneath her feet.

The elevator finally reached the top, and Leo led her halfway across the round restaurant. She struggled to focus on anything but the beauty of the lights outside.

Near a table with only two occupants stood the bodyguard from outside the diner that morning. "This is Frederic," Leo said, indicating the large man.

Frederic nodded at Anna, his mouth forming something that might be a smile, at least among the high-security set. He was as large as Andre, but his hair was sandy blond and messy.

They stepped around the bodyguard and Leo gestured to the couple seated at the table with the spectacular city view. "Anna, I'd like you to meet Celine Engel and Zane Kremer. Celine is my chief of staff, and Zane is my security director."

The two staff members stood and shook hands with Anna. Zane had lightly tanned skin, brown hair, and brown eyes. He looked to be in his mid-thirties, maybe younger. Celine was average height and petite. She had very fair skin, shoulder length light brown hair, and grayish green eyes. She didn't look a day over twenty, but Anna got the feeling that she was one of those people who, like Stacia, looked deceptively young.

After the formalities, Leo seated Anna across from Celine. After informing the waitress of their selections, Anna did her best to make small talk about the city and the weather as they waited for the food to arrive.

Having exhausted the lighter topics, Anna figured she could start getting some information from them. "So, how long have you two worked for the prince?" she asked.

Zane spoke first. "I started as a special security agent for the Grand Ducal Family about ten years ago, working various assignments for Prince Léopold and his siblings. I was promoted to the director of security for His Highness when he came here seven years ago for university."

That was a very satisfactory answer. Anna turned her attention to Celine.

"I have always worked with Prince Léopold. First as an administrative assistant while he was in secondary school, then as chief of staff when he moved to the United States."

Anna nodded. "And how large is Leo's staff here in the states?" she asked Celine.

Celine glanced at Leo who gave her a subtle nod. "Because Prince Léopold has his own residence in Miami, we have about twenty staff made up of housekeepers, cooks, attendants, and gardeners, not including members of the security detail."

"And how many security staff do you have?" Anna asked Zane.

Zane scowled slightly before taking a breath to answer. He probably wasn't used to discussing security matters so openly. "There are eight Luxembourger security guards protecting the grounds of the prince's Miami villa, two personal bodyguards." Zane nodded toward Frederic and Andre. "Plus three—or rather two—close agents."

"Close agents?" Anna glanced at Leo.

The prince smiled. "That's what Zane calls the female agents who go to parties with me."

Anna nodded slowly. "Down to two because one was injured in the attack?"

The grim looks on their faces was answer enough.

After a short silence, Zane spoke. "Given that you'll be temporarily stepping into that role, Miss Rivers, you'll report to me for daily assignment."

The prince held up a hand. "Actually, Zane, she won't be employed as part of the staff. Of course, she's welcome to attend your security briefing and volunteer for close agent assignment any time she feels it's appropriate. But ultimately, Miss Rivers will be running an independent investigation, and she can give us appropriate updates at her discretion."

Zane's mouth was a tight line, but his face showed no other emotion. "Yes, Your Highness," he said.

Anna relaxed back into her chair as some of the stress of the mission dissipated. Prince Leo had just made sure she had complete freedom during her investigation. That would make her life so much easier.

Their food arrived, and Anna was happy to return to small talk about the beautiful view of the city and the delicious taste of the food. Between bites of lemon rosemary chicken, she glanced in Leo's direction and caught him staring at her. He didn't seem to be concerned about hiding his interest.

She assumed the novelty of her presence would wear off at some point. In the meantime, maybe she could come up with something to distract his attention. She turned to Zane. "Have you been able to learn anything about the identity of the attacker?"

She had caught him mid-swallow, but he quickly recovered. "Unfortunately, no." He glanced at the prince. "The harpoon was untraceable. No distinguishing marks on it."

"How in-depth was the investigation at the scene? Any opportunity for forensic analysis?" Anna pressed.

Zane looked like he had been caught unprepared for a midterm. "Well . . . the scene of the attack was rather . . . chaotic. We did our best, but the tide and the shifting sands made things difficult."

She would need to tread carefully if she was going to avoid injuring the ego of Leo's head of security. She'd certainly need Zane's help during the investigation. "I'd love to get your input on possible suspects," she said. Then, turning to Celine, she added, "Both of you, actually. I'm sure you have more knowledge of the prince's personal interactions and family background than anyone."

Hopefully that was deferential enough.

"Uh, except for me, maybe." Leo gave her a small wave of his fingers. "I might also know about those things," he said sarcastically.

"You're too biased." Anna retorted.

Leo smiled knowingly. "That is certainly true, but I think I can still give objective observations about the facts. Here, I'll give you an example." He gazed at her. "I think your government picked the perfect woman for this assignment."

Prince or no, this guy was coming on strong. He was so sly with his compliments that the only defense Anna could think of at the moment was banter. "Okay, maybe we should talk about what you're looking for." She held up one finger, ready to tick off the requirements of the female security agent in the most ridiculous way possible. "So you need an agent who can't even keep a scrawny faux-assassin out of a private meeting." She challenged him with a raised brow.

"You were wonderful," he said.

Ignoring him, she held up a second finger. "And obviously we won't even talk about my physical appearance because—"

"It's perfect," he interjected.

"—it's such a dumb requirement." She finished her sentence, barely believing he could be saying these things with a straight face. She held up a third finger. "What about my partying skills?

36

Are you just going to trust that those are up to par?" She waggled her eyebrows at him.

Leo scrutinized her playfully. "Are they?"

A broad grin spread across Anna's face. "You'll have to wait and see."

"You know, the interesting thing about being a prince is that I usually don't have to wait to get what I want. I think we need to test your partying prowess right now." He arched a brow as if daring her to contradict him.

Anna stared back, unwilling to back down. "Unless you're planning to ask the restaurant to play some club music and manually strobe the lights, I'm not sure how we can possibly—"

"There's a club right there." Leo pointed out the window at a brightly lit section of street far below them.

"How could you possibly know that's a club?"

Leo pointed to himself with a smile. "Party Prince. Remember?"

Anna rolled her eyes and returned to the last few bites of her dinner. When the prince stood from the table, she looked up at him in surprise.

He held out a hand to her. "Let's go," he said.

"Are you serious?" she asked.

"I never joke about my party life."

"Your Highness, I don't think this is a good idea," Celine said.

Zane nodded. "I agree, sir. We haven't had time for security sweeps of any kind. It's too dangerous."

"But no one will be expecting us, either," Leo replied. "An assailant can't prepare an attack for an event that wasn't planned until ten seconds ago. It will be fine. I'll have Andre and Frederic—not to mention Miss Rivers—with me the entire time. You two can take the second car back to the hotel, if you please."

That left Zane and Celine both speechless, and neither appeared happy.

Looking up at the prince's expression, Anna could tell he was serious. And determined. She considered the situation. It *was* a surprise visit. Plus they would have his bodyguards with them. And she would presumably be at his side the entire time. The security risk was minimal.

Most of all, though, Anna wanted to get a full understanding of her role with the prince while she still had a chance to back out of the mission.

As she stood, Leo took her hand and tucked it in the crook of his arm. He led her across the restaurant toward the elevator, leaving Zane and Celine sitting at the table, dumbfounded.

In the elevator ride down, Leo gave his bodyguards instructions about his plan to go out for a little partying. They were to stay nearby in the club, but he told them to keep a low profile. Anna stifled a grin as she imagined either of the stocky men trying to blend in at a dance club. Maybe they could pretend to be the bouncers.

Once out on the street, Anna watched as the stiffness of Leo's posture and the stress in his shoulders melted away. Of course, he had already been agreeable and polite, but now he seemed happy. And somehow . . . lighter, almost carefree.

As they approached the club entrance, pulsing lights and a bone-rattling bass line spilled out through the front doors. Andre approached the bouncer and had a brief, whispered conversation. Andre flashed an ID badge and pointed back at Leo and Anna. The bouncer, who looked like a featherweight next to the bodyguard, nodded his approval and ushered the group into the club.

The music enveloped them as they stepped inside. Dozens of dancers bounced and flailed on the central floor, seeming to randomly appear and disappear as the lights shifted around them. The smell of perfume, alcohol, and sweat wafted through the air.

Leo placed his hand on the small of Anna's back and guided

her to the floor. Anna glanced over her shoulder to see that the two bodyguards had indeed, surprisingly, melted into the shadows.

At the edge of the floor, the prince pulled her to a stop. "How's this?" he yelled in her ear.

Anna nodded, not sure whether their position on the floor really mattered. She just needed to make sure the prince was safe while they danced. Switching into security mode, Anna scanned the surrounding crowd. None of the nearby dancers appeared to pose a threat to them. In fact, none of them seemed to even notice they were there at all. Leo said something unintelligible, and Anna turned her attention back to him.

"Dance," he repeated, moving his arms in a horrible pantomime of dancing. Hopefully that wasn't the way he really danced.

Anna half-heartedly moved side to side, watching the shifting mass of people around them as it slowly enveloped her and the prince. The crowd bumped and jostled them, pressing Anna and the prince closer together. Anna tried to push back, but it was a losing battle.

A guy in a bright purple shirt banged into her. Instinctively, Anna shoved him in the chest, knocking him onto the seat of his extremely tight pants. He looked equal parts apologetic and frightened. Reaching down, Leo helped the guy back to his feet and offered a quick apology. After the man nodded and moved eagerly away, Leo turned his attention back to Anna.

"Nobody here wants to hurt me," he said in her ear. "Or you, for that matter."

"Sorry," she said. "That was a reflex."

Leo brows inched up. "Remind me to keep my distance." There was a laugh in his voice.

"I will," Anna quickly replied. Leo probably thought she was joking.

"You need to relax and enjoy yourself."

Anna shook her head. "I'm not here to have fun. I'm here to protect you."

The prince gave her a regal glare that had probably been passed down through generations of European nobility. Anna was unmoved. Her mother had given her a much worse look the time she tried to glue her bedroom door shut with a concoction of peanut butter and laundry soap. Leo's royal stink eye wasn't even in the same league as her mother's.

The prince frowned at her stubbornness. As a concession, Anna began to step rhythmically side to side, but she refused to let out her full club dancer. She was on a mission, after all. Glancing side to side, she continued scanning the crowd for dangers.

Leo rolled his eyes and let his shoulders slump dramatically.

Was he going to pout like a four-year-old child?

His mouth slowly grew into a mischievous grin which had Anna worried. She was already sort of dancing. She was even snapping her fingers occasionally. What more did he want from her?

When the prince had her attention, he lifted one arm, holding it out at head level.

Anna recognized the dance pose, but there was no way a prince would do it. Would he?

His other arm came up behind his head and the first arm began snapping side to side like a giant, man-sized sprinkler.

Anna choked on a smile and looked away, not wanting to give the prince the satisfaction. She did a quick check of the dancers closest to them. When she finally allowed herself to look back, hoping the prince had stopped that ridiculous dance move, Leo had both thumbs tucked under his belt and his legs bowed outward like a cowboy who'd just stepped off his horse. He sauntered toward her, swinging his hips. Lifting one hand like he was twirling a lasso, he threw the imaginary rope toward her and pretended to pull her in.

After the first silly dance move, Anna was prepared for the prince's antics. She clamped her lips together to prevent a giggle from surfacing and simply shook her head. Needing another distraction, she glanced over her shoulder, checking the corner of the room to see if Frederic was still at his post. Maybe if she ignored Leo, he would stop embarrassing himself. After all, how much awkwardness could one prince have inside him?

Out of the corner of her eye, a sudden movement caught Anna's attention. She turned back in time to catch Leo in the middle of his running-man dance—sideways for full effect. A quick hand to her mouth was the only thing that kept the prince from seeing her laugh out loud.

Did the prince only have bad, decades-old dance moves? She shuddered to think what else he could come up with if this went on much longer. She had to do something to not indulge him any further in this embarrassing exhibition. Anna spun slowly around, using her dancing as a cover for a quick sweep of the area.

When she had completed her turn, to her absolute horror, Prince Leo was in full Carlton dance mode. His hips and arms were swinging side to side, and his hands were snapping enthusiastically. Anna's eyes went wide, and she rushed forward. "Okay, okay. You win. I'll have a good time. Just please stop embarrassing yourself." It was the best move, security-wise, that the prince not draw any excess attention to himself. But more than that, Anna couldn't endure any more of his openly public awkwardness.

Leo smiled and took Anna's hand, pulling her closer as they danced. Even though she tried to fake it, her muscles refused to relax. She was essentially on duty. That wasn't the sort of thing that could be turned off so easily.

Leo opened his mouth, presumably to chide her for not having enough fun, when a blonde girl, who looked barely old enough to be in the club at all, touched him on the shoulder.

"You're Prince Léopold!" she shouted.

The prince's mouth snapped shut. Anna wondered whether he would try to deny his identity.

It wouldn't have mattered what he said because the girl immediately turned to her group. "Look! Can you believe who's here? It's Prince Leo!"

Her friends gathered around her, and Leo gave what could only be described as a bashful wave. He glanced at Anna with an apologetic smile. She simply shrugged in response. She assumed this was a common occurrence and that the prince would know how to deal with a stray groupie or two.

The first girl sidled up to him, moving her body to the beat as she pressed against him. The other nearby admirers of the prince took their cues from the first girl and moved in closer, forming a circle of dancers around him. Fortunately, since Anna was there in a professional capacity, she wasn't jealous; it did suddenly make her job a lot more difficult, however.

A girl in a short red skirt pushed forward, bumping Anna in the shoulder. "I want to dance with the prince," she said in a high-pitched whine.

Another girl in a skin-tight neon blouse cut her off with a well-thrown elbow.

The girl in the red skirt stumbled into Anna, knocking them both backward. They tumbled into a heap on the floor that barely caused a stir in the dancers around them. Anna unceremoniously shoved the girl to the side and jumped up. Back on her feet, she glanced toward the prince, but the crowd had carried him out of sight.

She pushed toward where she'd last seen him, but progress through the swarming girls was slow. Even after shoving her way through half a dozen fans, Anna still couldn't see him. She had a sense where the prince was because of the direction everyone was facing, but she couldn't seem to get to the center of the cluster.

In her mind, a mental clock ticked away the seconds since she had been in sight of the prince. Anna doubted that even Leo's enormous bodyguards could have pushed their way through this horde. She couldn't actually see either security agent, but she hoped they were making themselves useful.

If brute-force wasn't going to get the job done, she'd have to use a little finesse. With a well-aimed poke to the back of the knees, the girl in front of her stumbled to the side, leaving a gap for Anna to slip through. Repeating that same technique, plus a few sharp knuckles to the ribs and a short tug on a ponytail that she wasn't really proud of, brought her close enough to see Leo.

When she caught sight of him, Anna saw mild panic in Leo's eyes. He had one girl hanging with her arms around his neck and another locked around his waist. Despite Anna's confidence that they wouldn't really pull him limb-from-limb, she wanted the prince to think well of Atlanta, so she fought through the horde to save him from the would-be princesses.

By the time she reached Leo, the girl around his neck had already planted half a dozen kisses on his cheek and was working her way around toward his lips. Anna yanked the girl away from a lip-lock just in time and tucked herself under his free arm. Once solidly attached to him, Anna pried the other girl's arms off his waist and began dragging him through the throng.

The closest exit from the dance club was the back door. She gave up all pretense of manners as she knocked girls out of their path right and left.

The back door clanged open onto a small alley as Anna and her royal sidekick spilled out to safety. As an added precaution,

Anna slammed the door shut and leaned against it. Their heavy breathing and sighs of relief echoed in the narrow space.

Leo gazed at the alley wall, as if he could still see through the brick to the crowded dance floor. His laugh was equal parts relief and resignation. "I've heard about your southern hospitality, but that was much more than I ever expected."

Anna smiled. "Well, can you blame them? It's not often a real-life prince waltzes so willingly into a southern belle's trap. Especially a prince with such killer dance moves," she added, grinning.

With a short laugh, Leo proceeded to give an encore performance. Anna shielded her eyes. "No, please, no more torture."

Leo only danced harder. "You cannot stop moves like this. They are a force of nature."

Anna doubled over with laughter until she nearly cried, the anxiety of a few minutes earlier quickly dissolving with the prince's humor. He finally stopped his silly show and moved toward her, his laughter diminishing to a soft chuckle. With his hand propped against the exit door, he leaned toward her.

Anna knew that look, and she was sorely tempted to remind the prince to keep his distance. Instead, she opted for another distraction. Ducking under his lean, she said, "So, did I pass the test? Or do you have another one set up for me here in this dark alley? Maybe an assassin will be jumping out from behind the dumpster any second." She turned and gestured toward the nearby garbage container.

The prince looked around them, almost as if suddenly becoming aware of where they were, and his expression darkened.

A single lamp cast a weak pool of light immediately around the club's back door, but otherwise the unfamiliar alley was dark. Distant noise filtered in from the street at the far end. It was like any other alley she'd chased bad guys into. But when she glanced back at the Leo, he looked different somehow. It might have been the harsh overhead light, but Leo's face seemed suddenly paler.

Unsure what could have caused the change, Anna tried to make a joke. "You can face a horde of fan-girls ready to literally smother you, but you can't handle a quiet alley with just one girl?"

Leo stared directly at her, but didn't seem to really see her. He stepped to her but turned his body toward the rest of the alley, almost as if shielding her from danger. "Can we get out of here?" he asked softly.

No bravado. No witty quip. All of the Party Prince had evaporated. He looked legitimately alarmed. Anna considered the handsome man standing in front of her, protecting her from some unseen bogeyman. Whatever had triggered his reaction was obviously deeper in him than Anna felt entitled to pry.

She touched his arm, hoping to bring him back to the present, to the fact that he had a very capable spy girl at his side. "Yeah. There's a great little coffee shop just around the corner."

Leo nodded, took a fortifying breath and offered Anna his arm. Though some of his color had returned, he continued glancing into the shadows as they made their way quickly back onto the bustling downtown street.

Anna wasn't sure if Leo's opinion of her partying skills—or her abilities in general—had changed that evening. But she had caught a glimpse of a more private and vulnerable side of him, and she was intrigued.

Anna knew two things for sure. There was certainly more to Prince Léopold than met the eye.

And he definitely needed her help.

Chapter 4

"What time is it?" Anna asked as she tossed another sundress into her third suitcase. Leo had said that he and his entourage had flown up to Atlanta in his private jet specifically to meet her—which was incredibly flattering—so they weren't likely to leave without her. But she still wanted to make a good impression on her first day on the job, so she didn't want to be late.

Hannah glanced at her watch. "It's eight forty."

Anna grabbed two more pairs of sandals and a set of black pumps and stuffed them in next to the clothes before standing back to admire her handiwork. "Well, that ought to be good enough."

"I still can't believe you're going to Florida with a prince," Mari gushed. "I would be totally freaking out."

Anna stopped and looked around at her luggage chaos. "I'm freaking out on the inside."

"You'll break the zipper if you add any more," Hannah said, pointing to the suitcase.

"Then be a dear and go get me another one," Anna said.

Hannah frowned. "Four suitcases? Are you sure you need this much stuff?"

"She is going to be with a prince," Mari observed.

Hannah shrugged and walked out.

Susan limped into the room as regally as she could manage, her back ramrod straight, her chin high. "Would it be ever so agreeable to your royal espionage-ness if we go over the equipment list?" Susan asked in very broad, pompous tones.

Anna rolled her eyes. Ever since reading up on the Grand Ducal Family during Anna's dinner with Leo, Susan had taken to strutting around Club Banana like a queen, speaking in oddly formal phrases and waving lightly with the back of her hand.

Anna put her hands on her hips. "Suze . . ." she warned.

A smile spread across Susan's face, and she plopped onto the bed. "Okay fine. But you take all the fun out of things."

Susan pulled a suitcase across the bed and opened it. This was the important suitcase, the one that didn't contain any clothing or shoes except the ones with built-in gadgets. "So, you have the basic overnight kit: wireless bugs—both stationary and remote controlled, encrypted laptop with secure satellite connection, door sensors, room monitors, tranquilizer heels and refills. Plus Hannah and Katie have been working on nail clippers that can also strip and splice wires."

Hannah walked back in the room dragging a suitcase. "It's a prototype, so make sure and bring it back." She plunked the suitcase on Anna's bed. "Would you be taking this much if the prince wasn't so handsome?" Hannah asked.

Anna felt the need to defend herself. "It's not about the prince at all. One of these suitcases is just for my textbooks. Plus, I'm going to be in Miami for who-knows-how-many weeks. I need to be prepared."

"Actually, Stacia just sent a message that you only have two weeks," Hannah said.

"Two weeks? I'm supposed to investigate the attack, figure out who's behind it, then track down and capture them in two weeks?"

Hannah shrugged. "Stacia said that his parents are going to bring him back to Luxembourg if things aren't resolved by then. Something about his American escapade being over."

That changed things. Anna wondered if Leo knew about his parents' ultimatum.

Hannah stepped closer to Anna and lowered her voice. "Be careful. Don't forget to check in every once in a while. And, blech, I can't believe I'm going to say this . . . don't forget Rule Number One."

Anna giggled and hugged Hannah. The girls all helped Anna stuff everything else into the suitcases and wheeled them out to the elevator.

Anna gave quick hugs to each of them. "Tell Katie goodbye for me," she said as she stepped into the elevator.

"Send super detailed status updates, and I'm sure she'll be happy," Susan said.

Anna hit the down button and waved as the doors closed.

Thomas was waiting for her when the doors opened in the enormous lobby. He helped her roll the luggage out to a large black SUV with tinted windows and small Luxembourg flags on the bumpers waiting in the porte cochere. Another black vehicle—a large sedan—sat behind the SUV with Andre in the driver's seat and Celine on the passenger side. The side door of the SUV opened and Leo beckoned her in. Frederic sat behind the wheel with Zane in the passenger seat.

"You must pack like I do," Leo said, eying her luggage being loaded into the back.

Anna thought about the weapons and surveillance equipment stuffed in the mission suitcase. "Just be glad we don't have to go through airport security," Anna muttered under her breath. The gadgets were designed to look like normal items one might take on a trip, but that didn't mean they could survive the scrutiny of an x-ray scanner. More than once they'd been forced to bribe or distract or just plain pull rank on unsuspecting airport security personnel.

"What was that?" Leo asked.

"Never mind," Anna answered.

Frederic expertly guided the vehicle onto the freeway and through several interchanges until they reached the regional airport, northeast of the city. Ten minutes after driving through the airport gates, she was stepping into the luxurious cabin of a private business jet. Anna supposed that was one of the perks of private jet ownership. Maybe Hannah's father would be open to the idea. Or perhaps the Banana Girls could make a case with Stacia.

In the space that commercial airliners could have crammed at least thirty rigid seats, this small jet had only eight, plus a compact sofa. As Anna sat down in the wide seat in front of a large window, the soft leather enveloped and cradled her body. She sighed. It wouldn't take much to get used to this type of travel.

As Anna wasn't actually in charge of the prince's personal security, she didn't feel the need to track his every movement. But she did watch him as he moved about the cabin. After visiting briefly with the pilot and copilot, whom he seemed to know very well, Leo walked through the galley area, greeting the stewardess with a light touch on the arm and a smile.

He reached the empty seat facing Anna. "I'm glad you saved a seat for me."

"It's your plane. I'm sure you could have any seat you want," she said.

He sat across from her. "True. But I would have felt badly

depriving someone of your company," he said with a gleam in his eye.

If she didn't do something soon, his flirting was only going to get worse. She'd simply have to force him to stay on task with the investigation whenever they were together.

Anna watched out the large portal as the jet taxied along the side of the runway and lined up for takeoff. The business jet was surprisingly smooth and quiet as it raced down the runway and leaped into the air. The towering high-rises of Midtown passed quietly beneath her. She could just barely make out Club Banana's rooftop terrace. Too bad she couldn't drop a goodbye note to the Banana Girls. She settled for a quick picture of the view that she could send them when she got to Florida.

A few minutes later, when they reached cruising altitude, Leo stood from his seat. He tilted his head toward the back of the plane. "Come on. I want to show you something."

Anna rose and followed him toward the aft of the plane.

They weaved among the other cabin occupants toward the back of the jet. If any of the members of Leo's staff thought this was uncharacteristic behavior on the prince's part, they didn't show it. He touched Celine's shoulder as he passed, and she glanced up with a broad smile.

Maybe Leo wasn't as much of an incorrigible flirt as Stacia had implied during the mission briefing. Maybe he was just overly friendly with everyone. Anna decided to observe his interactions a little closer, but in the meantime, she wouldn't take his flirtations too seriously.

"Take a look at this," Leo said as he pulled back the bulkhead door. A compact stateroom took up the entire back third of the plane. It had facing divans, a small work desk, and a big screen TV.

Leo plopped onto the bench that faced the TV. "Should we watch something while we fly?"

"Don't you have some princely business to catch up on?" Anna asked as she sat on the opposite divan.

"There are a fair number of events and appearances that keep me busy." He searched the nearby cubbies until he found the remote control. "In fact, we'll be going to one tomorrow. My friend Kyle is having a party at his mansion. He's invited the whole crew. It's going to be great."

"You could introduce me to the ones who were at the sandbar party," Anna said.

"I'd be happy to," he replied.

Anna settled back into her couch. Leo must have realized that she wasn't planning to watch the TV above her head. He set the remote aside and focused on her with those deep blue eyes. In an effort to continue thinking straight, Anna glanced around the stateroom. "So is this your family's jet?"

"The royal family has the use of several jets as needed. I've had this one since coming here for college."

"What can you tell me about your family?" Anna asked.

The prince leaned back and spread his arms out on the back of his couch. "What would you like to know?"

"Would any of them want to kill you?"

He barked out a short laugh. "You want to get right down to business." Leo grinned at her, but when she didn't reply, he continued. "I suppose I've aggravated my mother enough over the years; she might be tempted to. And my father has promised, in no uncertain terms, that I will die a very slow death if he ever finds out I've mistreated any of the women in my life."

Anna went along with his casual playfulness. "And they say chivalry is dead."

"Not in my family." He smiled that beguiling smile and Anna was forced to focus on the notes she was making on her phone.

"What about siblings?" Anna asked in her most professional investigator voice.

Leo held his arms out wide. "I'm the baby in the family. They all love me."

Anna arched an eyebrow in his direction, hoping it conveyed that she was trying to be serious about this.

"Honestly—aside from being loved by my entire family— what would they have to gain? I'm the youngest in the family. I'm number eight in the line of succession. What motive would any of them have to kill me?"

"Okay, let's go that direction." Anna tapped her phone screen. "How many people are there below you in the succession?"

"Two aunts, one uncle, seven cousins, and probably hundreds of great-great-uncles and fifth cousins twice removed."

"Who is next in line after you?"

"My Aunt Marianne."

"Does she like you?" Anna asked.

"You certainly are direct, aren't you?" Leo observed.

"It's part of my job," she replied.

"Yes, she does like me," he answered. "She's my godmother. I don't think she wants to kill me. You might need to cross her off your list."

Anna's brow lifted. "Really? Are you the investigator now?" She wasn't sure what possessed her to be so forward with him.

Leo chuckled and shook his head. The smile remained as his gaze returned to her. Anna did her best to hold his stare, but the longer she continued looking at his handsome face, the more mischievous his smile became. Guys this attractive and self-confident were either hiding behind a facade or they were as shallow as a kiddie pool.

Anna didn't really have the time or patience to figure out

which it was in Leo's case. She finally broke eye contact, glancing down at her phone to gather her thoughts for the next question. "So your family all loves you, and they'd probably do anything for you. That brings up the possibility of kidnapping," Anna said.

"Kidnapping? I'm twenty-four."

The prince's playful expression told Anna that he was only teasing her about the turn of phrase. "Is your family's ability to pay a ransom public knowledge?"

"I doubt it—aside from the general understanding that royal families usually want their princes back." Leo leaned forward, elbows on his knees, brow furrowed. "But think about it, why would someone attack me with a harpoon if they wanted to kidnap me? Were they planning to drag me onto a whaling boat and make their getaway?" His face broke into a wide smile.

Anna couldn't help but smile back at the ridiculous image. Doing her best to ignore his playful grin, Anna pressed on. "So besides any delusional members of the nobility, is there anyone else who might want you gone?" she asked.

Leo spread his hands wide, his face had lost its humorous aspect. "Honestly, it's like I told my parents when they insisted on contacting your government; I really think it was just a random act of violence. Maybe directed at me because I'm a prince, or maybe not. Sometimes these things just happen."

Anna tilted her head at him. "Unfortunately, I can't go back to my boss with the conclusion of 'sometimes these things just happen.' There must be more to it than that."

Leo shrugged and leaned back against the cushions.

Anna looked down at the notes she'd made from their conversations. "No one in your immediate family. Extended family is still a possibility—" Leo opened his mouth to protest, but Anna held up a hand. "—just a possibility. We're not ruling anything out." She glanced at her phone again. "You said no disgruntled business partners. What about former friends?"

A frown creased Leo brow. "What do you mean by *former*?"

"Like someone you've had a falling-out with. You know, like a big fight about something."

Leo shook his head. "I don't think I have any *former* friends."

"You've never had a fight with a friend?" Anna thought she was easygoing, but even she got into it with Hannah on occasion.

"Nope. I don't like to argue with people. Having fun is much more . . . fun."

"What about ex-employees? Have you ever had to fire anyone?" Anna asked.

Leo squinted and stared at the ceiling. "I know some staff members have been let go because of performance issues, but it's never been at my insistence. You'll have to ask Celine about that."

Anna made a note to talk to Celine later. "I guess that brings us back to the ex-girlfriends."

The prince's mouth went tight and his posture stiffened. "I'm telling you, I think it was just a random attack."

Anna nodded slowly, waiting. He didn't say anything more. He didn't even look at her. Instead, he grabbed the remote control and turned on the TV above her head.

Clearly that meant the conversation was over.

The only time Anna had seen his behavior shift so suddenly was when the topic of his ex-girlfriends came up. That and the few moments in the alley behind the dance club. Was there something else about the ex-girlfriends that he wasn't telling her? And did it have anything to do with alleys?

———————

With her luggage stowed in the beautiful coral-themed guest room with its spectacular views of the property's private beach and the wide ocean beyond, Anna walked through the villa meeting various staff members and familiarizing herself with the layout of the home. Once she was satisfied that there was no immediate danger to the prince from any of the staff—not that she'd expected there to be—she made a wide circuit of the grounds, checking the barrier along the edge of the property.

She was pleased to find that the eight-foot hedge that surrounded the property on three sides was actually growing over—and concealing—a high-security fence with a spiked top rail. The fence also included an intrusion detection system—a fact she discovered when she tried to test its scalability and was met thirty-four seconds later by Andre and two security guards. No worries about someone climbing in.

Her walk along the beach had been equally informative. Fifty feet out, barely visible in the waves, Anna could see the top of a security barrier submerged in the water. It extended from the spot where the hedges met the beach, and was marked by warning buoys every few feet. No risk of attack from the water, either.

Seagulls squawked overhead as Anna made her second round of the expansive villa grounds. She told herself she was trying to be thorough, but in reality, she wanted to walk around for pure enjoyment this time. That and to make sure the whole thing was real.

She strolled along the winding front lane, lined with dozens of tall palm trees, and stopped at the small guard hut set back from the main gate.

The young guard stood as she approached. "Hello again, Miss Rivers," he said.

Noah was a young Luxembourger in his early twenties—cute in a guy-next-door type of way. But also a little nerdy and overly-enthusiastic. "Noah, after I've fought with an adversary, they either call me by my first name, or they don't call me anything," Anna said.

"Well, after I've fought with a beautiful CIA agent, and she has let me live, I address her respectfully," Noah said with a wry smirk. "So are you here to finally exact revenge on me for elbowing you in the nose?" the guard asked.

Anna smiled. "You've already apologized at least a dozen times for that. It was your assignment to get into the meeting. You could have done much worse to me and I wouldn't hold it against you. My fellow agents and I beat each other up all the time."

Noah nodded and smiled. "Then are you going to accost me with more questions instead?"

"Are you ready to tell me what I want to know?" Anna said in her best mean-spy voice.

Noah grinned. "For the American spy sent to save our prince? Definitely."

The rumor that Anna was an agent with the CIA had quickly spread throughout the staff upon her arrival. Anna had initially considered squashing it, but, ironically, it came with a fair amount of respect, so she decided to wait to correct them if the need arose.

"In fact, I do have another question." Anna said. "How much advance notice do you get when a visitor is coming to visit the villa?"

"Standard procedure is twenty-four hours. It gives the security team a chance to vet them. Though we do sometimes get last minute guests," Noah replied.

"And what do you do in those cases?" Anna asked.

"Biometric security tied in with the Interpol database," he answered in a matter-of-fact tone.

Anna nodded, impressed. No sneaking in through the front

gate either. "Thanks, Noah," she said with a wink. "I'm sure I'll be back to interrogate you again soon."

He dipped his head. "I look forward to it, Miss Rivers."

She walked back along the red-tiled lane, past the patinaed Mediterranean fountain, up to the grand stairs of the front entrance, its red steps and white banisters matching perfectly with the white walls and Spanish tile of the villa.

When she reached the main doors, a villa staff member stood waiting for her. "Miss Rivers? Mr. Kremer asked me to inform you that the morning security briefing will begin in five minutes in his office."

"Thank you," Anna said as she swept past the attendant into the entry foyer. She wasn't technically required to attend the briefing, but it would be a great way to get to know the other security agents she'd be working with. Maybe even gain their trust.

Anna hurried across the broad entryway and turned toward the staff wing. Zane's security office was the first on the left. Inside the large room, Zane sat behind a robust wood desk with four security agents sitting in front of him.

Zane stood when Anna entered. "Welcome, Miss Rivers. Let me make some introductions." He pointed first to the men. "You know Andre and Frederic from our trip to Atlanta."

Anna offered the two familiar bodyguards a friendly smile.

Zane turned to the women. "These are the prince's close security agents: Kaitlynn and Jessica."

Jessica held out her hand. "You can call me Jessie, actually." Her handshake was firm and confident. From the tone of the muscles that Anna could see, she guessed that Jessie took great pride in her workout routine. She had hazel eyes, fair skin, and chin-length hair colored somewhere between auburn and brown.

The other woman, Kaitlynn, stepped forward and took

Anna's hand. Her grip wasn't nearly as strong, but she looked naturally athletic. She was tall, nearly Anna's height, and built like a fashion model. She had long, bleach-blonde hair, light blue eyes, and sun-kissed skin that pinked on her cheeks. Her smile was polite, but not overly warm. Anna had no clue about the woman's security experience, but if anyone fit the prince's expectations of gorgeous and ready to party, Kaitlynn did.

Zane turned back to Anna. "Given that you just arrived today, I assume you won't want to take any close security assignments right off the bat."

"Leo mentioned a party tomorrow. Is that the next thing on his schedule?" Anna asked.

Zane nodded. "It's a small event with a restricted guest list. Frederic will be on perimeter security, and Kaitlynn will have the close security assignment." He eyed Anna. "Unless you wanted to jump in right away."

Anna shook her head. "No, I'll mostly be there to observe. It might help if I could be close to Leo from time to time. Can more than one agent be on close security?"

Kaitlynn's nose went up a little. "Uh, you know, at parties like this, it works best if the prince only has one agent at his side the whole time."

Anna stared at her, trying to gage Kaitlynn's personality. Right off the bat, she seemed overprotective of Leo's company.

"I'm sure we can work something out that will facilitate your investigation," Zane said finally.

"Fine," Kaitlynn said with a sidelong glare at the newcomer.

Anna couldn't tell from one interaction if Kaitlynn had any particular emotional attachment to Leo, but if the prince's attractive party agents didn't have their own version of Rule Number One, they probably should.

Following the briefing, Anna decided a quick exploration of the interior of the villa was in order. She checked the hallway from her room at one end of the residence wing down to the weight room at the end of the other wing. The villa seemed to hum like a well-oiled machine. Back on the ground floor, Anna stopped by Celine's office, which was adjacent to the main entryway. One of the first things she needed to schedule was a visit with the injured agent. Anna hoped Celine could arrange everything. She had also been wanting to get a second opinion about possible suspects among the royal family.

Anna knocked lightly on the open door.

"Come in, Miss Rivers."

Anna smiled. The prince's chief of staff was a model of prim and proper behavior. "I need to visit with the agent who was injured in the attack. Can you tell me how to get in touch with her?"

"Certainly. She's in the Venetian Terrace Recovery Center." Celine tapped and swiped on her computer screen searching for the information. "Room 129. I can message you the center's contact information too if you would like."

Anna nodded and waited. Celine was so helpful, Anna decided to ask for a little more help. "Celine, you're familiar with the Luxembourg nobility, aren't you? Who would be next in line after Price Leo?" Anna asked.

If the question surprised her, she didn't show it. "The next in line is Prince Léopold's godmother, Her Royal Highness Princess Marianne of Nassau."

"Could she have orchestrated an attack on the prince?"

"Princess Marianne adores Léopold," Celine said. "You'd be hard-pressed to find another member of the family who thinks more highly of him. In her eyes, he can do no wrong. Frankly, she still spoils him rotten."

"Okay." Anna smiled, imagining a small Leo with an

enormous lollipop. "Are there any others in line after Princess Marianne?"

"Various uncles, aunts, and cousins until you get number eighteen," Celine explained.

Anna nodded. That confirmed what Leo had said.

Celine's brow furrowed as she continued. "Also, I'm not sure if the prince explained his place in the family. As the fourth child of Their Royal Highnesses the Grand Duke and Duchess of Luxembourg, Prince Léopold is below his three older siblings *and their children.* Anyone wanting to jump to the front of the line of succession would have to kill Prince Léopold, his older brothers and sister, and his young nieces and nephew." Celine stared at Anna, letting the information sink in.

Anna's mouth tipped into a sort of apologetic grimace. "So, not very likely."

Celine shook her head then continued, "You should also know that the Grand Duke and Duchess are the most connected family in all of Europe. They trace their lineage to noble families from Portugal, Belgium, Sweden, Italy, France, the Netherlands . . . shall I go on?"

Anna held up her hand. "Nope, I'm convinced." Suspects in the royal family definitely sounded like a dead end. "What about a kidnapping plot?"

"Kidnap the prince?" Celine asked.

"Yeah, you know, hold him for ransom. I'm sure his family would pay well to have him safe."

Celine tilted her head. "Hmm, I hadn't really considered that. But unless there was an accompanying threat or demand for safety money communicated to the Grand Duke and Duchess, it doesn't seem like a very wise plan. The attack at the sandbar party was almost certainly meant to hurt, not capture."

"True," Anna said. She stared at a blank patch of office wall as she continued to consider other alternatives.

After a long pause, Celine interrupted her pondering. "You know who is a much more likely suspect?"

"Who?"

"The prince's last girlfriend, Heather."

From the look on Celine's face, Anna could tell she wanted to share something more but wasn't sure if she should. Anna pulled a chair closer to Celine's desk and sat. "Really? What did she do?"

Celine glanced out the door and leaned forward, lowering her voice. "It wasn't anything specific that she did. But the rumor is that she ended their relationship when the prince wouldn't endorse her new startup business."

That was certainly an important tidbit of information. "How long ago was this?"

Celine tilted her head and squinted. "It was about a year after he graduated from college. So probably about two years ago."

"Do you think she could hold a grudge long enough to want to hurt him now?"

"She always seemed like such a nice girl." Celine's shoulders lifted. "But possibly. That startup was very important to her."

"I'll visit Makenna first." Anna held up her phone, the therapy center info still on the screen, "But I'd love to visit the ex-girlfriend later if you can help me arrange it."

Celine nodded. "I'll see what I can find out."

Thirty minutes later, Anna turned north and crossed the last bridge over the winding waterways of the prince's upscale neighborhood, trusting that the zigzagging directions of the Lexus' GPS would eventually take her to Makenna's recovery center.

Anna had tried to order a rideshare, but Leo balked, saying

she would cause an international diplomatic incident. He explained that if she was seen leaving the villa in a rideshare vehicle, it would be a black eye on the Grand Ducal Family, not to mention the tedious offers from all of the high-end car manufacturers to donate a vehicle for the prince's use. He said it was far more hassle than it was worth, and Anna believed him.

In the end, Leo insisted that she take the luxury white SUV. Anna hadn't argued too hard.

The range of vehicles in Leo's garage rivaled the Banana Cave's, though not quite as technologically advanced. She doubted any of his cars had instantly customizable paint jobs, high-end engines, or dashboards bristling with cutting-edge gadgets.

Nothing could beat a banana-mobile.

It turned out the navigation system did know what it was doing because it delivered Anna to the rehabilitation center without a hitch. At the front desk, a smiling young woman greeted Anna and asked for the name and room number of the resident she was planning to visit.

The receptionist checked her computer. "It looks like Ms. Sorensen is receiving guests today. If you'll go through these doors and take the second hall, her room will be the fourth one on the left." The young woman inconspicuously activated a hidden switch that opened the doors to the residential wing. She smiled politely as Anna turned and walked through.

The decor of the therapy center felt much more like a posh hotel than a hospital. On her way to find Makenna, Anna passed an entertainment room with comfortable chairs and large-screen TVs and an activity room with board games on tables and video game consoles against the walls. Residents recovering at this facility would never want to leave. Either that, or they were used to a certain standard of living that they were willing to pay for even during rehabilitation.

Anna found Makenna's door and knocked.

"Come in," an alert voice said.

Anna pushed open the door into a comfortable sitting area. A young woman with dark red, chin-length hair sat in a large leather armchair with a book in her lap. She wore a bright yellow blouse and blue athletic shorts. Her right thigh was bound in a thickly wrapped bandage. She turned when Anna entered, and Anna wasn't surprised to notice that she was quite beautiful in both figure and natural looks.

"Makenna?" Anna asked.

"That's me." The girl gave her a questioning look.

"I'm Anna Rivers, I'm working with Prince Leo's staff to investigate the attack on him—or really you—" she indicated Makenna's leg, "at the sandbar party last week."

Makenna waved her to sit in a nearby chair. "I'm normally a better hostess, but I just got this leg comfortable."

Anna sat across from her. "How is your leg doing?"

Makenna shrugged. "The doctors say I'll make a full recovery. Just some minor muscle damage. I'm already walking again without much help."

"That's great news," Anna said with an encouraging smile. "I'm sure the prince and the staff are looking forward to having you back."

"Yeah, I'll go stir-crazy if I don't get out of here soon." Makenna smiled. "And Leo came to see me the other day. He's so sweet." A look of concern suddenly crossed her face. "I hope they don't replace me while I'm recovering."

"I'm sure they'll still have a spot on the team when you're ready."

"But they'll be short-handed while I'm out of commission," Makenna replied with a frown.

"Actually . . ." Anna hadn't really meant to explain her strange, dual role during the investigation, but Makenna looked like she needed the reassurance. "I'll be filling in for you while I'm here investigating."

Makenna's eyebrows went up, and she gave Anna a quick visual assessment. "You've got the looks. Do you have any security experience?"

"Not as a bodyguard, but I do have a little personal combat training." That was the understatement of the year, but Anna didn't want to get into the details of her spy training. "Hopefully that will be enough for a temporary substitute."

Makenna considered Anna through slightly narrowed eyes. "You don't plan to stay on with Leo's security staff?"

"No." Anna shook her head. "It's just a short-term assignment. Once we figure out who attacked you, I'll be heading back to Atlanta."

A much more natural smile spread across Makenna's face, and she leaned back into her chair with a quiet sigh.

Anna waited a moment before continuing. "Can I ask you some questions about the attack?"

"Sure," Makenna said with a lift of her shoulder. "I doubt I'll be much help, though."

"Just tell me what you remember."

She shrugged. "It was a normal sandbar party, like a million others the prince has gone to. Things were winding down, and we were getting ready to leave. Everyone in our group was piling back into the boat. I was with the prince at the aft ladder, and he motioned for me to go first."

Makenna paused and squeezed her eyes shut, a grimace on her face. Anna waited.

"Then a searing pain shot through my thigh." Makenna pointed to her bandaged leg.

"You were facing the boat, and the speargun bolt went into your leg from the front, correct?"

Makenna nodded.

Anna tapped a quick note on her phone. "So the shooter must have been under the boat," Anna observed. "You didn't see anyone going under the boat before the attack, did you?"

Makenna shook her head.

"Do you remember seeing anyone suspicious at the party?"

She raised an eyebrow at Anna. "You've never been to a sandbar party, have you? They don't exactly have a guest list," she said dryly. "Basically it was Leo's entourage and security in his boat, plus Leo's friends in their boats. Plus half the population of Miami Beach. It's just a wide-open party. Like any public beach, only more fun."

"So someone could get pretty close in the water, if they wanted to," Anna said.

Makenna nodded. "Those sandbar parties are a security nightmare. Zane hates them."

"Then why does he allow the prince to go?"

"Leo loves them. He says they bring him into contact with the common man," Makenna said. Her smile turned to a mischievous grin. "But that's just his excuse to Zane. Really, they bring him into contact with friendly women." She laughed.

Anna rolled her eyes. That certainly fit what she knew about Leo so far. At least the reputation Katie had told her about. "And after you were shot, did you see anyone come out from under the boat?"

Makenna shook her head. "I don't remember much of anything except needing to get Leo safely in the boat. The ride to the hospital was a blur." She took a deep breath and stared out the window. Apparently, she didn't have any other details that would be helpful.

Anna hadn't really thought she'd find the attacker on her first day, but she had still hoped for a little more information.

After thanking Makenna for her time, Anna stood and moved toward the door.

"Hey," Makenna called after her. "Keep Leo safe for me, okay? He's a special friend."

"I'll do my best," Anna said with a polite smile.

Leo certainly had no shortage of people who cared about him.

Now if she could only figure out who his enemies were.

Chapter 5

The rising sun had just touched the tops of the palm trees the next morning when Anna took the final turn back toward the villa. The streets surrounding the prince's villa were unfamiliar, but Anna always enjoyed the calm of her morning run, so she had been willing to risk it. Finding the jogging path had been a major bonus.

The beat of her feet against the pavement and the steady, complimentary rhythm of her breathing helped clear her thoughts. She still had plenty of time to make it back before the broadcast of her thermodynamics lecture started. If she was lucky, she might even get in a shower and some breakfast, too.

Despite repeated attempts to use her morning run as a brain cleanser, as usual, her mind started running through her schedule for the day: breakfast, lecture, homework, the party with Leo.

The party with Leo.

In many ways, the assignment would be just like one of a dozen others where she had to play a part, to pretend to be someone she wasn't. But in those situations, she'd had the luxury of being completely undercover, where no one knew who she was or what she was really like. Attending an extravagant party with Miami's rich and famous as just plain Anna Rivers was mildly terrifying.

She'd need to focus on her mission. Keep Leo safe. Find out who had attacked him.

Through her mind flashed the vision of Kaitlynn dressed for a high-society party, draped all over Leo, feeding him grapes or some other silly, rich-person food. The image jolted Anna's middle with a sudden flash of envy.

Where had that come from?

She shook the thought from her head and sprinted the final hundred yards of her run. Stumbling to a slow walk, she rested her hands on her waist, chest heaving. She shook out the muscles in her arms and legs as she gradually cooled down.

In one quick motion, Anna bent down and grabbed her ankles, her face nearly touching her knees, long black braids brushing the ground. It was a stretch she had done immediately after her run ever since junior high.

The upside down street behind her only had a handful of morning walkers and cyclists, but one particular jogger caught her eye. He looked like he was also finishing up a run and cooling down, but he hastily turned the opposite way the moment she bent over to stretch.

And had he been pointing his phone camera at her?

Anna was proud of her butt. It was definitely in her top five favorite parts of herself, but that didn't mean she wanted some creep-weirdo taking pictures of it. She stood and continued her cool down walk, much more alert now to the sounds of the people around her.

Why would some guy by tailing her taking pictures? And how long had he been tracking her? Was it part of a plan to scope out the villa and sneak in for an attack on Leo? Had the assailant planned to find out her weaknesses and plot the perfect opportunity to exploit them?

The thought made her blood boil.

She turned at the next corner, walking away from her planned route back to the villa, and cast a quick look over her shoulder. Mr. Creepo was still following her, snapping shots with his phone.

Surveying her surroundings, Anna searched for the ideal place to lay a trap. Even though she wasn't in any immediate physical danger, her tired muscles tensed for action. She turned the corner at the next street and searched the road ahead. She needed to find a nearby hiding spot before the guy made it to the corner.

A scraggly tree stretched out from a low brick wall, encroaching on the sidewalk. It wasn't ideal, but it was probably the best she was going to get on such short notice. She hurried forward and ducked behind the tree, doing her best to hide her nearly six-foot frame.

She heard the creep round the corner and slow. She imagined his confusion as he stared down the empty road. Even at a full run, there was no way she could have made it to the end of the long street that fast.

He must have known that, too. Anna's only hope was that his rational brain wouldn't kick in until it was too late. If he stopped or turned back, she would miss her chance.

Keep coming.

His steady pace continued forward. The job he was clearly so intent on doing must have drowned out his ability to sense a trap. All the better for her.

Keep coming.

Anna focused on her breathing, forcing it to slow.

The instant he came into view, Anna lunged forward and caught him by shoulder. She wrenched his arm behind his back.

The man cried out in pain.

Anna dragged him toward the brick wall and pushed him chest-first against it. "Why are you following me?" she demanded.

He aimed a backward kick in her direction but missed. "It's my job," he squeaked.

Whoever he was working for certainly hadn't picked him for his fighting skills.

"Who hired you?" She pressed a little harder against his back.

"Idolize," he wheezed.

Anna wasn't sure if that was code for something, maybe a gang kingpin. "Well, if this was meant to be a scare operation, you can tell your boss you failed."

The man said something that sounded like, "Gossip column."

Anna frowned and let up on the pressure on his back. Remembering the phone he was carrying, she snatched it from his captive hand and released him. The man turned around, shaking out his recently freed arm.

Anna considered the phone in her hand and the semi-fit, thirty-something guy in front of her. He certainly didn't seem like hitman material. "You weren't sent to intimidate or attack me?"

The man's eyes went wide. "What? No!" He eyed her warily. "I'm a photographer for *Idol Eyes* magazine. I'm just supposed to get pictures of Prince Leo's new girlfriend for the weekly royalty column." The man straightened and glanced around. "But since I've got you talking to me, could I ask you a few questions? I'd be the hero back at the office."

"Wait. I'm not his girlfriend."

"Uh, you were seen at breakfast, dinner, and a dance club with him during his trip to Atlanta. Then you flew back with him and moved into his villa. Plus, he lets you drive his car . . ."

Anna opened her mouth to explain, but divulging her mission was out of the question. She couldn't even adequately explain Leo's arrangement with his close security agents, so that was no help either. She glared at the man and pointed her finger at him. "I'm not his girlfriend. I'm definitely not giving any interviews. And if I catch you following me again . . ." She let whatever unspoken threat he could imagine hang in the air before stalking away.

"I am going to need my phone back," he called after her.

Anna glanced down at the phone and quickly swiped through his album of recent photos, deleting the pictures of her bent over. She walked away from him, tossing the phone over her shoulder in his general direction. She didn't hear a crash, so she assumed he caught it.

A moment later, he called out. "Hey, you deleted the best ones."

Anna turned and took a threatening step toward him. He scurried backward and his hands went up immediately in surrender. "Okay, okay. I'll work with what I've got," he said.

A satisfied smirk spread across her face as she whirled around and continued down the sidewalk.

Apparently one of her best features wasn't going completely unnoticed.

The prince and his security entourage arrived at the mansion of Kyle Morgan fashionably late. With Kaitlynn on close security duty, and with the crush of friends swarming Leo, Anna slipped away into an adjoining corridor and then upstairs.

From a small hidden nook in the open balcony overlooking the main living room, Anna watched as Leo moved from group to group, greeting friends and being reintroduced to

71

acquaintances. Katie's insistence that Anna wear her red floral midi dress on the first occasion had been spot on. If Anna had been down mingling among the affluent guests, she would have fit in perfectly. Their clothes were in a mixture of beach casual and yacht party attire. Sandals, shorts, and spaghetti straps as far as the eye could see.

Leo walked casually among the clusters of guests, never staying too long with any particular set of friends. But as he moved from group to group, he appeared distracted, frequently glancing around as if in search of someone. There were plenty of attractive women attending. Did he have a favorite?

Anna wasn't really ready to take the close security assignment—not that Kaitlynn seemed ready to relinquish it—so keeping a vigil from the balcony seemed like the best plan for the moment. Though she couldn't deny the enticement of joining in with the laughter and conversation. So much decadence and luxury. How fun would it be to plunge whole-heartedly into that lifestyle?

In her revere, Anna lost sight of the prince. A moment of panic swept through her before she realized that Kaitlynn had the primary responsibility to stick close to him. Not that there appeared to be any threats at this particular gathering, unless you counted death by caviar.

She leaned forward, trying to find him in the small crowd. There were only twenty or thirty guests in the room; why couldn't she see Leo? Not knowing where he was formed a knot in the pit of her stomach.

At the sound of soft footfalls from the staircase landing, Anna quickly spun around.

"There you are." Leo approached her. Broad smile and easy manner. And charm. "Why aren't you downstairs keeping me company and meeting my friends?"

"I . . ." She glanced around, hoping to find some explanation.

"I need to observe your friends as part of my investigation." It wasn't the lamest excuse ever, but close.

Leo looked pensive in an overly dramatic way, his deep blue eyes boring into her.

Anna wondered if the prince knew how easily his friendly, confident mannerisms could be mistaken for flirting.

"You'll blend in much better down there mingling with my friends than up here like a hawk waiting to swoop in for the kill," he said with a grin.

He did have a point, but Anna wasn't ready to concede yet. A change of topic might help. "As proof of my power of observation from my perch, I couldn't help noticing that you seemed distracted. Were you looking for someone?"

The prince leaned against the wall and looked around casually. "Yes, but I found her."

"Anyone I should put on my list of suspects?" she asked. "Is it someone I should be protecting you from?"

"No, and I hope not." Leo continued in his casual tone. "But actually, she is quite important to the investigation. And she is, in fact, giving me quite a bit of trouble."

Anna arched an eyebrow in his direction. He wasn't exactly making sense. "Well, let me know if I can help," she said with a shrug.

"Oh, you can definitely help." He smiled. "You see, I'm having the devil of a time getting this woman to come down from the balcony and join the party."

Heat rose in Anna's cheeks. She looked away from the prince's charming smile and tried to regain her composure. He was just being friendly, she reminded herself. "Are you sure standing next to you at a party and socializing with your friends is in the job description?" she asked flippantly.

"Oh, most certainly," he said with a grin. "And being your radiant, stunning self. That's part of it, too."

Despite years of training to stay calm in dangerous situations, Anna felt her heart pound and her temperature rise. She took a deep breath and focused her thoughts. She could be friendly to the prince and pleasant to his friends without getting emotionally involved.

She had a mission to perform, and she had a duty to show the other Banana Girls that it could be done without swooning. After a few moments, she nodded—mostly because she didn't trust herself to say anything at the moment—and followed Leo downstairs to join the party.

Anna watched as the guests flowed in and out of Prince Leo's circle of conversation. She tried to remember names and match faces, but it was hopeless. They all looked rich and beautiful and popular. She tried to focus on a unique mannerism or item of clothing for each one she met. But even the hot pink Bermuda shorts, high-pitched giggles, and fake hair started to blend together.

In the end, she watched their body language. Were they comfortable around the prince? Were they happy to see him? Were they excited to be at a mansion party with him? If the slaps on shoulders, pretentious kisses on cheeks, and spontaneous laughter were any indication, the answer was yes on all counts.

Not a single case of shifty eyes, uncomfortably tight collars, or nervous swallowing in the group. And Leo didn't seem the least bit concerned. Anna would have been aggravated by his continual nonchalance about the danger he might be in if it weren't for the fact that he was so infectiously good-natured all the time. After half an hour with the prince, Anna almost believed that everything really would be fine.

Meeting Leo's friends was not turning out as fruitful for her investigation as she had hoped. How much information was she expected to get out of these superficial interactions? Short of witnessing another attack and catching the criminal in the act, Anna doubted she would make any progress at all during the event.

As the evening cooled, the party moved out onto the patios and balconies facing the ocean. After finishing a conversation with some of his college friends, Leo led Anna up the stairs to the second floor of the balcony. Kaitlynn, who had been watching them from the upper level, passed them on her way down the stairs. She smiled and gave Leo a friendly greeting but didn't quite move to the side enough to avoid bumping shoulders with Anna.

Anna would have gladly given Kaitlynn her post back— something her fellow agent clearly wanted—except that Leo insisted on dragging Anna with him from conversation to conversation.

Once on the upper balcony, Anna tried to forget about her huffy coworker. She leaned against the balcony railing and sighed as she watched the mansion's shadow stretch out across the dancing waves of the Atlantic.

Leo sidled up next to her with a silly grin on his face. "You enjoyed yourself, didn't you, spy girl?" he whispered.

Anna glared at him out of the corner of her eye. "I suppose," she grudgingly conceded. "But with all of the visiting, I never got to try one of the cream puffs from the buffet table."

Leo perked up. "Shall we go get some?"

Anna laughed. "It's okay, Leo, I was only joking."

He stopped and dramatically placed a hand to his chest. "Joking? About cream puffs? How could you?"

Just as Leo was halfway through a comical slow-motion collapse onto the hard wood deck, Kyle came up the steps accompanied by Kaitlynn.

"Leo, you have to come see my new hot tub," Kyle said.

The prince got back to his feet. He pointed to Anna. "But we were about to—"

Anna waved both hands. "No, it's okay," she insisted. This was Anna's chance to play nice with Kaitlynn while also having the opportunity to move freely around the party. And it wouldn't be a bad idea to have a short break from the prince's charm. "Y'all go ahead. I'll get the treats and join you."

Leo looked at her with a questioning expression as if to make sure that's what she wanted. Anna nodded. "Really. It's fine. I'll bring some for everybody."

Before Leo or anyone else could protest, Anna ducked into the house through the balcony doors and hurried across the loft area where she had just recently hidden from the prince. She stopped at the top of the staircase and placed her hand on the bannister. She closed her eyes, and slowly let out a long breath. She needed to center herself. She needed to stick to the job she was sent to do.

She descended to the main floor and wound her way through the crowd to the buffet. There were so many other desserts on the table that it took much longer than normal to find the cream puffs in question. After all, handsome princes weren't the only thing that could distract a Banana Girl—Kyle's cook had made those fruit tarts that look like little mini cheesecake pies. Anna had tried to make them once and the crusts were nearly impossible to press into such small shapes. The result was a delicious disaster that she had yet to attempt again. The cook had also made half a dozen varieties of mini cupcakes with buttercream swirled on top as tall as the cupcake itself. Anna glanced around at the rest of the spread, scrutinizing the selection of lavish desserts.

Aside from multiple distracting desserts, another serious problem presented itself. She had said she'd bring enough for everyone, but there were only five left on the tray. Normally, she would have grabbed only four—one for each guy, plus Kaitlynn and herself—so she could leave at least one behind. But who knew how many people would be in the hot tub with them? Even though she felt guilty about it, she grabbed the whole plate.

A Banana Girl should always have a backup when it came to desserts.

Anna walked through the large French doors and rejoined the party on the back patio. Cream puffs in hand, she mounted the stairs to the upper balcony. The prince was nowhere to be seen. Of course, that wasn't a huge surprise. They had gone to see Kyle's new hot tub.

She glanced around, considering the balcony, the patio below, and the ornamental garden which stretched from the back patio out to the beachfront.

But where was Kyle's new hot tub?

A couple stood close together in the corner, talking. With a smile on her face, Anna walked over to them. "Do either of you know where the hot tub is?"

The guy saw the plate in her hand. "Ooh, those look good."

Before Anna could say anything to stop him, he snagged one and popped it in his mouth. He didn't even have the decency to savor it.

So much for her spare.

The girl shrugged. "I think it's by the pool."

Trying not to scowl at the guy, Anna nodded her thanks and proceeded down the balcony steps. Following the sounds of splashing and frolicking, she navigated her way through the crowded patio to the pool area.

She stopped on the edge of the pool and looked around. The hot tub was just on the other side. Several swimmers were enjoying the hot water, but none of them was Leo, or Kyle, or Kaitlynn.

"Thanks, Anna," a guy said as he walked past. He looked vaguely familiar. Someone Leo had introduced her to, no doubt. She glanced down at her plate.

Only three cream puffs left.

She blew out a frustrated breath.

That guy had swiped one of her puffs.

Oh well. Kaitlynn probably didn't want one anyway.

Anna made her way back to the patio, keeping the tray closer to her body for protection. Through an open window, she saw one of Leo's college roommates, Trent, standing against the wall inside the mansion's large living area tapping out a message on his cellphone.

Anna entered through the back doors and walked over to him. "Have you seen Leo?"

Trent glanced up from his phone. "I know I saw him a few minutes ago. Have you checked the pool?"

"I was just by the pool. He's not there." Anna glanced around the room, hoping Leo might suddenly come around the corner looking for her. "He was going with Kyle to see the new hot tub."

"That sounds like Leo," Trent said with a laugh. "But if it's the new hot tub, it wouldn't be out by the pool. That one's been the same since Kyle inherited the house. Have you checked the third-floor sunroom? Kyle installed one of those treadmill pools up there not too long ago." He looked longingly at the cream puffs. "Can I have one?"

Doing her best to hide her annoyance at the prince—and her ever-dwindling supply of pastries—Anna offered Trent the plate. Apparently, Kyle wouldn't be getting one either. That was fine. She and Leo had planned to get them before Kyle showed up.

With growing urgency, Anna climbed the winding staircase two steps at a time, passing quaint little pictures of lighthouses and beaches as she went. Despite her brain knowing that Prince Leo was probably fine, that he had his security agent—the one actually assigned to protect him at this party—right by his side, Anna felt driven to find him. She needed to know that he hadn't been harmed on her first day on the job with him.

Anna hurried toward the back of the house to the wide solarium doors. Stepping inside, she found two young women in the water lying on floating lounges tethered to the side of the small pool. With the flow jets cranked to maximum, they slid and bumped around as if they were in a river.

"Have either of you seen Kyle or Leo?" Anna said, interrupting their laughter.

The young woman in the aqua bikini turned to the other with a mischievous smile. "We wish," she said. Tittering laughter reverberated in the small room.

Anna scowled at them. Didn't they realize this was important?

"I'm sort of in a hurry." Anna raised her voice a little in an attempt to cut through the giggling. "Did Kyle show you his new hot tub, or not?" Her initial frustration with not being able to find Leo was quickly becoming full-blown anxiety.

The other young woman smirked and turned to her friend. "He showed us a good time once . . ." More riotous laughter.

It was like talking to two Katies, except they both acted ditzy even when no guys were around. Anna rolled her eyes. She didn't have time for silly girls.

As she turned to leave, the girl in the bikini called after her. "Actually, I do know where the new hot tub is."

Anna spun on the spot. "Where?"

The girl lifted her eyebrows in the direction of Anna's dessert tray. "Can I have one of those?"

Anna crouched next to the small pool and held out the plate.

As the girl reached for the puff, Anna shifted the plate barely out of her reach. "Ah, ah. Information first."

The girl's eyes went wide; she was practically drooling at this point. "He bought a new boat last week. The entire back half is a hot tub."

Anna swung the plate closer, but kept it far enough away. "And where would the new boat be?"

The girl shrugged. "In the water, I assume."

Anna eyed her, considering whether that information was worth the next to the last cream puff. If this had been a real interrogation, she would have expected more, but she supposed it would be enough for a civilian interrogation, at least one that didn't involve thumb screws. Anna held the plate out for the girl in the aqua swimsuit.

Leo wouldn't mind sharing the last one, would he?

The idea of sharing food with Leo gave her a fluttery feeling in her stomach. Better focus on finding him first.

After the girl grabbed a puff, her friend made for one, too, but Anna pulled the plate away. She wasn't about to give her last one to the girl who wasn't any help. With her newfound information, she bolted from the sun room, amid protests from the cream-puff-less girl, and flew down both sets of stairs.

She glanced around at the guests crowding the large living area. Which of them would know where Kyle kept his boats? An employee carrying a dessert tray—unfortunately, not more cream puffs—made his way across the room. Anna approached him as he set the tray on the buffet table.

"Can you tell me where Kyle keeps his boats?" Anna asked.

"There's a boat house on the beach, next to the main dock," he said, pointing toward the ocean. He glanced down at her nearly-empty plate. "I can take that if you're finished."

Finished? Who stops eating when there's still one left?

Swiping up the last dainty dessert, Anna handed him the

plate and hurried for the back door. She planned to make her way to the beach as quickly as she could manage in sandals, and the plate would only slow her down.

But what to do with the last puff?

Anna was sure Leo would be a gentleman and let her have the last one. She decided to take him up on his chivalry in advance. Waiting until she had crossed the patio out of sight of most of the guests, she popped the whole thing into her mouth, too preoccupied with finding Leo to even savor the taste. She took to the garden path at a purposeful pace, reassuring herself that Leo would be fine as long as he stayed with Kaitlynn and Kyle.

Unless Kyle was the one trying to hurt him.

Had Kyle been at the sandbar party? Probably. But what reason would Kyle have to harm the prince? And why wouldn't he have done it long before today or even the party last week?

These questions swirled around her mind as she took her clunky sandals in hand and continued barefoot down the cobbled path. Usually running helped clear her mind, but at the moment, her thoughts churned with possibilities of how Kyle could overpower Kaitlynn and hurt Leo.

Maybe the pastry had addled her brain.

Even before reaching the boathouse, she could hear the sound of the ocean waves slapping against the hulls of various boats. She could also hear voices and laughter.

Bounding out onto the gangway, she reached the door and wrenched it open. In the semi-darkness of the boathouse, Anna moved along the access deck, past several high-performance speedboats, toward the sound of the voices.

Leo's happy laughter stood out. Anna paused momentarily, leaning against the wall. He sounded safe. It had all been a false alarm. Anna's shoulders relaxed, and she took a deep breath, trying to gather some semblance of normalcy.

Slipping her sandals back on, she strolled around the corner to the last berth. A stout-looking wood-paneled boat bobbed up and down in the waves, moored to the deck. Occupying the majority of the aft space of the boat was a huge hot tub. At first, it looked very wrong to see water inside a boat, but the dozen guests sitting around the sides of the tub looked perfectly normal.

"Anna! You found us!" Leo called. A jubilant cheer went up from the hot tubbers, and they all raised their drinks. "And look what Kaitlynn had the server bring us." Leo pointed to a huge tray of cream puffs next to the tub.

Anna couldn't help but noticed that Kaitlynn was now wearing a bright-pink swimsuit instead of the frilly purple skirt and white blouse she'd had on earlier. Apparently, her fellow agent had thought of everything.

After the wild goose chase around Kyle's mansion and grounds, Anna was forced to admit to herself that she didn't have the natural instincts of a bodyguard. She had utterly failed at staying close to Leo. She had also failed to deliver on the cream puffs, not that a silly dessert pastry mattered as much as the prince's safety. Fortunately for Leo, Kaitlynn had succeeded on both counts.

Anna glanced at Kaitlynn and nodded, begrudgingly acknowledging her success. By the smirk on Kaitlynn's face, she clearly knew she had won. Anna needed to stop worrying so much about getting the prince's attention or gratitude and go back to doing what she was sent here for. Kaitlynn was assigned to close security for this event, and she clearly had everything in hand. Leo didn't really need Anna there anymore.

She pasted a smile on her face. "Great. It looks like you've got everything." She jabbed a thumb over her shoulder. "I'm going to go check to see if"—she racked her brain for something that would take her away—"Zane needs me . . . to cover anything."

With that pitiful excuse hanging in the air, Anna turned and tramped back through the boathouse and down the gangway, doing her best to ignore the sounds of the impromptu hot tub party floating on the breeze.

Halfway back up the path to Kyle's mansion, she met Jessie heading down to the boathouse. Anna acknowledged her fellow security agent with a wry smile and a wave.

"Zane heard you were looking for Prince Leo. Did you find him?" Jessie asked.

Anna tipped her head toward the boathouse. "I did. He's checking out Kyle's new hot tub boat, and Kaitlynn's with him, so he's fine."

At that moment, raucous laughter echoed up from inside the boathouse. Anna turned away, unsuccessfully attempting to hide her disappointment in her own performance during the party.

Jessie considered her for a moment then nodded and turned back toward the mansion. They walked in silence for a few seconds before Jessie spoke. "You know, doing this job correctly can be difficult, but I always try to remind myself that it doesn't matter which of us is with Prince Léopold, as long as he's safe."

"Yeah, I guess." Anna let out a long breath. "Plus, I'm only in this assignment temporarily. I'll be gone as soon as I solve the case, so it doesn't really matter."

Jessie shrugged. "I suppose that's true." But her voice made it sound like she didn't believe Anna's assertion.

That wasn't surprising. Anna could hardly convince Jessie when she couldn't even convince herself.

Chapter 6

The morning after the hot tub incident, Anna went on her run early enough that she wouldn't feel rushed through breakfast. On her way toward the dining room, she saw Kaitlynn enter from the back patio. Now was as good a time as any to ask Kaitlynn some questions in private.

So much for not being rushed at breakfast.

"Hey, Kaitlynn. Do you have a minute?" Anna asked.

Kaitlynn's smile was not necessarily menacing, but Anna wouldn't call it warm, either.

"I wanted to ask you about the attack on Leo last week. I understand you were with the prince when it happened."

"Yes, I was at the party, but I wasn't on close security," Kaitlynn said.

"You've probably been asked this already, but did you see anyone suspicious that might have been involved?"

She shrugged. "We were about to leave the party. I had just gotten into the boat. Makenna was next to the prince at the back of the boat. Always the gentleman, he had her get in first. Just as she reached the ladder, she cried out and grabbed her leg."

"Makenna said the shot came from under the boat," Anna said.

Kaitlynn nodded. "Yeah. But there wouldn't have been any way to see someone under there at that point. The water filled with blood fast, and then the other guests all started screaming. It was mayhem."

When Kaitlynn didn't say anything else, Anna nodded for her to continue.

"I dragged the prince into the boat. He wanted Makenna to be taken care of first, but she refused. In fact, she was pushing him in from behind. While she had a harpoon sticking out of her leg."

It looked like Kaitlynn wanted some response to Makenna's bravery. "Wow," Anna said, shaking her head.

"Five seconds later, we had her in the boat, and we tore out of the harbor. We were halfway back to the villa before someone realized there was a hospital right on the edge of Biscayne Bay. We pulled up to the sea wall, and Leo and one of his friends carried her into the emergency room."

Anna took a deep breath. She knew it must have been a traumatic ordeal and wanted to let Kaitlynn know she appreciated what Makenna had done. "The prince told me about Makenna's heroic effort that day. Were you two close?"

"She'll be back in a few weeks."

"What?"

"You're talking about her like she's dead," Kaitlynn said. Her mouth narrowed in annoyance. "I'm saying Makenna's tough. She'll be back soon."

"Sorry. I hadn't meant to imply that—"

"Yeah, I'd say we're pretty good friends," Kaitlynn continued, brushing off Anna's attempt at an apology. "As close as you can be with a coworker, anyway. We spend time together at events and even off-duty sometimes."

"How long have you worked together?"

"I was hired after one of the previous agents had an accident."

Anna's eyes went wide.

Kaitlynn must have read Anna's concern because she airily waved a hand. "Not that kind of accident. The girl was clumsy. She slipped coming down the stairs at a party. Good thing she wasn't on Leo's arm at the time, or she would have taken the prince down with her."

Anna's brows went up. That would have certainly made the front page of the tabloids.

Kaitlynn continued, "Actually, that was the first thing Zane tested me on in my interview—after checking my security credentials, of course. He made me walk the length of the main hall with a stack of books balanced in each hand. I thought it was a test of strength or endurance. Only later did I find out he didn't want someone clumsy like the last agent."

Anna needed to bring this conversation back around to the investigation. "Are you familiar with Leo's last girlfriend, Heather?"

Kaitlynn shook her head. "I think the first female close security agents were hired around that time. Probably why she broke up with him. You could ask Jessie. She was the first one."

"So you wouldn't know if Heather had been around the prince's boat at the sandbar party last week?"

Kaitlynn considered her for a moment. "Listen. I know you have your assignment, and being on the security team is a means to an end, but you should know, we're not really private investigators. We don't look for suspects. Our main focus is on Leo; keeping him safe and doing what he needs."

"You sure were ready with a quick swimsuit change yesterday." That thought had been festering ever since the party, and the words slipped out before Anna could stop them.

Kaitlynn's eyes narrowed. She took a step closer to Anna and lowered her voice. "You seem like a nice girl, so let me give you a piece of advice about being on the prince's close security detail."

With her abject failure the day before floating through her mind, Anna bit her tongue, knowing she might need to swallow her pride when it came to taking advice from this glorified bodyguard.

"This was something I learned from Makenna, actually," Kaitlynn said. "The prince needs security agents who are able to keep him safe. Doing that means being part of his social circle at events. Yes, that requires gorgeous looks, which you have, but it also includes having fun. You weren't in a swimsuit yesterday, and you walked away from the prince. I came prepared so I could stay close to him. That's my job. And I enjoy doing it. There's certainly no crime in that."

Anna's fellow agent stared at her with sharp, green eyes for several moments before turning and walking away. Anna waited until Kaitlynn was out of earshot before letting out an annoyed huff.

Kaitlynn's comments stung, but that wasn't the worst part. Anna knew, deep down, that Kaitlynn was right. Anna hadn't done her job at the party; she hadn't even really known how to do the job right. That fact must have been obvious to everyone.

Trudging down the hall in the other direction, Anna continued to her original destination, the dining room. With a deep breath, Anna forced her shoulders to relax. Keeping a pleasant smile on her face was the hardest part, though.

A blast of smells accosted her as she entered the large room. She stepped over to the buffet table and scowled at the selection. She wasn't in the mood for any of it. In fact, what her mood really needed was half an hour in her own kitchen back at

Club Banana. She'd whip up a batch of her mother's waffles. That always made her feel better.

With some hesitation, she crept into the main kitchen area where Lara, the villa's resident chef, was ordering assistants around, preparing various dishes.

"Hello, Miss Rivers, what can I get you this morning? Maybe a special order?" Lara continued mixing as she spoke.

Anna didn't want someone to make her mother's waffles. She wanted to make them herself. "Actually, I'd really like to do some cooking of my own."

Lara spread her arms wide. "The kitchen and my staff are at your disposal."

Anna glanced around at the commotion. "I'd hate to be in the way. Are there any other places in the villa to cook? Like a kitchenette or something?"

A knowing smile spread on Lara's face. "You want to do some cooking away from prying eyes, yes?"

Anna shrugged. "Cooking relaxes me, but not if it causes stress for someone else in the process."

"Hmm." Lara tapped a finger to her chin. "There is a small kitchen with a bay window breakfast nook up on the third floor. As far as I know, it's never used."

"That would be perfect," Anna said with a grin.

"Feel free to take whatever ingredients you need from the pantry." Lara motioned toward the shelves tucked at the back of the large kitchen.

Anna walked across the room toward the food stores. "Thanks," she called over her shoulder.

"As long as you bring me a small taste of whatever you make," Lara called after her.

Anna grinned. "Deal."

Gathering the needed supplies into her arms, Anna set out in search of the third-floor kitchen. Knowing that it had a bay window made the hunt easier; she focused on the back of the house where the best views were.

When she finally found the kitchen and nook, she was dumbfounded. How could a space like that go unused? The view was spectacular. Better than her room's view and easily as good as the one from the second-floor balcony. The nook was high enough to see over the tops of the palm trees for an uninterrupted view of the ocean.

Anna sighed as she surveyed the small kitchen. She could get used to working here. Not that the views from Club Banana's kitchen weren't impressive. It was fifty stories up, after all. But it was nice to have a change of scenery every once in a while.

And who could ever get tired of gazing out at that cool blue water?

Setting her ingredients down on the counter, Anna went to work mixing. Only once she had her mother's delicious batter ready did the thought occur to her that the small kitchen might not even have a waffle iron.

"I suppose I could make pancakes out of it," she muttered to herself.

"There's one in the cupboard above the refrigerator."

Anna started and whirled around. Leo stood a few feet from her, smiling at her reaction.

In an attempt to regain the upper hand, Anna said, "How do you even know what I'm looking for?"

"Given that you know of my love for American waffles, I assumed you'd come up here to cook my favorite breakfast." He stood across the counter, peeking into the mixing bowl in her arm. He glanced at her, blue eyes full of anticipation.

"Well, you guessed right on the waffles, but they're not really for you," Anna said with a teasing look. "I like to cook when I'm frustrated."

89

Leo's brows went up. "And who gets to *eat* your frustration waffles?"

Anna shrugged. "I might be willing to share. If you ask nicely."

"I can do that. In fact, I can do more than that." He crossed the small kitchen toward her. Taking her hand, he bent over it in dramatic fashion.

Though she desperately wanted to, Anna couldn't bring herself to pull away.

With his lips hovering over her knuckles, the prince gazed up at her. "Dear Miss Rivers." He placed a long, lingering kiss on the back of her hand. "Might I please have one of your magnificent waffles?"

Now he had crossed over friendliness squarely into the realm of flirtation. She pulled her hand back and picked up the whisk to stir the batter again, though it was already plenty mixed. Anna hoped her pounding heart wouldn't betray the aloof expression she was attempting. "I suppose a request like that—especially from a prince—will be enough."

Leo grinned. "But I wasn't finished yet," he said, reaching for her again.

"No. Really—" In an attempt to keep him at bay, Anna instinctively swung the wire whisk up, brandishing it like a sword. In the process, she splattered the prince in the face with waffle batter. Her eyes went wide, but she didn't drop her weapon.

He wiped a dollop from his cheek. "I had also planned to heap lavish praise on the cook." He licked his fingers. "But I see the cook will be heaping things on me instead." A smile tugged at the corner of his mouth.

Anna tried to keep a straight face, but a tiny giggle squeaked out. She clamped her lips together, hoping to prevent any more giggling, but it was too late. As the prince's snicker progressed quickly to full laughter, Anna doubled over, trying not to let him hear her embarrassing belly laugh. Every time she looked back at his batter-splattered face, a fit of giggles would erupt again.

After the laughter had subsided, Anna wiped away several tears while Leo wiped away the messy batter.

"I'm fortunate you're on my side. If I'm ever attacked by a breakfast pastry, you'll have just the weapon to defend me."

Anna gave him a sidelong glare. "Watch yourself. That last one was a warning shot."

"What will you do next time, run me through?" His laughter threatened to spill over again.

She brandished the whisk in his direction. "No. I'll dub you Sir Waffle. How will you ever live that down with the royal family?"

Leo chuckled. "My brothers would have a field day with that one."

"Did you say there was a waffle iron somewhere?" she asked.

"I believe it's above the refrigerator."

Anna opened the cupboard door and searched through various pans and small appliances. She found a bright red waffle iron and plugged it in on the counter. The waffles would have a strange design—sort of like a five-petaled flower—but they would still taste the same. While the waffle maker heated up, she whipped up a small batch of buttermilk syrup.

As she worked, Anna asked Leo about his family and the brothers he'd mentioned. He told her about growing up the youngest of four, and the tricks his two brothers used to play on him.

"There is a lovely pastoral scene on the wall of the formal dining room in the palace. And my favorite character in the picture was a particularly cherubic-looking child. My brothers would wait until I was up close to the picture, then they would speak in a very high-pitched voice pretending to be this small child." Leo chuckled and shook his head. "For years, I thought I was the only one who could hear the painting speak."

Anna grinned, trying to imagine an adorable young Leo, eyes filled with wonder.

When the prince asked about her family, Anna shrugged. "I didn't grow up in a palace, I'll tell you that for sure."

Leo seemed unfazed. "All the more reason I'd love to hear about it."

She explained about the busy-bodies in her neighborhood—mostly friends of her mother—who would always catch Anna the moment she got into mischief. "It got to the point where I would purposefully get into trouble as a way to summon them if I needed something," she said with a wry smile.

Leo rubbed his chin, a contemplative look on his face. "A young, troublemaking Anna. I just can't picture it." His face broke into a wide grin.

The beep of the waffle iron saved the prince from Anna's witty retort. She opened the iron and dumped the waffle onto a plate. As she did, the waffle separated into five smaller pieces, each shaped like a heart. As heat crept up her neck, Anna opened the iron again and looked closer at what she originally thought was a flower shape. But it wasn't one large five-petalled flower; the petals were each individual little hearts.

She couldn't serve heart-shaped waffles to the prince. As if his flirting wasn't bad enough already. He would be intolerable if he thought she was making romantic overtures.

But there wasn't anything she could do now. If she made a big deal about it, he would only tease her more.

She decided to act normal.

Arranging the small heart waffles upside down on his plate, hoping he wouldn't catch on, Anna brought their food to the little table.

"Thank you so much, Anna. I can't wait to—" Leo looked at

the waffles and a broad grin spread across his face. He gazed across the table at her.

Anna forced her stern expression to stay in place. "Don't."

Leo touched a hand to his heart. "I had no idea, all this time . . ."

"We've only known each other three days, Leo."

". . . that you harbored such feelings . . ."

"It was the only waffle iron in the cupboard."

". . . of unrequited love." He reached slowly across the table for Anna's hand.

She pulled it out of his reach and met his sappy-sweet gaze with a glare. "Did you purposefully put a heart-shaped waffle iron in there just so you could tease me?"

The prince playfully waggled his eyebrows.

Anna pushed her chair back from the table. She had been looking for something to reduce her frustration and annoyance, not increase it.

"Wait." Leo held up his hands in surrender. "This wasn't a . . . how would you say it? A setup. That waffle iron came with the villa. The home used to be a vacation rental, and we bought it fully furnished. Honest. I simply have not gotten around to changing some things, like this breakfast nook."

Anna considered him with narrowed eyes. He seemed sincere in his explanation.

"Besides," he added. "These are Norwegian waffles. They're meant to be shaped this way."

With an exasperated sigh, Anna sat back down, and they both took bites of their waffles. Anna smiled at the memories it conjured.

Leo was more effusive in his feelings. "Mmm." His eyes rolled back slightly. "Mmmm. This is delicious."

They sat in companionable silence except for Leo's delighted groans. When Anna finished eating, she stared through the bay windows at the amazing view—palm trees swaying in the breeze and surf lapping at the sand. She glanced back at the adjacent kitchenette. It was perfect. "Don't change it."

Leo paused mid-bite. "I beg your pardon?"

"This." She swung an arm to indicate the breakfast nook. "Don't change any of it. I think it's perfect just like it is."

"You really like it?"

Anna nodded.

"Please feel free to use it anytime you would like. In fact, I'd be happy to eat your frustration food any morning you want to cook it."

"Is that part of the job requirement?"

"No. Unless you count having a happy prince as one of your requirements."

"Actually, I don't," Anna said with a thin smile. She tilted her head, contemplating his offer. "I'll think about it." She looked away when she saw the grin on his face, affecting an air of mock aloofness. "I may be back tomorrow solely based on how much you've already annoyed me this morning."

He dipped his head forward in a half bow. "I live to be of service."

If the morning's experience were any indicator, Anna would be fighting smiles and giggles a lot around the prince. At least, when they were alone.

"By the way, what frustrated you so much this morning that you had to make waffles?" Leo asked. "It couldn't have been me already."

"Oh, I was talking to Kaitlynn about the investigation, and some of her answers were annoying," Anna said as nonchalantly as possible.

"What a coincidence. I went for a walk on the beach with Kaitlynn this morning."

"Really?" Anna's chin went up a fraction of an inch. "A walk on the beach?"

Leo nodded.

This was good. In fact, it really was for the best. If Leo was happy to spend time with any of the women around him, then that meant his flirting was just friendliness. That should make it much easier for Anna to keep her own feelings in check. And she would have no problem keeping Rule Number One during the mission, despite how frustrating and flirtatious the prince was.

Or so she told herself.

Anna sighed. "Looks like I'll be cooking something again tomorrow," she muttered.

Chapter 7

I n the briefing the next morning, Anna was given her first close security assignment. Prince Leo had a ribbon cutting ceremony at a local hospital that afternoon, and Zane figured that the semi-controlled environment would make an ideal first opportunity for her.

Initially, Anna would have balked at being given a milk-run assignment, but after the cream puff debacle a few days earlier, she was willing to start slow.

Fortunately, being near Leo would give her more time to watch the people around him, and she was anxious to move the investigation forward. Unfortunately, being near him physically meant she also ran the risk of getting too close emotionally. But Anna told herself she had that under control at the moment. Besides, the sooner she closed the case, the sooner she could put some space between herself and the prince's charms.

Even though hospital security had swept the new wing of the medical center earlier that morning, Zane had insisted it be swept again prior to the prince's arrival. Because Celine, Zane, and the rest of the security detail had needed to go to the hospital earlier, and because Leo had thrown a small fit about hardly ever getting to drive his favorite car, Anna got to enjoy a breathless twenty-minute ride zipping past rows of businesses and palm trees on Route 1 in a red Ferrari convertible.

The third time Leo gunned it to seventy miles per hour between stop lights, Anna felt like she needed to say something. "I know it's a performance car, but don't you think that's a little much?" she yelled over the wind.

He flashed her a toothy grin. "This is Miami!" he yelled back. "Besides, haven't you ever heard of diplomatic immunity?"

Anna shook her head, gripping the door handhold as Leo swerved around a slow-moving delivery truck. She couldn't deny the thrill, even if she wasn't the one driving. Maybe she'd have to talk to Hannah about an upgrade after the mission. Hot Banana wasn't bad, but it was no Ferrari.

Leo slowed a little when they reached the access road that wound around the hospital toward the bay. He turned into the parking lot nestled between the water and one side of the hospital and quickly found an empty spot. They walked from the parking lot along the seawall to the main entrance where a small crowd waited for them. Given the excellent location, patients in this hospital might be tempted to stay sick just for the view.

An older woman in a gray business suit and flowing white lab coat came bustling out to meet them. "I'm so sorry, Your Highness. If you had brought your car here to the turnaround, one of the attendants could have parked it for you."

The prince waved his hand dismissively. "I love driving that car. Even in parking lots."

Anna could attest to that fact. She'd never seen someone leave tire marks skidding into their parking space. And if she had, it certainly hadn't been in the parking lot of a hospital.

Once inside the air-conditioned building, the head of the new maternity ward, Dr. Jameson, introduced several of the doctors, nurses, and administrators who would be part of the ribbon cutting. Leo graciously greeted each of them by name and asked how they were doing. Anna remembered the names just long enough to tap them out in her phone the first chance she got, though she wasn't sure she hadn't mixed up any of the first and last names. She'd have the Banana Girls run checks on them later, just in case.

The group was ushered up to the fifth floor where the ceremony would take place. Leo wasn't the only VIP in attendance. The mayor and several city commissioners, along with members of their staff, were also there for the ribbon cutting. The hospital had set up a lectern at the front of a small instruction room with a long red ribbon attached from one wall to the other.

Behind the lectern, there was a small stage for Leo and the other VIPs. As Leo's close security for the event, Anna was considered his personal guest, so she was seated next to him. She had to admit that working close security had its advantages. From her place at Leo's side, she could see everyone in the room: the requisite press on the front row, hospital employees and neighbors from the local community, even the various staff members—including Zane, Kaitlynn, and Leo's bodyguards—lining the back walls. She was in the perfect position to keep the prince safe.

One by one, the VIPs stood and delivered short speeches about the momentous nature of the event or their gratitude to the various sponsors or the good that the new maternity ward would do for the community. As another VIP stood to say a few words, Anna glanced around her and realized that more than half of the guests seated with her on the stage had already spoken.

She leaned over to Leo and whispered, half joking, "I won't have to stand up and say anything, right?"

He cocked an eyebrow at her. "You're not ready with a speech to give?" he whispered back. "Everyone else is." His face was dead serious.

A feeling of dread—not unlike her frequent nightmare of showing up to a class presentation unprepared—bloomed in her stomach. "No, no one told me I had to say anything," she hissed. It wasn't that she minded public speaking, but she preferred having the chance to prepare herself.

Without really thinking, Anna reached out and clutched Leo's hand. His fingers wrapped around hers and squeezed back reassuringly. Several seconds passed as the panic welled up inside her. She scanned the faces of the gathered crowd, trying to think of a few words of gratitude or hope that she could share. Maybe she could just borrow themes from the others that had already spoken. The room suddenly felt much hotter than before.

Leo leaned in close to her ear, his breath tickling her cheek. "Try not to react to what I'm about to tell you," he whispered.

Anna nodded ever so slightly.

Leo's soft voice continued. "If I'd known that putting you in an uncomfortable situation would make you want to hold my hand, I might have done it much earlier."

Anna resisted the urge to turn wide eyes on him. "This is your fault?" She made a subtle gesture from herself toward the lectern.

She could hear the laughter in his voice when he whispered again. "I'm not quite as guilty as you think." He let his fingers intertwine with hers. "The only crime I've committed is prolonging the chance to hold your hand by making you think you'll have to give a speech."

The blood rushed from Anna's head, and she felt a little dizzy. "I don't have to give a speech?"

"No. But unfortunately, I do." He squeezed her hand and

then released it to join in the applause for the speaker.

He stood and approached the lectern. At that moment, Anna was tempted to either hug him out of relief or take him down herself. This prince could be so charmingly aggravating.

In his speech, Leo talked about reaching out to help our neighbors and something about the growth of families. Anna really couldn't have given much more of a report on what he said. All she knew was that she didn't have to speak to a crowd full of strangers.

After the applause for Leo's remarks died down, the other VIPs all stood and moved toward the ribbon. Leo coaxed Anna to join them with a beguiling smile and an offered hand. They each took an oversized pair of scissors and posed in front of the red satin band for photos.

"Are you terribly upset with me?" Leo said through his smile.

"I haven't completely decided yet."

The clicking of camera shutters buzzed.

"Well, I have a confession to make. I'm afraid I'm not above petty ploys to get a beautiful woman like you to grab my hand or lean close to me." His smile never faltered as the flashes continued. "How do you feel about scary movies?"

Anna laughed through her fake smile. "I suppose I could watch a scary movie with you, if you need someone to protect you from the big, bad monsters."

The prince's smile grew even wider. "I'm not too proud to take you up on that offer."

At the signal, the VIPs all cut the ribbon and the crowd clapped politely.

Anna stayed close to Leo's side as guests and other VIPs thanked him for coming and made small talk about the hospital or Leo's family. She smiled and offered small comments where appropriate.

As the event wound down and the crowd filtered out of the room, Anna had an opportunity to speak to him without so many listening ears. Fortunately for the prince, her fury had faded. She hadn't been forced to give a speech, and a very small part of her had—begrudgingly—enjoyed holding Leo's hand for those few moments. She knew she was in trouble if such a simple gesture could have that effect on her. She needed to keep her guard up.

"So, the ribbon cutting ceremony at a maternity ward. That's a far cry from your typical pool party or night at the clubs," Anna said.

"Supposedly, it's good for my image. Or it makes me look responsible. Or something like that," the prince said with a grin.

Anna really did enjoy bantering with Leo. "True, but it doesn't quite fit with the young bachelor prince vibe. I mean, the majority of women in a maternity ward are either on duty, already in a relationship, or a little too young for you."

Leo let out a loud laugh. "You can blame my mother for the maternity ward part. It's a favorite cause of hers. Anytime she finds out about a maternity ward opening, whether or not it has anything to do with Luxembourg or the Grand Ducal Family, she will attend." He pointed to himself. "Or send a family member."

"Well, I agree with your mother. It's a good look for you." She glanced him up and down. "Especially in that suit. You look quite respectable."

He leaned a little closer and lowered his voice. "Looks can be deceiving, you know."

Anna rolled her eyes and looked the other way. "Don't spoil the moment."

Leo and Anna made their way out of the ribbon cutting room into the hallway, and Celine and the security detail followed. As they boarded the waiting elevator, they were joined by Dr.

Jameson. "Your Highness, thank you so much for being here for the ceremony. And I really would like one of our attendants to bring your car to the entrance."

"Really, it's no trouble. I quite enjoy acting like a regular American," Leo said.

Dr. Jameson's expression alternated between consternation and concern. Clearly she wasn't sure how to disagree with a prince. She just needed to spend more time with him. Anna found disagreeing with Leo came quite naturally.

As the group exited the elevator into the main lobby, Dr. Jameson continued, "But it reflects poorly on our hospital and the city of Miami. Really, Your Highness, I must insist."

Celine joined in the conversation. "I hate to contradict you, Your Highness, but I quite agree with Dr. Jameson, and I've already sent Kaitlynn to bring your car around."

Leo fished out the keys from his pocket and jangled them playfully in front of Celine. "How can she without these?"

"Spare," Celine deadpanned.

Leo sighed and turned to Anna. "Outsmarted again," he said with a shrug.

The group moved slowly through the atrium and out onto the sidewalk in front of the hospital's main turnaround drop-off area. The prince was gracious in his comments about the ceremony, though Anna could see in the lines near his mouth that he was frustrated by the fuss about him walking to get his own car.

A minute later, the deep growl of the Ferrari engine drifted toward them on the ocean breeze. Leo shot a look at Anna, and she could read the annoyance in his expression.

She leaned in and whispered, "Do you need to make some waffles with me when we get back to the villa? I hear it really helps."

His smile was warm. "Absolutely. You cook, I'll eat."

The Ferrari swung around the corner from the parking lot—engine purring—and glided along the waterfront road running to the hospital entrance. Kaitlynn revved the engine. She looked like she was having the time of her life, and Anna wished she'd been asked to go get the car. Without even braking, Kaitlynn hung the last turn into the hospital's drop-off area. With a broad grin on her face, she gunned the engine once more, and the roar echoed off the cement overhang. Now Kaitlynn was just showing off.

As the red sports car approached, Anna's muscles suddenly tensed.

It was coming too fast. What was Kaitlynn thinking?

Anna saw the moment when Kaitlynn's expression changed from concern to panic.

The car barreled toward the sidewalk and the gathered crowd.

Anna glanced from the car to Leo. Without any conscious thought, her brain judged the trajectory and the best place for escape. She grabbed Leo around the chest and tackled him into a nearby cluster of shrubs.

Screams echoed in the enclosed turnaround area as the Ferrari smashed into the yellow safety posts with a sickening crunch. A few seconds later, the belabored engine died.

Anna looked back at the chaotic scene, scanning for any additional threats. When she was sure they were safe, she helped Leo out of the bushes. His face and neck had a few scratches, but otherwise he looked unscathed.

Unfortunately, she couldn't say the same for the Ferrari. Leo's face fell when he saw what had become of his favorite car. It hadn't been moving fast enough to deploy the airbags, but probably just barely. The hood was crushed and crumpled from the impact with the bollard not two feet from where Leo had been standing.

Anna looked at Leo. "You okay?"

He nodded. "Yes. How's Kaitlynn?"

They moved to the side of the car. Kaitlynn was slumped over, clutching her shoulder.

"Are you okay, Kaitlynn?" Leo opened the door and knelt next to her on the passenger seat.

Kaitlynn looked up at them with wide unfocused eyes. She had a red mark on her forehead where it must have hit the steering wheel.

"She tried to kill the prince!" Dr. Jameson screamed, pointing at Kaitlynn.

Zane and the other bodyguards were close enough to the car to protect Leo, but really there seemed to be little danger from the injured agent.

Anna leaned closer. "Kaitlynn. Are you okay? What happened?"

"The brakes. Ow." She grimaced in pain as she moved her arm. "They were completely gone."

Several hospital employees had emerged from the front entrance, drawn by the commotion. Leo motioned to two attendants. "This woman needs medical attention, please."

They did a quick check on Kaitlynn's injuries then moved her gently to a wheelchair amid the fussing and protesting of Dr. Jameson.

Anna turned to Leo. "That doesn't make any sense. The brakes were fine earlier, weren't they?"

"You saw how often I used them on the way here." A guilty expression flashed across his face. "I hope my hot rodding didn't wear them out. What if it's my fault Kaitlynn crashed?"

"Are you completely ruling out the idea that she was trying to kill you?" Anna asked.

Leo frowned. "She would've had plenty of chances before

this." He gave Anna an incredulous look. "Do you think she was trying to kill me?"

Anna glanced out at the bay, eyes unfocused. "No, I don't think so. I saw the look in her eyes right before she nearly crashed into you. It was pure terror."

"Then what could have happened?"

"Assuming it wasn't just bad luck, someone must have tampered with the brakes. We'll need to have a mechanic check it out."

"I'll have him do that." He rubbed his arm—the one that had taken the brunt of Anna's tackle. "Thanks for the save. I'm glad I have such quick-thinking employees."

"Don't forget that I'm not technically your employee," Anna said.

"The job's still open if you want it," he said earnestly.

"If it includes fending off harpoons and dodging runaway cars to keep you safe, I think I'll keep looking."

In the security van on the ride back to the villa, Leo arranged to have the Ferrari delivered to a special body shop that could both inspect the brake system and repair the damage. The rest of the drive was quiet and somber.

As they walked through the front doors of the villa, Leo's cell phone rang. "It's past midnight in Luxembourg. Why is my mother calling so late?"

Celine averted her gaze from Leo. "I may have sent an update to the Grand Duchess about your incident this afternoon."

Leo took a deep breath. "Oh well, better get this over with." He answered the phone. "Hello, Mother." A long pause. "Yes, I'm fine." Walking into the front parlor, he shut the door behind him.

Anna decided it would be a perfect opportunity to make a call to Club Banana. She hurried upstairs to her room and sat on her bed in front of the TV she had repurposed as a secure video conference screen. The call request went through almost immediately, and a video of the Club Banana living room popped onto the screen. Anna had only been gone three days, but seeing the familiar room made it feel like three weeks.

Susan waved enthusiastically from the couch, her injured leg propped up on a nearby ottoman.

"Hi, Susan," Anna said.

"Hey, Anna. How's Miami life treatin' ya?" the redhead asked.

Anna shrugged. "Some fun, but mostly work."

"How about the investigation?"

"Yeah, that's the reason for the call. Could you put in a request for the security camera footage from Mercy Hospital? I need the video from the east parking lot."

"Will do," Susan said with a smile. "What do you need the security video for?"

"I'm trying to figure out who could have sabotaged the prince's Ferrari at the hospital today," Anna answered.

Susan sat up straight. "Wait. Rewind." She twirled her hands in front of her. "What was that about the prince's Ferrari sabotaging the hospital?"

Anna grinned. It was one of Susan's favorite things to do when she didn't catch something—to intentionally mix the items up in a silly way. "We were at the hospital for a ribbon cutting, and when the other agent brought the car around to pick him up, she nearly rammed into us."

"Is the prince okay?" Susan asked.

"Except for a few scratches and a bruise on his arm, he's fine. The other agent has a torn rotator cuff, though."

"What makes you think it's sabotage?" Hannah called from off camera.

"The other agent says the brakes were completely gone," Anna explained. "Leo is having the repair shop take a look at them."

"Hmm." Susan tapped her chin looking thoughtful.

"That still doesn't mean sabotage," Hannah said. "They might have just failed."

"Catastrophically? At that exact moment? I doubt it," Anna said. "Leo and I were driving up Route 1 just a few hours earlier, and believe me, the brakes were working."

"Wait, so you're saying someone sabotaged the brakes so that the other agent would crash into the prince?" Susan asked. "That doesn't seem like a very reliable plan for an attack."

Anna sighed. Susan was right. How would the saboteur know that Kaitlynn's driving style was to rev the engine in low gear, avoiding using the brakes?

Driving style.

"I think I've got it," Anna said suddenly.

Susan did an overexaggerated jump in her seat.

"What if the attack wasn't meant to be the car crashing into the prince in front of the hospital, but the prince crashing the car into the ocean?"

"Yeah, but again, how would the saboteur know that the prince wouldn't try to use his brakes until later, when he drove near the water?" Susan asked.

Anna thought back to the layout of the hospital and its adjoining parking lot. "Both the parking lot and the front of the hospital come right up to the edge of the bay, and there's a short road from the parking lot winding next to the water. The attacker wouldn't have to know when he would use his brakes. All they'd need to know is that Leo likes to hit his top speed in the car every chance he gets."

Susan frowned. "Even in a hospital parking lot?"

"He left skid marks on the way in," Anna said.

Susan's eyes went wide. "Wow. So if he had been the one to get the car, he would have laid rubber in the parking lot and then gone straight out into the water."

Anna nodded slowly, playing in her mind the way things would have gone if Kaitlynn hadn't gone to get the car. The woman really had saved the prince's life, and she didn't even know it.

"Okay, I'll get the security footage and send it to you. Hopefully it'll show something," Susan said.

"Thanks. And by the way, is Mari there?" Anna asked.

"Yeah, hang on." Susan walked off camera and yelled down the hall. "Mari! Anna wants to talk to you!"

A few seconds later, Mari came and sat next to Susan on the couch. "Hey, Anna. What's up?"

"I'm assuming since I've only been gone a few days that you're still on speaking terms with Trey."

Susan snorted. "Speaking terms? Is that what we're calling it these days? Just because Hannah gives him access to Club Banana for Mari's mission, he thinks he can come over all the time now. We can't seem to get rid of him. Not that Mari wants to get rid of him." Susan glanced at Mari, her eyebrows moving up and down suggestively.

Mari's cheeks flushed an adorable pink. She nodded. "Yeah, I'll probably see him tonight."

Anna tried to hide her smile at the girl's embarrassment. "Great. Can you ask him how hard it would be to disable the brakes on a Ferrari?"

"What model?" Mari asked without missing a beat.

Susan swung her head dramatically and stared wide-eyed at Mari. Anna felt the same way, but restrained herself on the theatrics.

"You've been hanging around with Trey long enough that you know the difference between the models of cars?" Susan asked.

Mari laughed. "No. But I've been hanging around him long enough to know that's the first thing he'll ask me."

Anna scrunched up her face, thinking about the car. "Um, let's see, it was engraved all over the interior. Porto-something? Does that sound right?"

Mari shrugged and Susan copied the gesture. "I'll ask Trey," Mari said. "And you need to know about disabling the brakes? Are you planning to start a life of crime?"

"No." Anna laughed. "We think the prince's car might have been sabotaged."

Anna heard the front door of Club Banana close. Suddenly Katie ran into view, eyes wide. "Leo's car was sabotaged?! Is he okay? What happened? Do I need to come down there to help?"

Anna held up her hands in a calming gesture. "It's okay. He's fine."

Katie looked visibly relieved. She glanced around before continuing. "But you're sure you don't need me to come down and help out? I don't even need the prince to send the private jet; I could fly commercial."

Anna laughed. "No, Katie, I'm pretty sure I've got things under control."

Katie shrugged. "So, what's he like in real life? Is he, you know, like a real prince?"

"Yes, he's definitely a real prince," Anna said.

Katie sat next to Susan on the couch and plopped her chin into her hands. "No, I mean, is he like a storybook prince?"

A grin spread on Anna's face. "Actually, he's just a normal guy. He sometimes makes dumb jokes, he definitely thinks he's smarter than he really is, and every once in a while, his hair is an adorable mess."

Katie just stared at her starry-eyed so Anna continued. "But he is very handsome, and occasionally he's even charming." She didn't dare tell the Banana Girls how the prince's charms were chipping away at her resolve.

Katie sighed and Susan mimicked her with an even grander sigh. Anna couldn't help but smile. After a long pause, Mari spoke up, probably trying to keep the call official. "Okay, so I'll check with Trey and let you know."

"And I'll forward the security recording when I get it," Susan added.

"And I'll check the close-up pictures of the prince's last beach party," Katie volunteered. "Just to make sure there aren't any clues hidden in his—"

"Thanks everyone," Anna said, definitely wanting to cut Katie's train of thought short. "Tell Hannah hi for me," Anna added.

Mari looked off screen. "Anna says 'hi'."

Susan waved in what was obviously Hannah's direction.

"Bye, Anna," Hannah's voice called. "Be a good girl."

Anna rolled her eyes and switched off the call before she got a lecture from her friend.

Chapter 8

When Anna returned from her jog the next morning, she saw messages from both Mari and Susan waiting for her. After a quick shower, she grabbed her tablet and stopped by the pantry on her way up to the breakfast nook. She only needed to bring a few ingredients this time, so it was an easy trip.

Leo was already waiting for her at the table inset into the bay windows. "Oh, good. I was hoping you'd be frustrated about something again," he said with a broad smile.

Anna rolled her eyes. "Actually, I'm not frustrated this morning."

"That's bad news."

"Sometimes I cook because it helps me think."

"Is your thinking food as tasty as your frustration food?" the prince asked.

"You'll have to wait and see," she answered with a teasing smirk.

The prince watched her as she arranged ingredients and set out mixing bowls. "So what is the cooking going to help you think about?" he asked.

"I've been thinking about Kaitlynn's accident yesterday." Anna cut butter into the flour and brown sugar mixture as she talked. "You know, Leo, that could have been us in the Ferrari when the brakes went out."

"I wouldn't have hit the safety post. I would have swerved," he said with confidence.

"Leo." Anna stopped her mixing and fixed him with a stare. "You would have floored it in the parking lot and gone over the seawall."

"Ah, you're still frustrated about my driving yesterday. That should help with whatever you're making."

"I'm not joking, Leo."

The prince nodded slowly, his flippant grin turning more serious. "I know. And you're right. It's a sobering thought that we very nearly had to escape a sinking sports car."

"Or very nearly drowned in it." She arched a brow at him.

"Yes. That's true." Leo sighed. "I think I'll be more careful about my driving whenever I get the Ferrari back."

They were both silent as Anna continued adding ingredients. After pouring the crumb cake batter into a pan and putting it in the oven, she grabbed the tablet and sat down next to Leo.

"Hopefully my friend sent me the surveillance video from the parking lot yesterday," she said as she opened the message from Susan.

Anna turned the screen toward Leo and they watched as various cars crossed the road in front of the hospital parking lot. Leo leaned toward Anna until their shoulders touched. It wasn't absolutely necessary to be close to see the screen, but Anna couldn't bring herself to put more distance between them. She promised herself she would as soon as the video was over.

A few seconds later, a red Ferrari zoomed into the picture,

took the hairpin turn into the lot, and screeched into a parking stall.

"That was some good driving," Leo said.

Anna wanted to glare at him, but with him sitting so close, she didn't dare for fear of their faces touching. Seeing it from an outside perspective, she had to admit that the prince was a skilled driver. Maybe it was the experience of sitting in the passenger seat with someone else completely in control that had her so unnerved the day before.

The Anna and Leo on the screen walked across the street toward the hospital's main entrance and out of view. Right as she wondered whether they would have to fast forward, the timestamp jumped ahead twenty minutes. A large supply truck pulled up to the stop sign on the small hospital access road. Right as it completely blocked the camera view of the Ferrari, it came to a stop. And it didn't continue forward after obeying the stop sign. In fact, the truck was still there a moment later when a white mid-sized car pulled up behind it, swerved past, and turned into the parking lot. The white car passed behind the supply truck, but didn't emerge into view on the other side.

Anna paused the video and glanced at Leo. "Where'd the white car go?"

Leo shrugged. "Maybe it parked."

Anna rewound the video to the moment before the supply truck blocked the view of the lot. There were no other open parking spaces near the Ferrari. "Where?" Anna held out a hand to the screen.

"Keep watching. I want to see what happens next," Leo said.

Anna let the video continue to replay. The truck stopped again and a few seconds later the white car drove by and disappeared behind it again. And then they waited. And waited.

After three minutes, the driver of the stopped truck finally looked up and pulled through the intersection, turning right toward the front of the hospital.

The white car was still there near the Ferrari. The truck had moved out of the way just in time to show a woman with short blonde hair and sunglasses getting back into the sedan.

Leo gasped.

Anna instinctively paused the video and jerked her head in his direction. She had to pull back to avoid brushing her nose against his cheek. "What?" she asked.

Leo stared at the screen, eyes narrowed, shaking his head. "I can't believe . . . it's not possible."

"What's not possible? Do you know that woman?"

He tilted his head and squinted. "Well, it almost looks like Heather. That's even the kind of car she drives."

Anna turned back to the screen. She resumed the video, and they watched the woman in the white car pull out of the parking lot and drive away.

Leo held out a hand toward the screen. "We couldn't see what she was doing. That doesn't prove anything."

The video jumped forward again to show Kaitlynn getting in the car and driving out of the parking lot onto the access road toward the hospital entrance at a nice, even speed, never braking. Then the video stopped.

"Leo, if something happened to your car, it must have been when that truck was blocking the camera."

"What about the rest of the video? What about the missing parts?" he asked.

"We can get the full video, if you would like. But my co-agents are pretty thorough. They would have sent the relevant portions."

He shook his head again.

"Besides," Anna continued. "Why would that truck driver

wait at the stop sign for so long checking his phone? Don't you think that looks suspicious?"

"He might have been lost."

"He stopped a full ten feet from the sign. He knew exactly where the truck needed to be to block the Ferrari from the security camera."

"Let's say, for a moment, that I believe you," Leo said, his mouth a thin, serious line. "If the truck guy was working for the woman in the sedan, why did he pull away two seconds before she got in the car? He sat there for three minutes. If he'd waited three more seconds, the woman would have been unrecognizable."

"That's a good question. I don't know," Anna said, frowning. "But I'll have my friends look a little closer at the car, maybe they can enhance the video to see the license plates."

Leo sat back in his seat and folded his arms. "Well, I don't care what they find, I refuse to accept that Heather would sabotage my car. She loved that car. We would drive around the city together all the time in the Ferrari."

Anna raised an eyebrow at him. "Did you usually drive like you did with me yesterday?"

Leo gave her a sheepish look. "I suppose."

"Then she would know your driving habits. She would know that a cut brake line in that particular parking lot would mean you being dumped into the ocean."

"You're suggesting that my ex-girlfriend knows how to cut the brake lines on a Ferrari Portofino?"

Anna clapped her hands together. "I knew it was a porto-something."

Pulling the tablet away—and completely ignoring Leo's look of confusion—Anna established a secure connection with Club Banana and opened the message from Mari. "I asked one of my co-agents last night to let me know how hard it would be to

115

sabotage the brakes on your car." Anna scanned Mari's reply. "See, look, she says that the brake system is not openly accessible, but it could be easily done if someone knew what they were looking for." She glanced at the prince.

"And why would Heather want to kill me?"

"I don't know, but I plan to ask her when I stop by her office this morning."

"Is it alright if I don't go with you to the interrogation?" The prince's smile looked more like a wince. "It might be awkward."

"I wouldn't have wanted you there anyway. You're too distracting."

Leo puffed up his chest and lifted his chin. "You just can't seem to concentrate when I'm around?"

"You'll distract the people I need to talk to, not me," Anna lied.

Leo's face sank into a feigned pout. "Fine. But that leaves me with Jessie and the muscle men for security at my lunch."

Anna remembered the anti-hunger event Leo was scheduled to attend. She patted him on the hand. "I'll try to be quick so I can meet you there."

Her assurance seemed to satisfy him. That and when the crumb cake came out of the oven.

With some help from the Banana Girls, Anna was able to track down the address of Heather Diaz's clothing startup business, Fashion East. The company's headquarters were on the third floor of a medium-sized office building north of the Miami river.

Anna found an open parking spot around the corner in front of a jewelry store and walked back to Heather's building. Once on the right floor, Anna pushed through the frosted glass doors and marched into the reception area.

"May I help you?" the receptionist asked with a fake smile.

"Anna Rivers. I'm here to speak to Heather Diaz please." Anna handed the woman her official federal identification.

The receptionist glanced at the ID and handed it back. "Heather isn't available at the moment. May I put you on her schedule?"

"I need to speak to her today. I can wait." Anna moved toward a comfortable-looking sofa when the receptionist spoke again.

"Ms. Rivers, Heather is actually not in the office. She had an event she needed to attend, but she's planning to be back later this afternoon, probably around two or three."

Anna considered the receptionist. Was she simply covering for her boss? Or was Heather really not in the office? Obviously Anna could wait her out. Maybe Heather would show up earlier—or maybe the receptionist would crack under Anna's withering gaze. She seemed sincere enough, but sometimes it was the most sincere-looking ones that were trouble.

After fifteen minutes of a one-sided staring contest on Anna's part, she decided that it would take more to get the receptionist to crack. Or more likely, Heather really was away from the office. Either way, Anna didn't want to waste any more time.

Not only that, but she had said she'd meet Leo at the anti-hunger event.

"I'll come back this afternoon. Go ahead and put me on her schedule for three." Anna figured she might as well make it official.

The receptionist's glossy fingernails tapped away on her computer. "I've got you down for three o'clock."

"Thank you." Anna turned and left the waiting area.

Back in the car, she navigated the tight city streets until she left the looming Miami skyscrapers behind. Following the car's navigation system, she drove through blocks of shops and apartments. The farther she went, the older the apartment complexes got and the more prevalent the graffiti became.

Under the shadow of a freeway overpass, Anna found the address for Leo's foundation event. She double checked the information Leo had given her. It was the right place. She just couldn't imagine why the prince would be holding a fundraiser lunch in such a seedy part of the city. Around the corner, she found the prince's security van parked next to a reclaimed wall of community art. She must be in the right place.

Anna parked near the van and walked toward the entrance of the building. What had looked like a crowd of less fortunate citizens milling around in front of the building was actually a line of people waiting to get inside.

She bypassed the line and stepped through the doors into a cavernous space that must have been a small warehouse in a former life. The area was clean and well-lit, with long tables spaced in even rows, about half of them filled with people eating. Laughter and conversations echoed off the walls, giving the large room a happy atmosphere.

This was not at all the event she had anticipated. Instead of hardwood, the floor was cement painted in chipped gray. Instead of crisp, white linens, the tables were spread with well-worn red gingham. Dixie cups instead of champagne flutes.

A long cafeteria-style serving line stretched across one end of the room. Anna walked in the direction of the serving line, still somewhat in a daze. Then she saw something that surprised her even more. Leo stood in the middle of the buffet counter, wearing an ugly T-shirt and a frilly yellow apron, serving up hotdogs with a pair of tongs. Jessie stood next to him, also working the buffet.

When Leo saw Anna, he waved his tongs which—much to the dismay of the lady waiting for her food—still held a hotdog. "Anna! Come help serve the food," he called.

Anna walked around the buffet and stood behind him and Jessie. Below the apron, he wore frayed jeans and sneakers. Jessie was also dressed sensibly for working in a soup kitchen. Anna wished she'd been told about the casual dress code.

"What's on the menu?" Anna asked cheerfully.

"Grab an apron and join us." Leo pointed—with tongs and hotdog again—toward a nearby closet.

Anna selected a flowery pink apron and returned to the buffet, fastening the ties around her waist. She wondered what the prince wanted her to help serve given that there was no extra serving station near him. Anna hovered near Leo and Jessie watching the procession of guests file through the food line.

Jessie glanced over at Leo who continued serving hotdogs. He was completely oblivious of the awkward situation he'd placed them in. She turned to Anna and held out her tongs. "I'll go see if they need any help at the dessert station."

"Thanks," Anna said, smiling warmly at her fellow agent.

Jessie didn't return the smile with quite as much warmth. She cast one more quick glance at Leo's back before moving away to another part of the serving line.

Anna stepped up to the buffet next to Leo. "I had no idea this was what you meant when you mentioned the anti-hunger event," she whispered.

"What did you think I was talking about?"

She shrugged as she worked diligently to capture a hot dog from the water of the serving tray. "I thought it was going to be an upper crust luncheon or something."

Leo stared at her as if she wasn't making any sense. "Why? Those people don't need any help finding food."

Anna couldn't argue with that logic.

As various men and women came through the line, Leo served them all with a happy smile, always offering a second hotdog whether they had grabbed two buns or not. Sometimes he asked the person's name, sometimes he called them by name like he would a longtime friend. He always introduced them to Anna as if they were welcomed guests of honor.

Despite her initial shock, she couldn't help but admire Leo's ability to converse with people who were clearly outside his social sphere. Maybe it came with wearing jeans and a cheap T-shirt, maybe it was just in the prince's nature, but he seemed to have a gift for making people feel special.

"Princess Viviana!" the prince suddenly shouted.

Anna looked down the serving line and saw a little girl with blonde hair and pink cheeks who looked about six or seven years old.

"Prince Leo!" the girl called back, bouncing up and down on her toes. "Bonjour!"

"Bonjour. Ça va? I can tell you've been practicing your French," Leo said as he placed a hotdog on her plate.

The little girl nodded vigorously, pigtails bobbing.

"Viviana, I want to introduce you to my friend Anna," Leo said.

"Bonjour, Viviana." Anna imitated the greeting.

"Do you speak French, too?" she asked.

"No, but I'm a fast learner," Anna replied. "Maybe you'll have to teach me."

The adorable girl considered Anna for a moment then cast a furtive glance at Leo. "Maybe we should learn something besides French so we can talk about Prince Leo and he wouldn't understand us." She had a conspiratorial glint in her eyes.

"That's true," Anna said with a very purposeful nod in Leo's direction.

She kept staring intently at Anna. "Did you know our names end with the same sound?" Viviana asked.

Anna smiled as she leaned forward and whispered. "It's like we're in a special club together."

The little girl giggled.

"So, Viviana, why are you learning French?" Anna asked.

"I want to be ready when I meet a handsome prince someday," the girl answered very matter-of-factly.

Leo's brow went up, and he pointed to himself with the tongs.

Vivian shook her head. "No. I mean a *young* prince."

The prince's shoulders sagged as he looked over at Anna. "I guess I'm too old now," he said with theatrical dejection.

Anna patted his arm consolingly.

"Well, you're too old for me," Viviana said. "But you might be just right for Anna."

With a nod of agreement, Leo turned to Anna. "Did you hear that? I'm just right for you."

"She said 'might be'," Anna corrected.

Viviana's mother stood behind the young girl, apologizing to the other people in the serving line, though none of them seemed annoyed. They just held their plates out for Leo to serve them as he continued his conversation with the precocious girl.

Viviana tilted her head and considered Anna. "Are *you* a princess?"

Anna choked on a laugh.

Leo leaned over and whispered. "Do you want to be?"

Anna brandished the tongs at him, brow arched. "Don't joke about that sort of thing."

Leo did have the decency to pretend to look frightened as he placed a hotdog on the next plate.

Anna turned back to Viviana. "Do I look like a princess?"

The little girl nodded. "You're beautiful like a princess. And you look like Tiana from *The Princess and the Frog*." Viviana put a hand to her mouth as a tiny gasp escaped. "Tiana . . . her

121

name ends like ours. Can she be in the club, too?" she whispered.

Anna nodded. "She's definitely in the club."

That seemed to satisfy Viviana. Her mother smiled shyly at the prince and Anna then tugged on Viviana's shoulder. "Come on, sweetie."

"Goodbye, Prince Leo. Goodbye, Anna, my secret club friend." Viviana waved as she walked away.

"Bye, Viviana," Anna said.

"Goodbye, Princess Viviana," Leo called out in a regal tone. "Rule your subjects with grace and kindness."

They continued serving the line of visitors, and Anna's gaze lingered on Leo's increasingly handsome face as he smiled and greeted the guests to his soup kitchen.

He must have noticed her attention, because after a few moments he glanced over at her. "You claimed to be immune to my incredibly distracting charisma, but I would say that doesn't seem to be the case."

Her smile grew as she returned her attention to serving.

Leo inclined his head, catching her eye. "Anything you would like to share? I am currently giving audience to girls named Anna." He glanced in the direction Viviana and her mother had gone. "Actually, to any girl whose name ends in -ana."

Anna shook her head and smiled. "I was just thinking how much my impression of you has changed."

Leo leaned toward her. "In a good way, I hope."

She nodded. "I probably shouldn't tell you this, but this side of you"—she waved her tongs to indicate the converted warehouse full of normally hungry people having a good meal— "is actually quite . . . attractive." Anna cringed at the admission. She hoped the prince wouldn't tease her for it.

A mischievous grin spread across his face. So much for that hope. He opened his mouth to say something.

At that moment, Celine stepped up between them. "Your Highness, have you seen Jessie? I thought she was working at this station with you."

Leo glanced around as if expecting Jessie to be nearby. "She was, but then Anna took her place."

Celine frowned. "And I wonder if it wouldn't make more sense to have you standing at the front of the line greeting the needy as they enter."

He replied with a quick shake of his head. "I'm greeting the people here. Besides, I want to be useful, not just a pretty face." He shot Anna a knowing look over Celine's shoulder.

Celine looked around at the gathered crowd and frowned. "I only thought, given your mother's desire that you improve your image, that you would want to make the most of the opportunity to look good in the public eye."

"I would rather be useful," the prince said firmly.

Celine dipped her head in acknowledgment of his wishes.

"In fact," the prince continued, pointing to their serving bins, "it looks like we're almost out of hotdogs. I'll go get some more."

"Your Highness, I really must protest. Let Anna go get the hotdogs. Fetching food is not an appropriate activity for a member of the royal family."

"Celine, this is my foundation. I do all of this to feed people who are hungry. If they need more hotdogs, I should be allowed to get the hotdogs. Also, you're implying that it's too lowly for me but not for Anna. I think that is very—"

"It's okay, Leo," Anna interrupted. "I can go get them. Besides, you should stay here greeting your guests."

"Thank you, Miss Rivers," Celine said.

With a sigh, Leo nodded. "Fine. There's a large walk-in

freezer down this hall and to the left." He pointed with his tongs. "The boxes of hotdogs should be on a shelf straight to the back."

Anna handed her tongs back to the prince and started down the hall.

"Oh, and the handle on the freezer door sticks sometimes. You might have to jiggle it," Leo called after her.

The prince's instructions were perfect. She walked down the main hall and turned left at a branching corridor. The freezer was easy to spot; it was the only stainless steel door in the hall. She peeked in through the inset windows and saw the rows for frozen food stacked on shelves. Anna tried the handle. It wouldn't open. She jiggled the handle, but still nothing. As she wrenched it to the left, she thought she heard the latch almost catch, but not quite. She was about ready to try swearing at it when she heard footsteps approaching.

"I should have just come with you. It's a very tricky latch. Bob and I are the only ones who can get it open," Leo said. He took hold of the handle and jiggled, pressed, pulled out, then turned.

Anna pointed to the now-open door. "You didn't say that. All you said was 'jiggle it'."

With a broad smile, the prince bowed her into the spacious freezer. "I must guard some secrets. Why else do you think they keep me around?" Leo joined her, letting the door close softly behind him.

"I bet it would be nice to sneak back here on a hot summer day," Anna said.

He grinned. "I've done that once or twice."

"How many more hotdogs do we need?" Anna asked when she reached the correct shelf.

"Two more boxes? That's a hundred hotdogs. We can always come back for more."

They each hefted a box and walked back to the door of the freezer. Leo grabbed the interior handle and twisted, but the door didn't open. He tried twisting the other way, but nothing happened.

"Is there a trick to getting it opened from the inside, too?" Anna asked with a small laugh.

Shaking his head, Leo frowned at the handle. "No. I've never had any trouble with the handle on this side."

Anna set her box on a nearby shelf. "Let me try."

The prince stepped aside, and Anna twisted and jiggled and turned the knob to no avail. She huffed her defeat and looked back at Leo. "Now what?"

"Fortunately, there's a panic button." Leo pointed to a white box that looked sort of like a fire alarm. He pulled down on the latch.

"It looks old. Does it still work?" Anna asked.

"I don't know, I've never had to use it," Leo said.

Anna glanced at the shelves lining the freezer. "Is there something we can use to bang on the door?"

They both looked around for something solid. "Nothing but frozen food and cardboard boxes, unless you want to take a shelf apart," Leo said.

"Well, I'm sure Celine will come and find you pretty soon. It's sort of her job to follow you around," Anna said.

"She won't find us for a while," Leo replied. "I told her I was going to the bathroom."

Anna gaped at him. "Why would you tell her that?"

"Because I *was* headed to the bathroom when it occurred to me that you would never be able to get the door open on your own."

Anna put her hands on her hips. "I would have gotten it eventually. I might have gotten it even sooner if a certain prince

125

had given me better instructions." She leveled a playful glare at him.

Leo spread his arms wide. "But then you would have been stuck in here alone without a certain prince to cuddle with for warmth."

Anna laughed, her breath swirling in frosty clouds between them. "Do you just hang out around women waiting for the chance to use lines like that?"

He shrugged. "Some might call it a superpower."

A second later, Celine's eyes peeked over the edge of the door's inset window. Her voice was muffled through the glass. "Your Highness, what happened?!" The outside handle jigged and turned, but the door didn't budge.

"The latch must be broken," Leo yelled to his chief of staff.

The woman pulled and twisted and jerked on the handle, her eyes wide and wild.

"She's going to hurt herself," Anna observed.

"Celine, go get help," the prince called through the glass. "Have Zane call the fire department."

Celine nodded and hurried away.

"I guess all we can do now is wait." Anna looked around the frosty space for a place to sit. Nothing but cold metal shelves and a colder cement floor. She grabbed an opened box of meat and dumped the bags of seasoned diced chicken on the shelf. Then she broke out the bottom of the box, folded it flat, and handed it to Leo.

He took the box with a confused look.

"That's for your royal butt," she said.

He laughed and sat in front of the door on the makeshift seat. Anna repeated the process with a box of ground beef and sat on the ground next to him. After a few moments, his shoulder brushed against hers. She leaned into him, enjoying the tiny bit of extra warmth. He glanced at her, a small smirk tugging at the corner of his mouth.

"It's for warmth," she explained defensively.

Leo nodded. "Of course." He took her hands in his. She resisted. "For warmth," he repeated back as he rubbed his hands over hers.

After a few minutes, she returned the favor and rubbed the outsides of his hands. The colder her hands got, the easier it was to rationalize holding hands with the prince. "If I had known Miami was this cold, I would have brought my winter coat."

Leo smiled, his teeth beginning to chatter. "I don't even have a coat here in Miami. My good winter coat is back in Luxembourg."

"Fortunately for me, I got trapped in the freezer with a prince," Anna said.

"Is that because I have such strong arms to wrap around you? Or because I have such a warm personality?"

"No. Because the fire department will work extra hard to rescue a prince." Anna rolled her eyes. His flirting was just as bad as ever, but she was starting to see through some of his bravado.

Leo chuckled, but it quickly set his teeth chattering.

After a minute or two more of pressing closer together and shivering, Anna spoke, "Why do you hide this side of you?"

"You mean this other side of me that's cold?" He gestured to his side that wasn't huddled against Anna. "You can have that side, too, if you want it."

Her attempt at a laugh through her shivering sounded slightly scary. "No, I mean the side of your personality that I'm finally getting to see today. Why don't you let everyone see that?"

"Most of the people in my social circle see what they choose to see." His voice was quiet, almost pensive.

Anna considered the prince's declaration. Maybe she had misjudged him as well. She had just assumed that he was a stuck-up party prince with no real depth. And it might have stayed at that if it weren't for the small glimpses at something deeper.

A sudden bang on the door drew their attention to the small window. Celine had returned with a firefighter at her side. "Are you still alright, Your Highness?" she yelled. Her eyes went wide when she saw them huddled together on the floor holding hands.

Leo waved to let them know they were still fine. The sounds of more twisting and wrenching of the outside handle was followed by tools rapping and scraping on the door.

The prince cleared his throat. Anna could see his breath in the air in front of them.

"You mentioned earlier that your impression of me had changed," he said.

They had scooted together close enough that her head was now on his shoulder. She assumed he felt her nodding in response. "At the beginning of the week, I thought you were nothing more than a self-absorbed, rich prince who didn't care about anything but his next party or how beautiful the people around him were."

He puffed out a fogging breath of air but didn't reply.

"Now I know that's just a facade. Or maybe, like you said, it's what people choose to see," Anna said. "But deep down, I think you're caring and thoughtful." She squeezed the prince's hand—for warmth, or course.

Leo was quiet for several moments. "When I was young, my father took me on a trip into the mountains, just the two of us, and explained what was expected of me as a prince. He listed manners, and duties, and service. It sounded like hard work.

But the part that stuck with me was when he said, 'You must always be what the people need you to be'."

When he didn't continue, Anna ventured to ask, "And the people need a Party Prince?"

He chuckled. "I've embellished the role somewhat." He switched to holding and rubbing her hands in his. The only thing interrupting the tranquil silence was the incessant scratching and banging on the door.

After a minute Leo said, "Thank you."

"For what? Saying that you're a fake who wears a mask?" They shared a shivery laugh.

"No. For seeing me. I mean, for seeing me for who I am. Most people only see my title or my money."

"I meant what I said earlier—it really is quite attractive. Don't be afraid to show that side of you more often."

Leo turned toward her, their faces only inches apart. He gazed at her, those deep blue eyes searching her face, glancing at her lips. "Attractive to women in general? Or attractive to you specifically?" he asked softly.

Her heart raced. If she'd had any feeling in her fingers or toes, she was sure they would have been tingling. This was the danger of growing close to someone, emotionally, on a mission. And now that she knew the kind of man Leo was, it would be so much harder to be indifferent to him. Anna opened her mouth to tell him they needed to keep their distance, or that she couldn't let herself fall for him, or that he was far too charming for his own good, or anything. But all she could do was shake her head.

A sudden grinding sound reverberated through the freezer walls and pulled their attention back to the door.

Leo's mouth spread in a wide grin. "Being trapped in a freezer with a handsome prince is probably a pretty romantic experience, isn't it?"

There it was. He had slipped behind the mask again. Behind the jokes and the flirtation. Well, two could play that game. And it would probably be safer for Anna in the long run. She forced a playful smile. "It might be, except for the frostbite and the drilling."

The door shuddered with an earsplitting clang.

Anna quickly pulled back from Leo. He also leaned away from her, though not as quickly.

The door swung open to reveal an axe-wielding firefighter smiling proudly. Leo stood and helped Anna to her feet. The prince escorted her out into the welcome warmth as they thanked all of the firefighters and other well-wishers for their assistance during the rescue.

Leo glanced back at the mangled door. "I guess I'll have to finally replace that stupid handle."

As Anna drove back toward downtown Miami and her appointment with Heather Diaz, she rolled over the possibilities in her mind. Could someone have sabotaged the freezer door handle? Certainly possible, but unlikely.

That wouldn't have been a very solid plan to harm the prince. He was watched constantly. Anna was surprised it had taken Celine a whole five minutes to notice he was missing. So Leo had never been in any real danger. Besides, how could the attacker have known that Leo would end up in the freezer? It was nearly Anna in there alone. It was much more likely that the latch had simply failed. It had obviously been problematic already.

On the other hand, Leo said he was one of the few who knew how to open that latch. Maybe it wasn't such a longshot that he would have ended up locked inside. And it would have been the perfect cover given the fact that the latch was already failing.

But that still didn't solve the issue of how easily he could escape unharmed.

Questions about who could have done it turned Anna's thoughts back to Heather. What was the event that had taken her away from her office that morning? Could the ex-girlfriend have snuck into the soup kitchen and sabotaged the freezer handle without anyone noticing? That was a much more difficult challenge than blending in at a sandbar party or parking next to the prince's car in a public parking lot. A better question was: could Heather have done all three of those things? Anna intended to take a measure of her abilities during their interview.

A few minutes before three, Anna walked into the Fashion East waiting room. The receptionist immediately showed her to Heather's office. As Anna entered, the woman behind the wide, glass-topped desk stood and offered her hand.

"Heather Diaz," she said with a firm handshake.

"Anna Rivers." Anna produced her official identification. "I have a few questions for you about Prince Leo."

Heather arched an eyebrow before inviting Anna to sit in front of her desk. "What would you like to know?" She was slim, medium height, with deeply tanned skin, light green eyes, and dark brown hair

"You were in a romantic relationship with the prince, correct?"

Heather nodded.

"How long ago?" Anna asked.

The woman tilted her head and glanced out the window. "Let's see, Leo and I started dating about two years ago. I had just opened Fashion East a few months earlier, and I had the misguided notion that if I could get my foot into the Miami nightlife, I might find a celebrity who would love my clothing line and want to endorse it for me."

"And did you?" Anna pressed. "Find a celebrity to do endorsements for your company?"

"No. I met Leo. We started dating. I sort of got distracted." Heather smiled as if Anna should understand how easily that could happen.

Anna nodded and made a few notes on her phone. The only thing the note page said so far was "two years ago," but she pretended to write more as she formulated her next question.

"And when was the last time you saw Leo?"

"We ran into each other about a year ago at the home of a mutual friend. That is if you don't count seeing him on the news. I saw a video about the attack at the sandbar party. That was awful."

"Did you go to that particular party?"

"When Leo was attacked? No. I haven't been to any of those beach parties since we broke up," Heather said.

"Do you remember where you were on the day of the attack?" Anna asked as casually as she could.

Heather frowned and considered Anna. "No. That was a few weeks ago, right? I mean, I could look that day up in my schedule to see if—"

"What about something in more recent memory?" Anna abandoned all pretense of the polite investigator. "Where were you yesterday afternoon around two?"

Heather was taken aback by the sudden shift. "Uh . . . I was here at the office."

"Can anyone verify that you were here the entire time?"

"Only about two thousand people around the world," Heather said with a smirk.

It was Anna's turn to be surprised.

Heather tapped her keyboard and turned the monitor in Anna's direction. "Here's the livestream product launch I did yesterday at two. We had over two thousand attendees. It lasted about forty-five minutes." Heather pointed to the time stamp and duration.

Anna leaned forward, looking at the details of the video stream. They seemed authentic. "You livestream your product launches?" Anna wondered if that was common. She wasn't an expert in the fashion industry—that was more Katie's area of expertise.

"Crowdfunding got Fashion East off the ground. Even now that we've grown, we still want our backers to feel like they're a part of what we do. It's in our company culture."

Anna nodded. She could easily check that detail with Katie later, but for the moment she believed Heather's explanation. "What about this morning? Can your whereabouts be verified?"

"I attended a fashion show in Miami Beach. I'm sure I can be seen among the crowd in the video shots. I was on the third row." She paused for a moment. "What's this all about Ms. Rivers? Is Leo okay?"

"The prince is fine," Anna said reassuringly.

"What happened yesterday? Or this morning?"

"I can't really discuss the investigation, but there have been a few incidents," Anna said.

"And you think that I might have had something to do with them?" Heather's voice was steady which Anna found interesting considering that she just found out she was a suspect in an investigation.

"It's been suggested that you and the prince didn't part on amicable terms. That you broke up with him because he refused to endorse your new clothing line."

"Leo broke up with me," Heather said flatly.

Anna stared back at her. "He broke up with you?"

"Yes. He said he couldn't go through the same pain twice."

Anna frowned. "What did he mean by that?"

"You know, like he couldn't go through the same pain as he did with Amy," Heather said.

"Amy dated Leo before your relationship?"

Heather nodded. "And you know how that ended, right?"

It was painful to admit that she didn't know something, but Anna couldn't see any other way in this situation to get the information she needed. "No. What can you tell me about that?"

"Well, none of the prince's recent interactions with women will make any sense if you don't know about Amy Fulton." Heather sat back in her chair. Anna took it as a cue to make herself comfortable.

"Leo and Amy started dating during their senior year at the University of Miami. I didn't know him at the time, and he never talked about her much, but based on what I've gathered from mutual friends, he was madly in love with her. They dated for almost a year, and were getting pretty serious."

Anna smiled politely. A day ago, she wouldn't have believed the story of Leo in a committed relationship, but things had changed that morning.

"One night after a party, they were leaving a nightclub walking toward Leo's car, when they were attacked. It was probably a mugging gone wrong, but in the confusion, Amy was shot. Leo had a bodyguard trailing half a block behind them, but he wasn't close enough to stop the shooting, and the mugger got away."

"What happened to Amy?" Anna asked.

"The bullet must have grazed her spinal cord. She was in the hospital for several weeks and then in long term care and physical therapy for months after that."

Anna's distress must have shown on her face because Heather added, "She did eventually recover and learn to walk again. I think she's doing fine now."

"And what about the prince?" Anna asked, starting to understand the direction this was going.

"I think he wanted to stay close to Amy, to see her through everything. But her family insisted on being the ones to care for her and to help her through the recovery. Leo paid for everything she needed, but in the end, I think he sort of got squeezed out. Eventually, Amy told him he needed to go on with his life without her."

"That must have been tough," Anna said.

"Yeah. Plus, I don't think Leo ever really forgave himself for Amy's injury. I know he thought the attacker had targeted him personally, and that being with a prince had put Amy in danger."

Anna nodded. That sounded like Leo. "But how did that affect the end of your relationship?"

"It came to a head one day when we were walking around downtown after a party. We were accosted by a mugger. Nothing happened. Leo's bodyguard, Andre, was right behind us, and the mugger ran off. But it really shook Leo. He was a complete wreck for about a week. Finally, he broke up with me, saying he didn't want to put me at risk anymore and that he couldn't go through that pain again. Honestly, given the similarities in the two attacks, I'm not surprised that he decided to end things. Leo was seriously traumatized."

"How long after the attack on Amy did you start dating?" Anna asked.

For the first time, Heather looked slightly embarrassed. She dipped her head and glanced away from Anna. "I was the rebound girlfriend—though I didn't know it at the time. We met the week after Amy told him to move on with his life."

Leo's experience with Amy's shooting and then the attempted mugging with Heather explained so much about his current situation. Even his abrupt mood shift behind the dance club in Atlanta suddenly made sense. Anna was beginning to understand why he employed female close security agents instead of bodyguards, and why he hadn't been close to any women besides his agents since Heather. Maybe he figured they wouldn't be in as much danger as regular girls because they were trained for security and combat.

"I do still care for him," Heather said with a small shrug. "But in the end, it was probably for the best. I'm so involved in my startup and he's . . . a prince. It wouldn't have worked out."

"Thank you for your time, Ms. Diaz," Anna said as she stood.

"Please, call me Heather . . . assuming I'm not still a suspect."

Anna smiled and shook her head. "I'll check your explanation and verify your alibis, but I think what you've said makes sense. It certainly helps me understand Leo a lot better."

"He's kept his distance from women, emotionally-speaking, for a while now," Heather said. "Hopefully he won't be that way forever."

Anna hoped that as well. She just wasn't sure she wanted to be around to see it.

Chapter 9

The next morning, Anna skipped her usual run in order to get caught up on her school work. Most of her classes were video recorded, so she had stayed up the night before watching as many lectures as her bleary eyes could handle. Even still, it hadn't been enough. For the first time in the mission, she was almost grateful that Stacia had given her a two-week deadline. There was no way she could keep up in her classes if things continued much longer.

She sat at a patio table next to the villa pool, glad to at least be enjoying the morning sun and the view of the ocean while studying. Between the distraction of the view and the distraction of her thoughts on the investigation, she obviously wasn't as productive as she could be, but she was doing her best.

"Good morning, Anna," Leo's voice called out from the patio steps behind her.

Add one more distraction to the list.

He came and stood next to her cabana "What are you working on?"

"Thermodynamics." She tapped the screen of her tablet to show the textbook graphic.

"Well, let me know if I can be of any help," he said as he walked toward the pool.

Anna watched him remove his shirt and sandals, adjust his nicely-fitting swimming suit, and dive into the cool, blue water. Apparently Leo was making the best of a difficult situation, given that Zane had basically confined him to the villa for the weekend.

After he resurfaced, she called out to him. "Aren't you a bit too far away to help?"

"I have exactly zero experience with thermodynamics. It's really just moral support." He rolled onto his back and stroked across the pool. "Why don't you skip the studying and come join me?"

That would certainly not help her get caught up in her classes. But she convinced herself that she could use a short break from her studies. There would be plenty of time to get caught up later.

Anna stood and walked over to the swimming pool.

"Aren't you going to need your swimming suit?" Leo asked.

She sat on the edge of the pool deck. "No, why?"

The prince's brow furrowed. "I may not be an expert on all of your American customs, but usually a bathing suit is required for getting in the water, isn't it?"

"Going swimming with you—alone—is definitely not part of the job description." Anna needed to hold on to this. She needed to be good. She had always tried to set a good example of not breaking Rule Number One, even when it was tempting. And she was hanging by a thread as it was.

"Perhaps a rogue assassin is lurking in the deep end, and I'll need you to throw your body in the way to save my life."

Anna raised a brow.

"Fine. I really just want the company," he said. "Does that qualify?"

Anna swung her feet around and dangled them into the refreshing water. "I'm here, aren't I?"

"What if I want to start a water fight?" He moved slowly toward her, a small smirk on his lips.

Anna swung a well-aimed kick across the top of the water, splashing the prince full in the face. He counter-attacked with both hands, sending streams of water her way. Anna squealed and ducked while doubling her kick-splashes. He definitely had the advantage of already being wet, but eventually her superior firepower was too much for him.

"I surrender. I surrender," the prince yelled, holding his hands in the air.

Anna ceased her onslaught but eyed him warily as he sneaked over toward her. When he reached the side of the pool where she sat, he flicked a tiny bit of water on her leg.

"I'm sure somewhere in one of your college history classes, they taught about arms races, didn't they?"

"Yep," he said with a nod.

He looked unrepentant. Anna needed a distraction. "By the way, you'll be glad to hear that I don't think your ex-girlfriend is trying to kill you."

Leo suddenly became serious. "You mean Heather?"

"She has a solid alibi during the sabotage at the hospital."

"What about the car? Did your spy girl friends find out if it was Heather's?" he asked, drifting away on his back.

"The license plate wasn't visible for long enough to be sure, but what could be seen matches Heather's plates. But given that Heather's real car can be seen at the same time on some traffic footage my friends were able to track down, I figure the attacker must have faked the plates."

He smiled. "See, I told you she would never sabotage the Ferrari—or me, hopefully."

"We still don't know who *did* cut the brakes, though." Anna stared out at the ocean beyond the beach, deep in thought. "It has to be someone who knew you and Heather were dating."

Leo continued floating lazily around the pool. "Why do you say that?"

"Because the person in the security footage intentionally dressed up to look like Heather, drove a car like Heather's, and was sure to be seen for just a second even after going through all the trouble to not be seen for most of the sabotage. Whoever it was wanted us to think it was Heather."

"So where does that leave us?"

"Lots of dead ends, unfortunately," Anna said with a sigh. She sat in silence, watching Leo swim small circles nearby. She felt like that was how her investigation was going, too.

"The only constant so far is that you seem to be safest here at the villa," she finally said.

Leo turned toward her, suddenly alert. "If you're suggesting that we should be sequestered at the villa," he said, waggling his eyebrows. "I think that's an excellent idea, and I'd be happy to get started right away by kicking out all of the staff so we can be alone."

"I didn't say *we*. I said *you*," Anna corrected.

"Oh, then I don't like your idea at all." He went back to his lazy swimming stroke.

His outrageous flirtation made Anna smile, but it quickly faded. "I'm worried, though, Leo. I've been here for a week, and I don't feel like I'm any closer to figuring out who attacked you than I was when we first met. We only have one more week."

"So, you have one more week. You'll figure it out."

Anna wasn't sure if Leo was aware of his parents' threat to bring him home if she didn't succeed, but now was as good a time as any to tell him. "Leo, you're not going to like this, but it's not just *I* have one more week. It's *we* have one more week."

"What do you mean? I love the sound of *we*."

He could make her smile even when she was trying to deliver bad news. "If we can't solve the case by the end of the week, your family is going to insist that you leave the US and move back to Luxembourg."

Leo quickly stood up in the waist-deep water, skin dripping. "What? I haven't heard anything about this."

Anna shrugged. "It might be an idle threat, but that was the ultimatum communicated to my boss."

He dropped back down in the water, a clouded expression on his face. He floated a few circles in the water near her, muttering something unintelligible. Finally he turned back to Anna. "Fine, then what do we need to do to solve the case?"

"I've already hit a dead-end with the attack at the sandbar party. I'm not sure we'll ever know who did it. Same goes for the sabotage on your brakes. Basically, I think we'll have to wait for another attack."

"Great, let's tell Zane that we're going to start hanging out at the roughest bars in downtown Miami until someone attacks us. Maybe we can even pick a fight. I've always wanted to see an American bar brawl, and this might be my last chance."

Anna raised a brow at him. "You would be on your own—there's no *we* on that one," she said. "Besides, we don't need a random—and especially not provoked—attack from a stranger. We need to figure out who is behind the harpoon attack and the brake sabotage."

"Do you have a better way to bait the person into attacking me again?" Leo grinned, his playful personality firmly back in place. "I still think the bar fight is a good idea. I can just imagine you grabbing some huge guy by the throat—" Leo began an absurd pantomime of body slamming an invisible foe into the water.

Anna spoke over his antics. "Even if we consider the freezer incident a sabotage instead of an accident, all of the attacks so

141

far have happened when you were out at an announced event—one that was a part of your official schedule. We need you to get back out in public doing your normal activities."

Leo considered her for a moment. "Celine has already cancelled all of my events for the weekend. Zane didn't think it would be safe. Should I have her un-cancel them?"

"It wouldn't do any good this late. The attacker is probably planning things in advance. But if she hasn't canceled your Monday schedule, that might be a good place to start."

"I'll make sure Celine plans and announces the full schedule for Monday." The prince swam over next to her. "Just as soon as we're done with our swim." He leaned against the side of the pool, his chin propped on his hand, and stared up at her. "How do you make all this spy girl stuff look so easy?"

Leo had perfected the art of the confident come-on, which made her all the more hesitant to mention the next part. "There is one more thing." With an internal cringe, she pressed forward. "I'll need to stay close to you anytime we're out."

His eyes went wide with excitement. "I love this idea. In fact, why wait until Monday? You could start staying close to me right now."

Anna tried to glare at him, fighting the smile tugging at her lips. "You are impossible sometimes. Did you know that?"

With a sly grin, the prince nodded knowingly.

Chapter 10

Anna spent the rest of the weekend getting interrupted from finishing her homework by a cooped-up prince who was bored out of his mind. It wasn't all bad. Leo helped her prepare for an upcoming midterm by quizzing her on events in early US history. He was rather snobbish about the fact that US history began in what would be considered very recent history for Luxembourg. Anna pointed out that he didn't live during his country's ancient history anyway, so it hardly mattered. Leo also entertained her by translating her ethics essay into French, German, and even Luxembourgish.

Monday morning, after an uneventful run and morning routine, Anna stopped by Zane's office to check the day's itinerary. Apparently Zane and Celine had taken Anna's advice on letting Leo out of the villa for official royal family business because he was scheduled for a morning meeting and luncheon downtown at the Jamaican Consulate followed by a visit to a local software company looking to expand its European operations.

Now they would have to wait and see if the plan worked.

"Miss Rivers." Celine approached the security wing from her personal office nearby.

"Celine, it really is okay if you call me Anna," she said.

Celine smiled. "Thank you, Anna. Do you have much driving experience?"

Anna didn't think it would be appropriate to brag about her recent use of Hot Banana—the Banana Girl's color-shifting, convertible BMW sports coupe—to evade a pair of goons trying to kidnap Mari, so she kept that to herself. "Yes, I'm a good driver."

Celine's gaze fluttered upward, relief visible in her tired expression. "Oh, thank goodness. The chauffeur seems to have gotten his days mixed up and drove to the airport to pick up Minister Klein who isn't coming until next Thursday. On top of that, he got a flat tire on the way back, so Zane has gone to help him, and I don't know who else to ask to drive Prince Leo to the Jamaican Consulate," Celine said in one breath.

Anna put a hand on the woman's arm. "It's fine, Celine. I'm an excellent driver. And I was already scheduled to go with the prince to his meeting."

"Thank you, Miss Rivers. You are a lifesaver," Celine said with a sigh.

Anna smiled at the kind words. "Which car are we taking?" she asked. "Obviously the Ferrari is out of commission."

"Yes, and that's fortunate as well. It means I don't have to argue with His Highness about driving himself to an official consulate visit. I've told him so many times that he must be chauffeured on official visits, but he never listens to me."

"Don't I know it." Anna rolled her eyes in solidarity with the prince's overworked chief of staff.

She smiled knowingly at Anna. "Take the Mercedes. And you'll need to leave in"—she checked her watch—"fifteen minutes."

Anna hustled to the kitchen to grab a quick bite to eat. Who knew if she would be invited to eat at the consulate luncheon? She grabbed a small pastry and stuffed it—in a most unladylike way—into her mouth as she headed for the front foyer.

Leo stood at the bottom of the grand banister wearing blue chinos and a light pink dress shirt. He cleaned up pretty well for a Party Prince. For a split second, Anna's mind flashed to what he might look like in a tuxedo, or even better, full royal regalia.

Unsure of where that thought had come from, she shook her head and approached the prince. "You should probably be paying me double today because I'll be working two jobs," she announced.

Leo turned with a smile and an inquisitive brow. "I'm not even paying you for the first job, remember? Unless you're finally willing to take me up on the offer."

Anna gave a non-committal shrug and continued. "You're short one chauffeur today, and I happened to be available on short notice."

"Do you even know how to drive a stretch limousine?" he asked.

Anna put her hands on her hips and pushed out an offended huff. "I do, but it's got a flat, so we're taking the Mercedes."

Leo straightened. "If we're taking the Mercedes, then I can drive."

Anna shook her head. "Sorry. Official Ducal Family business means official Ducal Family rules. Celine says you have to have a chauffeur."

The corners of his mouth turned down in a faux pout. "As the resident prince, you would think I'd get my way around here every once in a while."

Anna reached out and touched his arm. "If I promise to drive fast and take sharp corners, will you be a happy prince?" she said in a sing-song voice.

His gaze shot to her, mischief in his eyes. "Are you patronizing me? Are you patronizing your prince? The penalty for—"

Anna cut him off. "You're not *my* prince."

Without missing a beat, he cocked his head to the side and shot her a wicked grin. "Would you like me to be?"

He was a sly one, no matter how princely he sometimes acted. She rolled her eyes and turned toward the garage. She needed a little breathing room from his charming wit.

The tire-squealing might have been a little bit over-the-top, but Anna enjoyed the feel of the Mercedes taking the corners. Not to mention the fact that Leo was clutching the handle grip in the back seat, hanging on for dear life.

"Remember when I implied that you might not know how to drive the Mercedes?" he said as they swung another tight turn. "I take it back. You could probably make a minivan fly like a bat out of—"

"Hang on!" Anna yelled as she slammed on the brakes at a red light. Leo hit the back of the passenger seat with a soft thud.

Of course, the prince was correct in his estimation of her abilities, as evidenced by her feats of skill on the mission last year when they acquired Family Banana—the Banana Girls' minivan.

"I think we can both agree you've proven your point, Miss Rivers." He was trying to use his authoritative princely tone on her, but his grin told her he wasn't really angry.

Maybe she should ease up.

A very little bit.

"When we get the Ferrari back, you'll have to take me out for a drive so I can enjoy all this from the front seat."

"Is that in the job description?" Anna said with a smirk.

"It certainly is, in your case."

The light turned green, and Anna guided the sporty sedan forward at a more reasonable speed.

"Did that American spy agency of yours teach you how to drive like that?" Leo asked with a voice clearly in awe. "And do you think there's any possibility they'd give me a few lessons if we asked nicely?"

"Why? Is international spy on your backup list in case the prince thing doesn't work out?"

Leo laughed. "Sure. You make it look pretty easy. Plus I've seen a few spy movies."

Anna fought a growing smile. She really did love spending time with Leo. He was so energetic and full of life. If she didn't find his attacker soon, she ran a real risk of getting in way too deep with this charming prince. Unfortunately, the mission would be over at the end of the week, whether she found the attacker or not. Anna wondered what Stacia's policy was on a Banana Girl taking some time off for a freelance job.

Two blocks from the consulate, Anna noticed a red sports coupe closing fast in the next lane. Right when she expected to see the small car flash past, it slammed on the brakes and pulled in behind them.

She'd driven performance cars enough to know that some drivers were out looking for the thrill of someone to race with. But they weren't in the Ferrari; the red coupe wouldn't have any reason to think she was a speed demon unless they had been following her.

Could they possibly have drawn out Leo's attacker this quickly?

With that thought, Anna took a sudden turn away from the planned route to Leo's meeting. The red coupe matched her turn exactly.

It was possible that the other car had abruptly pulled in

behind them so that it could make that turn. Anna did another quick turn, back toward their original destination, and slowed way down. Assuming it wasn't intentionally following them, the red coupe should get annoyed and breeze by. But the red coupe didn't pass; it slowed to match Anna's speed, staying a few car lengths back.

"Anna, I didn't mean to slow down this much," Leo said. "We do need to make it in time for my meeting."

She gave him a dirty look through the rearview mirror, then turned her attention back to the red coupe. It was accelerating now, moving up on the right. The windows were tinted so dark that the driver was invisible. As the car moved into Anna's blind-spot, she had that familiar deep-in-her-gut feeling of impending danger.

It was another attack.

She mashed the accelerator and the car's engine roared to life.

A second later there was a loud pop and Leo's window shattered to bits.

"Get down!" she screamed.

Leo ducked flat against the seat.

Anna continued accelerating after the initial shot, and she had no intention of slowing down anytime soon. She pulled around to the left of a slow-moving van plastered with the name of a local plumber. Fortunately, many of the streets in this part of downtown were one-way, so she didn't have to worry about head-on traffic at the moment.

The red coupe sped around the plumber's van on the other side.

Anna was sure that the speedometer on the dash must be measuring her heartbeat racing faster and faster. Buildings flew by in a blur as she searched for some way to get Leo to safety.

"Did you happen to bring a gun with you?" Leo yelled over the air rushing in through the broken window.

"What do you need my gun for?!" Anna yelled back.

"Well, I can see you're busy driving, and I don't know whether your spy instruction included simultaneous driving and shooting." Leo sounded amazingly calm, considering the situation. "I figured I could shoot back while you drive."

Anna jerked the wheel to the side to avoid a truck. "This isn't some spy movie. You'll get yourself killed!" Her fingers clinched hard on the wheel as she drifted around a tight corner, tires squealing.

The car reached fifty before Anna was forced to slow for the next turn. A second later the rear window shattered in a cascade of glass.

"Stay down!" she ordered as they careened into another turn.

"I really could be much more helpful if I had a gun!" he yelled over the screeching tires.

"You're not a secret agent, Leo! Your only job right now is to stay alive." Anna floored the accelerator and swerved around a chicken and waffle food truck. She was tempted to distract Leo from his fixation on her gun by mentioning the waffles, but she didn't want to risk that he'd poke his head up to look.

"How far back are they?" Leo asked.

"What?"

"How far behind us is the shooter's car?" Leo repeated.

"About fifty feet." Anna veered as a slow-moving SUV shifted into her lane.

"What's that in meters?" Leo called back.

"I don't know! It's about five car lengths."

A second later, a fiery poof came from the back seat accompanied by the smell of fireworks. Anna glanced over her shoulder to see the prince with a brightly burning road flare in his hand and a silly grin on his face.

"I'm being helpful," he said as he tossed the flare, grenade-style, out the shattered back window.

The bright, arcing flare left a trail of smoke behind them. Leo's wild aim hadn't been good enough to hit the red coupe, but it was close enough to force their pursuer to dodge the unknown projectile.

Anna needed something else to distract the prince. Too bad the waffle truck wasn't still around. Then she hit on an idea. "Leo, we need the police. Call 911." She sped under an elevated rail station and through an intersection as the light turned red.

"Good idea," Leo said.

The red coupe raced after them, running the red light and narrowly missing a taxi cab. Anna was slowly increasing the gap between them. If only she could find a place to hide.

"Yes, our emergency is that we are being chased and shot at by someone," Leo spoke into his phone.

Without slowing, Anna forced the Mercedes into a tight right turn.

"Where are we? I'm not sure, let me check."

With a quick glance over her shoulder, Anna saw the prince attempting to look out the broken window. "Don't sit up! Get down lower!" Anna commanded.

"The dispatcher needs to know where we are! How am I supposed to be helpful from the floor of a car?" Frustration was evident in Leo's voice.

"I'll tell you. We're on—oh crap—" Anna swerved to avoid an oncoming car.

What was that tow truck doing driving on her side of the street? As they bumped over a set of railroad tracks, Anna looked at the white lane markings in front of her. She smacked her forehead. "This is a one-way road!" she yelled at herself.

"We're on a one-way road," Leo repeated to the operator. "And I think we just crossed some railway tracks. Is that helpful?"

Anna jerked the wheel hard, skidding the big Mercedes in a one-eighty. No sense helping the assassin do his job by plowing head-on into traffic. The wheels skidded along the asphalt and up over a curb onto the sidewalk. Oncoming cars slammed on their brakes and honked. She had definitely made a scene with that maneuver. As the world stopped spinning, she saw the red coupe headed straight for them. She gunned the engine and swerved completely onto the sidewalk, zigzagging behind traffic signs and light poles as protection.

The red coupe continued toward her, angled across the three-lane road on a collision course. At the last minute, it swerved away, narrowly avoiding a steel light post. Anna watched in her rearview mirror as the coupe executed a similar one-eighty, zeroing in on them again.

"Now we've turned around," Leo said loudly into his phone. "No, we're still on the same one-way road that I told you about before, but now I presume we're going the right direction."

They whizzed past cars doing the speed limit and sailed through another intersection. Anna glanced at the street sign. "Tell them we're on Miami Avenue crossing 5th Street." She glanced at the compass readout on the electronic dashboard. "Heading south."

Leo repeated the location to the dispatch controller. "She said they're sending officers to help."

Anna surveyed her surroundings. It looked like the road would be one-way for a while. So unless the police timed it just right and caught them at a cross street, or decided to drive into head-on-traffic, she was on her own until they could catch up to her. Hopefully the police would catch up before the attacker did.

The Mercedes was powerful, but it couldn't compete with the small, unmarked red coupe for agility. Anna knew she needed to find somewhere she could open up and let the big engine run free, but her swerving was probably the only thing keeping them alive at this point.

"Thank you so much; that's very kind of you," Leo said to the dispatcher. "I'll call back if we have any more trouble. Goodbye." He sounded as though he had just set up an appointment for tea.

"Leo, you're supposed to stay on the line until the end. How long have you lived in the states?"

"I've never had to call 911 before! She said they were on the way, so I figured we were done."

With a resigned head shake, Anna glanced in the mirror. The red coupe pulled up in the right lane. Anna jerked the wheel sideways, forcing the coupe back. It swerved around behind them and came up on the left. Another shot rang out, and Anna instinctively ducked and swerved away again, pouring on the speed. No broken glass this time, though. Their attacker must have missed.

She couldn't keep up this game of cat and mouse; eventually the shooter in the red coupe would find their target. She'd need to lose them permanently.

Checking for the one-way sign this time, Anna pulled a hard left at the next intersection, forcing the coupe to slow to avoid hitting the light pole on the corner.

"Wait, don't turn!" Leo yelled. "The dispatch woman thinks we're on that road." He pointed backward.

"That's why you're supposed to stay on the line with them." She quickly evaluated the new road, watching as the red coupe negotiated the turn behind them and accelerated again.

This road had only two lanes, and the Mercedes was

definitely the bigger and heavier of the two cars. Perhaps she could use that as an advantage.

Just as the front of the coupe was nearly even with the Mercedes' back bumper, Anna veered suddenly towards it, smashing the left headlight. She'd take the small car apart piece by piece if she had to. As the coupe accelerated and switched sides again, Anna slammed the brakes for a split second. The front of the coupe smashed into the Mercedes' substantial bumper.

Scanning the road ahead, Anna caught sight of a row of thick support columns for the city's elevated tram. She left a small space in the lane next to her and slowed a bit, inviting the coupe to come up beside them. It was a risky move, considering they would be at point blank range.

"I am definitely going to give you a raise after this. I don't care if you aren't on the payroll. I can easily fix that," Leo said.

Anna's mouth tightened in a thin line as she watched the coupe maneuver behind them. She squeezed the steering wheel so tightly that her knuckles hurt. The seconds felt like minutes as she willed their attacker to fall for her trap.

Finally, their pursuer took the bait and moved forward into the narrow gap. Anna watched for her opportunity, counting the quickly dwindling number of cement support columns that she could use as a weapon. If she moved too soon, the driver of the coupe would see the trap. Too late and . . . it would be too late.

Anna left off the accelerator. She needed the coupe just a few more feet forward.

Through the barely lowered passenger window, Anna saw a muzzle flash followed immediately by a loud impact against the left side paneling of the Mercedes.

That would have to be close enough.

She wrenched the steering wheel to the left, slamming the

black Mercedes against the red coupe. The small sports car was no match for the large sedan. Anna had timed it perfectly; she even managed to hook the coupe's bumper with the sedan's wheel well.

The small car fought her efforts to push it off the road. Hopefully that meant the occupants were too busy to shoot at them anymore. Even at this close range, Anna still couldn't see the driver or shooter.

The coupe's tires squealed as it tried to break free of the entanglement. Anna bent forward over the wheel, aiming to wipe the little coupe off the side of her car with the support columns. The rubber squealing stopped for a split second and both cars lurched to the left, putting the Mercedes on a collision course with the column. The coupe was attempting to oversteer and force Anna and Leo into the large supports. Anna quickly corrected, hoping it would be soon enough to avoid a collision. The coupe slammed on its brakes again. The cracking sound of the bumper tearing off the front of the small car quickly followed.

The coupe skidded to a crash into the tram's support as Anna steered the sedan back onto the road, missing the column by inches. She would have preferred a larger margin of safety, but at least they were finally free of their pursuer.

Anna couldn't tell whether the crash had been serious enough to put the little car out of commission. It couldn't have done any favors to the radiator with the bumper missing.

Half a block later, Anna saw the flashing lights of two police cars at the cross street. They'd either have to drive the wrong way on the road or they'd have to circle around the block to pick up the occupants of the coupe. She hoped they got to the accident before their attacker got away. But instead of pulling through the intersection to circle the block, both squad cars turned to follow the Mercedes. As nice as a police escort was, Anna would rather they catch the prince's attacker.

An unpleasant thought occurred to her. "Leo, did you tell the emergency dispatcher which car we were in?"

Leo turned around in his seat, watching the flashing lights growing closer. "Uh, probably not. You don't think they suspect us of being the perpetrators, do you?"

Anna sighed. "It appears so." She pulled the Mercedes to a stop in the striped loading zone of a small corner cafe. "I'm sure we can get everything straightened out quickly enough, but you might be late for your lunch."

Leo laughed. "That's okay. The Jamaican Consul General always tries to overfeed me at our lunches. I think she's trying to fatten me up for some nefarious purpose."

Several seconds passed with only the sound of nearby foot traffic and approaching sirens coming in through the broken windows.

"Thank you, Anna. You very likely saved my life."

Relief flooded through her as the adrenaline subsided. She turned around in her seat and considered the grateful face of the handsome prince. Her stomach sank at the thought of how close she had come to losing him, or to being a casualty herself.

She nodded in acknowledgement. "You're welcome." Then in an attempt at humor, she added, "It's definitely part of the job description."

Chapter 11

T he next morning after her run, Anna wandered down to the garage, a scrumptious danish pastry in hand. She wanted to go over what was left of the ballistic evidence on the Mercedes. She couldn't shake the niggling feeling that something wasn't quite right.

The Mercedes was back in its usual place between the limousine and the empty spot reserved for the Ferrari. Anna walked up to the damaged sedan. This was as close as she'd been to the vehicle since the police had ordered her and the prince out of the car the day before. It had taken some skillful negotiation—along with her federal agency identification—to convince the local police that Leo really was a prince from Luxembourg. Leo had offered to call the nice lady at the dispatch center to verify his identity, but Anna thought that the poor woman had already been through enough.

The police had swarmed and inspected the car, removing the bullets and recording the ballistics information. But when they sent a team to the scene of the crash, the only thing the coupe had left behind were a few flecks of red paint embedded in the concrete support column and an errant bumper in the middle of the road.

Leo had—understandably—missed the rest of the events on his schedule. And when they had all arrived back at the villa, Zane placed the prince on lockdown again—for his own safety, of course.

Anna moved carefully around the sedan, inspecting it from various angles. She had complete confidence that the local police had conducted a thorough ballistics investigation, but she didn't trust that she could get her hands on the results quickly enough to be of any use in solving the case. She would need to see what she could learn on her own.

Closing her eyes, she tried to recreate the attack in her mind. The first bullet had shattered the right passenger-side window. She crouched next to the car, placing herself where the shooter would have had. It only took her a few seconds to see the hole. The bullet had lodged in the back of the driver headrest—only inches from her head.

Adrenaline surged in her gut.

She had nearly put her friends in the market for a new Banana Girl.

Good thing she hadn't slammed on the brakes any harder or that shot would've had her name on it.

Wait.

Had she slammed on the brakes?

She took a deep breath and tried to go back to that moment. Fear for Leo's safety surged through her again as she pictured the red coupe closing in from the side. Her leg flinched.

Her instinct had been to protect Leo, to get him away from the danger.

She hadn't slowed the car. She'd accelerated.

What had the attacker been aiming at?

Anna opened her eyes again, imagining Leo sitting on the

right side of the back seat. He had claimed to have chosen the rear passenger-side seat so that he would have a better view of the road. But based on how often she had caught him glancing her way, she knew it wasn't just the view of the road he'd wanted to see.

Anna bit her lower lip at the butterflies his attention still caused in her stomach. She forced herself to focus on the investigation. She had to keep the prince safe. That was her assignment.

A rush of realization flooded over her. This wasn't just about the mission anymore. The growing feelings for the prince that she'd been fighting for the last week had defied all of her efforts.

She cared for Leo.

Her desire to protect him didn't come from her duty to the assignment. She needed to keep him safe because she didn't know what she would do if anything ever happened to him.

Anna took several deep breaths, letting each one slowly out.

She had certainly made a mess of Rule Number One, hadn't she? But now wasn't the time for emotional attachment. If she was going to keep Leo safe, she needed to figure out who was behind the attacks and make them stop.

Refocusing her attention on the car and the mysterious bullet hole, she backed up a few feet, raised her fingers, and pointed—gun-like—at the battered Mercedes. She switched her aim back and forth between where Leo would have been and where the bullet ended up. She even shifted backward and repeated the exercise, wondering if she had misjudged where the coupe had been when the shooter had fired.

The only way she could make sense of it was if she was wrong about the coupe's position *and* about her memory of accelerating right before the shot was fired.

She shook her head. Could she be wrong on both counts?

Maybe she should check more of the car.

Anna circled to the rear and crouched low. The second shot had broken out the back window. She gazed through the jagged gap in the glass searching for the second bullet hole. Several minutes of staring and she still couldn't find it.

She closed her eyes, going back to the moment the back window had been shot out. At this point—despite his desire to play super-agent—Leo had already dutifully hunkered down in the backseat.

Why had the attacker shot at all? There's no way Leo would have been visible, and they couldn't possibly have known where in the back seat he was hunched over. Not to mention the fact that angled glass was notoriously difficult to shoot through accurately.

The niggle of a suspicion began to grow in her gut.

Those were the only windows that had been shot out, but Anna knew there were two other shots, and she was absolutely certain she'd heard one of them impact the left side.

She walked around to the driver's side and scanned the body of the car. The last bullet had left a hole in the pillar between the front and rear doors.

Anna tilted her head, considering the hole's placement. This one didn't make any sense either. The coupe had been at point blank range when the last shot was fired. She leaned back against the limousine, unable to position herself in the exact spot the shooter would have been. She shifted from the bullet hole in the pillar to the approximate location the prince would have been.

No way someone missed that shot.

It just didn't make sense.

Anna pulled out her phone and connected to the Club Banana video conference line.

Mari answered. "Hey, Anna. If you're calling for Trey's information on the mystery coupe, I didn't get a chance to talk to him about it yet." She pushed out the apology in one long, flustered breath.

Anna smiled. "You didn't get a chance to talk to him because you haven't seen him since I called yesterday? Or because you were doing other things when you saw him?"

The young woman's cheeks pinked even more. "Sorry, Anna. I promise I'll ask him about it tonight, though."

"It's okay, Mari," Anna said. "I actually called for a different reason. I have a puzzle for Susan, is she there?"

"Sure, hang on." Mari stood from the couches and walked down the hall. She seemed understandably anxious to pass the call off to someone else.

Several moments later, Susan hobbled on-screen. "Hi, Anna." Her bright red hair was poofier than usual. She must have barely woken up.

"Have y'all been sleeping in late because I'm not there to wake you up with a hot breakfast?"

Susan flopped back into the couch cushions and held her stomach. "Anna, I'm starving. Where are you when my tummy needs you?"

The girls both laughed.

"Actually," Susan continued, "no school yesterday or today. Fall break."

Anna had forgotten. The stress about school that had been gnawing at the back of her mind lightened ever so slightly. At least those were two days she wasn't getting any further behind in her classes.

"Whaddya got for me?" Susan asked.

"Somebody was shooting at us yesterday," Anna replied

"Yeah, I heard. You and the prince both okay?"

Anna shrugged. "Leo's ego took some bruises, but otherwise, we're fine. What I need is someone to double-check my rough ballistics analysis. I can't figure out what the shooter was thinking."

"I can do the mathematical calculations," Susan said. "But if it's rough, that might be more Hannah's department."

"Is she there?"

Susan nodded and pointed off screen.

"I'm here, Anna," Hannah called out.

"Don't I get to see your pretty face?" Anna teased.

In the very bottom corner of her screen, Anna saw her blonde friend lean into the range of the camera, give a begrudging smirk, and disappear again.

Anna laughed. "Good enough, I guess."

She switched to her phone's front camera and showed Susan and Hannah the bullet holes and shot angles.

"So the shots were all off by a few inches, that's not surprising," Hannah said.

"What do you mean?" Anna asked.

"Most people don't train shooting from one moving vehicle to another. The shots from the side would have drifted because of wind drag," Hannah replied.

Anna frowned. She hadn't thought of that. She stepped back and considered the car again. "That would explain two of the shots," she said. "What about the shot from behind? That one had no chance of hitting Leo."

"Maybe they wanted to shatter the window to scare you or to have a more accurate follow-up shot," Hannah offered.

"Maybe . . ." Something still felt off to Anna. Something about the drift from the side shots. She moved to the driver's side of the car. "Wait a second. When wind drag pushes the bullets off target, it pushes them backward from the direction the car's moving, right?"

"Yeah," Hannah answered.

"So where would the shooter have been aiming to hit this

spot?" Anna placed her finger over the bullet hole in the center pillar. She backed up to give the Banana Girls a better view of the entire car.

"The driver," Hannah answered curtly.

Susan looked back at the camera, eyes wide, a hand over her mouth.

The nebulous dread that Anna had felt floating in her gut over the past few days slowly coalesced into a solid rock.

Susan lowered her hand. "Anna, they weren't aiming for the prince . . ."

Anna nodded. Finally understanding why so many of these attacks hadn't made sense.

She finished her friend's thought. "They were aiming for me."

There were plenty of places that a prince could spend his time while he was locked down in his personal mansion villa. He could be out at the pool enjoying some morning sun. He could be down on the beach, wading through the Atlantic Ocean surf. He could even be playing tennis or basketball on the outdoor court. But Anna was fairly certain she knew where to find this particular prince at this particular time of day. In fact, her stomach made it unanimous. It was breakfast time, and she'd find him in their favorite breakfast spot on the third floor.

On her way there, she passed Jessie on the second-floor landing. Anna was tempted to share her recent discovery with her fellow agent, but Jessie had been giving Anna the cold shoulder lately, barely acknowledging her when they crossed paths. Anna knew they hadn't been incredibly close before, but there had definitely been a chilling of their working relationship in the past few days.

Ever the optimist, Anna tried again. "Good morning, Jessie," she said with a wave.

The woman cast her a passing look of disdain. Anna shrugged and continued to the breakfast nook.

As she hustled up the last set of stairs, details of the other attacks tumbled through her brain. Makenna, the close security agent who had been shot with the harpoon, had probably been the target all along, not Leo. And the Ferrari's cut brake lines could have been meant for Kaitlynn, or perhaps Anna herself, not the prince. What about the freezer incident? Was Anna the target there, or could that have simply been an accident?

She also wondered how Leo would take the news.

"You've been arriving later and later to our morning breakfast date." Leo said as she entered the small kitchen. He stood at the counter mixing a delicious-smelling batter in a bowl. He even had on an apron.

Anna's brain tripped over the word *date*. "Are we making this official now?" she said in as light a tone as she could manage. "I don't remember breakfast dates being in the job description."

He stopped stirring but didn't look up. After a moment, he grabbed a handful of nuts and added them to the bowl. "Actually, I had hoped you'd want to do that one on your own," he said softly. Finally he glanced up at Anna, his gaze intent on her.

She had been around enough guys to recognize that look. Despite his usual bravado and his current nonchalance while making breakfast, she saw in the prince's eyes that he was very serious danger of falling for her, assuming he hadn't already.

To make matters worse, Anna was pretty sure she was falling for him, too.

They stood there staring at each other across the small

kitchen for several long moments, Anna's stomach doing flip-flops all the while.

She wasn't ready to deal with her feelings for Leo. She didn't know how a relationship between them could even work.

She needed something to distract the prince.

Or herself.

Or maybe both.

She took a fortifying breath and walked over to the counter. Seating herself on a bar stool facing him, she leaned forward and glanced into his mixing bowl. "So, what brought you to the kitchen this morning?"

Thankfully, Leo seemed willing to move on to lighter topics. "Caramel pecan muffins."

"I'm not sure that's a thing. Maybe you mean caramel pecan brownies?"

"You Americans eat brownies for breakfast?!" he asked in shock.

Anna laughed. "No, I mean, I've never heard of caramel pecan muffins but I *have* heard of caramel pecan brownies."

"Oh, of course you haven't heard of them. I'm making up the recipe as we speak."

Doing her best to cover a smile with her hand, Anna nodded. "Well, I'm sure they'll be delicious."

As she watched him stir, his face screwed up in concentration, Anna remembered why she had come looking for him in the first place. "Leo, I think I discovered something about the attacks. I still need to visit with some of your former close security agents, but I have a theory."

"Really? What is it?" he asked as he turned in search of another ingredient. He grabbed a stick of butter from a nearby tray.

"Well, there's good news and bad news. Which do you want first?"

Leo stopped and stared at the ceiling as if pondering the question. "I think I want to hear the bad news first," he said with a finger on his chin. "It's like eating. You never want to finish a meal with the worst food. Always save the best for last."

Another comparison to food. Anna supposed she was lucky he hadn't compared her to food yet. "Actually, I lied," she said. "You have to have the good news first. It's much more dramatic this way."

The prince arched an eyebrow at her in a very regal manner. Maybe he wasn't used to the way she handled him. Finally, he waved a hand for her to proceed.

"Well, the good news is that I don't think anyone is making an attempt on your life. These attacks weren't meant to hurt you," Anna said.

His eyebrows went up in surprise. "Really? So a high speed shoot-out through downtown Miami, or having my brake lines cut, or a spear gun attack at a party, those were simply for my health?"

"I didn't say they weren't meant to hurt. I said they weren't meant to hurt *you*."

"Wait . . ." Leo frowned, his brow knit in concentration. "You mean . . ."

Anna saw the moment the truth hit him. The cube of butter slipped from his hands and thudded to the ground.

Leo shook his head in disbelief. "You mean the attack at the sandbar party was meant for Makenna? And the cut brake lines were meant for Kaitlynn? But that means the car chase and shooting was . . ."

". . . meant for me," Anna finished his sentence.

Leo's eyes went wide. His face lost all of the fun, joking it usually had. "Truly?" he asked.

Anna nodded. "It's just a hunch right now, but all of the evidence points that way."

He stared at her. "You're in real danger."

That was the understatement of the mission.

"Apparently so." She shrugged. "Remember that mission thing I was sent her for? This sorta falls into that."

Unfazed by her attempt to keep the mood light, the prince shook his head emphatically. "No. This is unacceptable."

"I suppose you could fire me," Anna suggested with a laugh.

"I can't fire you because you refuse to let me hire you." His expression was completely earnest.

"I was kidding, Leo. I mean this is just—"

"We need to get you out of Miami!" He turned and started pacing the small kitchen, running a hand through his hair. "But would that keep you safe? Would the attackers continue to target you if you left?" His gaze flitted past her as he started another circuit through the narrow kitchen.

"Leo . . ." Anna said lightly.

He glanced her way but didn't really see her. "And even if you're not here, how can I know for sure that you're safe? If you go back to Atlanta, how can I protect you? What if next time they—"

"Leo!" she said more forcefully. He stopped pacing. She waited until she had his full attention. "This is part of my job," she explained gently. "It literally *is* in the job description. I've dealt with this kind of thing before. It's okay."

The prince leaned down and reached across the counter, firmly grasping her hand. "No, it's not okay. I can't let anything happen to you, Anna."

Anna squeezed his hand back. "I'm a big girl. Plus, I'm the one who's supposed to be protecting you, remember?"

All of the bravado of the Party Prince was gone. Leo was just a man desperately worried about a woman he cared for.

About her.

His gaze continued riveted on her, deep blue eyes so full of concern that it was almost her undoing. "I can't lose you," he whispered.

She stood and moved around the counter. Katie had once told her that men need hugs just as much as women, they just pretend not to. Anna cautiously approached him and slipped her arms around his middle. He pulled her so quickly into a crushing embrace that it took her breath away.

His chest felt as solid and strong pressed against her as it had looked from a distance. Anna melted into his arms. Nestling her cheek against his shoulder, she inhaled the scent of his warm skin. A countdown started somewhere in the back of her brain, telling her she only had a few more seconds before shattering Rule Number One into a million bits.

Three.

Two.

One.

Reluctantly, she slowly pulled away from his arms. He didn't protest. Perhaps he recognized the dangers as well.

She gazed at his handsome face, regretting what she had to do. "I have to go," she said softly. "I can't do any investigating while I'm standing in your arms."

A mischievous grin spread across his face. "It could be an investigation. Of sorts."

Anna felt her cheeks heat.

This prince was charming. Or a charmer. One of the two.

She pushed firmly on his chest and he begrudgingly released her.

"I don't suppose you'd take me with you?" he asked.

Anna shook her head. "Until I have more evidence about what's going on, you might still be at risk."

Leo rolled his eyes. "Ironic that I'm not the one being targeted, but I'm stuck inside for my safety. While you're the one in real danger, but you're free to come and go as you please."

"Life is full of injustices," she shot back. "Besides, you're too distracting, remember?"

His mouth tipped into a grin. "I do my best." After a moment, his expression turned somber. "You'll let me know what you find out?"

Anna nodded.

"And please be careful." He took her hand and lifted it slowly to his lips, placing a long, gentle kiss on it.

With incredible self-restraint, Anna forced herself to step back and pull her hand away. She took a deep breath. "I'll be careful," she said. She glanced at the strange assortment of ingredients he had on the counter and in the bowl. "Good luck with the muffins."

He shook his head. "I can't believe you're leaving before they're done."

"As entertaining as it might be to watch this"—she waved a hand at his work—"learning experience you're about to have, I really need to go. You could save one for me."

He must have heard the skepticism in her tone. "They have caramel and pecans. How could anything with caramel and pecans turn out badly?"

"We'll see," she said with a grin.

On her way out of the small kitchen, she saw Celine walking down the third-floor hall. "Celine," Anna called out. "You're just the one I wanted to see."

Celine stopped and waited for Anna to catch up. "What can I do for you, Miss Rivers?"

"Anna," she corrected.

"Anna," Celine amended.

"Can you tell me the names of Leo's former close security agents?"

"Certainly, let's walk down to my office."

When they reached her office, Celine looked up the names of the former agents and wrote them on a small piece of paper. It wasn't a long list; only three names.

Anna thanked Celine and left her office, nodding to Zane as she passed him on the way to her room. She might need to call the Banana Girls and get some help tracking down the agents' contact info. As she mounted the grand staircase, she glanced at the paper again and realized that Makenna wasn't on the list. Of course, Anna had only asked for former agents, so naturally, Celine hadn't included Makenna, or Kaitlynn either for that matter. Come to think of it, Anna hadn't seen Kaitlynn around the villa since the Ferrari accident. Even though Anna's last visit with Kaitlynn hadn't gone terribly well, she had new insight now and, hopefully, better questions, too. She was probably still in the hospital or at a therapy center recovering. Anna wondered if she would be at the same facility as Makenna.

Anna doubled back toward Celine's office. Maybe the chief of staff would know where Kaitlynn was staying during her recovery.

Rounding the corner a few doors from Celine's office, Anna slowed at the sound of voices, not wanting to interrupt Celine if she was in the middle of a phone call.

". . . but that seems like so long to wait," Celine said.

Anna wouldn't have thought much of the comment, except for something about Celine's voice. It wasn't the normal prim and proper tone she was used to hearing from Celine. It sounded teasing and almost . . . seductive.

The next surprise was when Anna heard Zane's voice reply, "It could be sooner." His voice was soft and suggestive. "If you happen to be down at the boathouse in about ten minutes when I finish my security rounds."

"Hmm, that would be perfect," Celine replied with a flirtatious giggle. "We just have to make sure no one sees us."

"Why do we still have to keep this a secret?" From his tone, it sounded like a question Zane had already asked her. "I'm sure if you tell the prince, he'll understand."

Were Zane and Celine involved romantically? Anna had *not* seen that one coming. But it made sense; they probably spent a fair amount of time together. Anna didn't know what the royal family's policy was on relationships between coworkers, but she didn't imagine Leo would be too strict about it.

When Celine didn't respond—at least, not audibly—Zane continued. "Think about it, Celine. What's the worst that could happen? It's not like you want to be at this job forever, do you?"

Anna frowned. She didn't know Zane well enough to gage whether he wanted to permanently be the head of the prince's security, but she had seen Celine and the pride she took in working for Leo.

"Don't worry, love, everyone will know soon enough," Celine cooed. "I want to wait until the attack investigation is all cleared up."

Zane grunted in response, but he didn't sound happy.

"Just be patient." Her voice was sugary, completely unlike what Anna was used to hearing from her. Maybe being in love did that to a person.

It sounded as though the conversation was about at an end, so Anna ducked back around the corner into the main hall and proceeded to her room, thinking about Zane and Celine's exchange as she went.

Of course, the mystery of a budding romance between Leo's top staff members wasn't nearly as important as interviewing the former agents for her investigation, but Anna was definitely tempted to hang around the villa to find out more. She would have to content herself with watching them in the future to see if there were any little signs of romantic involvement that she'd missed earlier.

Back in her room, Anna made a quick call to Club Banana to ask the girls to look up the addresses of the former agents on her list. Susan promised to have the information sent to Anna's phone before she made it past the villa gates. Katie even offered to call ahead and set up the visits.

Anna couldn't help but smile at that. She knew how her friends felt. Though it was much less stressful, life at Club Banana was never as fun knowing your fellow agent was out on a mission. Helping a fellow Banana Girl was the best way to feel involved. After finishing her chat, Anna went down to the garage and borrowed the keys to the Lexus from the chauffeur, promising to take incredibly good care of it, given his dwindling fleet of vehicles.

Chapter 12

The interviews with the three former close security agents took most of the morning. All three had reported growing closer, emotionally or romantically, to Prince Leo before their employment came to an end.

The first one had lost her job because of failing a random drug test. But the woman insisted that she had never taken drugs except for a traditional brewed drink that was common in her culture.

The second agent had been fired for stealing the diamond necklace of one of Leo's visiting cousins. And, though the necklace was discovered in her room, the woman denied having stolen it. She said it must have been planted there.

The third agent was the one Kaitlynn had referred to earlier, the clumsy one. She openly admitted being clumsy, especially after her mother had suddenly passed away. In fact, she cited her constant accidents on the job as the reason she had to quit. She was certain that Leo's safety was in jeopardy if she continued working for him. It was interesting, Anna thought, that the former agent hadn't experienced any new accidents since she left the prince's team.

As she drove back toward the villa, Anna struggled through a swirling fog of thoughts. It seemed too incredibly coincidental that all three girls had grown close to the prince and then lost their jobs shortly after. And setting aside the clumsy one, the other two agents had been removed under questionable circumstances. Illicit drugs and jewelry theft? It was possible. Or were the girls telling the truth about it being a set up?

But more importantly, who could be behind all of it? And why?

The most obvious reason Anna could think of was jealousy. If the agents were fired or quit as soon as they got close to the prince, then someone must be trying to keep these girls away from him.

But who besides a jilted lover would be this jealous?

Anna frowned. She needed to give that some more thought, and rush-hour traffic wasn't the best time. Maybe a lounge chair on the villa balcony later.

Plus, rush-hour traffic wasn't the only thing distracting her. Thoughts about Leo kept barging in.

How was she ever going to sort those feelings out?

From the very beginning, she had seen how friendly and playful the prince could be. It had only been a matter of time before those antics grew into something more.

A horrible thought suddenly occurred to her.

Had her failure to rebuff the prince's casual flirtation led him to think he had feelings for her? And had his constant attention led her to think she had feelings for him? And was it too late to put all of these feelings back into the Pandora's box they'd come from?

Anna shook her head, trying to clear away the distracting thoughts. She would need to deal with that later. For now, she would do her best to cling to the scattered shards of Rule Number One that she had left.

On her right, she caught sight of Makenna's recovery center. She braked hard and pulled into the parking lot. It was fortunate that the GPS had brought her right past the facility. In her rush to solve the puzzle, she had nearly forgotten that Makenna's interactions with the prince might be another important clue. She needed to ask Makenna whether there had been a budding relationship between them when she was attacked. At the same time, Anna dreaded what the answer might be.

She parked the sleek, white SUV near the facility's combo tennis-basketball-pickleball court and walked toward the beautiful building. As she entered the main reception area, Anna saw the same young woman who had been working there last week. She smiled politely as Anna approached the desk.

"I'm here to visit Makenna Sorensen again," Anna said in anticipation of the receptionist's question.

"Room number?"

Anna pulled out her phone and swiped through her notes to find the information from her last visit. "Room 129."

The receptionist checked the computer. With the same polite smile, she looked up and said, "I'm sorry, but that information doesn't match our records."

Anna frowned. "Is Makenna just not seeing anyone right now?"

The receptionist offered Anna a patient look. "If the information matches, but the resident is not receiving guests at the moment, I would tell you that they are not receiving guests."

Was this meant to be some sort of test of intelligence?

"So . . . did Makenna move to a different room?"

"Changes in our residents' status are protected by privacy laws. I'm not at liberty to disclose if there has been any change."

"Huh," Anna huffed. She wondered what had changed. She needed to figure out a way to get through the security doors. She casually reached into her purse and felt around for the tiny micro-bot that Hannah had packed for her. Palming the postage-stamp-sized device, Anna leaned forward and rested her hands on the edge of the reception counter. "Is there really nothing you can do?" she asked sweetly.

The receptionist flashed her a fake smile. "I'm sorry."

Sure that the micro-bot was securely in place on the underside of the counter, Anna returned the smile and sighed dramatically. "Okay. I guess I'll come back another time." She walked casually back out to the SUV.

Once situated in the front seat, she pulled up the bot's control app on her phone. The video feed showed an upside down view of the reception area. Anna forced her brain to think like a spider—she was crawling along an inverted ledge. Using the control arrows, Anna moved the bot along the bottom of the counter's ledge around to the side of the desk. She panned through the full video feed to make sure no one was visible as she moved the bot down to the floor.

From her previous visit, Anna knew the button for the security doors would be on the surface underneath the receptionist's desktop. The bot needed to get under there without drawing the attention of the receptionist.

With a quick check of the surroundings, Anna sent the bot scurrying around the edge of the desk into the dark shadows underneath. She switched the camera to low-light visibility and steered the small machine up the inside wall of the desk to the underside surface where she hoped the button would be. Squinting at the enhanced video feed, Anna caught sight of a small bump on the underside of the desk, just above the receptionist's legs.

The micro-bot had multiple electronic tools at its disposal, but only one physical implement—a short, stubby arm that could be extended and retracted. Anna moved the bot within a few inches of the hidden button and considered the feasibility of making it work. Given the relative size of the two objects, the bot's ability to activate the button didn't look promising. Plus, even if the bot successfully pushed the button, she'd need to be there in the lobby to sneak through. The receptionist would definitely see her.

As Anna sat contemplating the situation, the young receptionist shifted in her chair, and an object caught Anna's eye. With the bot inverted again, it took her a moment to sort out what she was seeing. The receptionist's ID card dangled into her lap from a long lanyard. Anna zoomed in on the card and saw the tell-tale signs of an embedded RFID chip.

Perfect.

If it had been a contact-chip ID, her plan would never have worked.

Anna moved the bot to the edge of the surface, as close to the ID card as possible, and opened the suite of electronic options the bot had available. From the list, she chose *RFID skim* and activated it. A few seconds later, the micro-bot transmitted the receptionist's RFID encoding to Anna's phone. She transferred the data to the RFID app and slipped out of the car.

Skirting the edge of the parking lot, Anna moved to the south wing of the facility—the wing with Makenna's room—looking for a side entrance with an ID scanner. She found one just around the corner of the building. Activating the RFID transmitter, she held her phone up to the scanner and heard the welcome click of the automated latch.

Soundlessly, Anna slipped through the door and walked down the hall toward Room 129 with the confidence of someone who was meant to be there. As she approached Makenna's room, Anna remembered that she would need to retrieve the micro-bot at some point. Despite its well-hidden location, it wasn't the type of technology she wanted to risk falling into unscrupulous hands. And she definitely had her doubts about that receptionist girl.

Anna pulled out her phone and activated the micro-bot's return program and geo-tagged the SUV, hoping that the embedded AI would be smart enough to avoid detection by anyone watching. She just couldn't risk another trip into the reception area without arousing suspicions.

Once the micro-bot had its marching orders, Anna knocked on Makenna's door and waited.

And waited.

And waited.

With more doubt than confidence, Anna tried the door handle.

Locked.

She checked up and down the hall, knowing that the longer she stood there, the more conspicuous she would be. The hallway was still empty, but it probably wouldn't be for long. She glanced at the doors of Makenna's neighbors. They were all closed. So much for casually popping her head in to ask after a friend.

But Anna wasn't ready to give up quite yet. She strode down the hallway toward the main corridor, trying to choose between the entertainment room and the activity room. She decided on the activity room because she figured it would be easier to interrupt someone in the middle of a card game than a movie.

She passed a few other residents and visitors as she wound her way to the activity room and stood just inside the entrance. The residents ranged in age from barely adult to barely alive. Across the room, she saw a pair of athletic-looking guys in their late twenties with nearly matching knee braces playing cards. If Makenna had caught anyone's attention during her stay, Anna bet it was these guys. She walked purposefully in their direction.

When the first guy saw her and nudged his buddy before she even made it halfway across the room, Anna knew she had picked the right people to talk to. "Is there room at this table for one more?" she asked once she'd reached them.

The extra once-over by the two muscle-boys was completely unnecessary; they had both had plenty of opportunity to ogle her on her walk toward them. Plus, from the looks of things, they didn't really have any other options in this facility. But Anna knew it made them feel more secure about themselves.

"Sure," the lean one with the stubbly cheeks finally said. "You know how to play poker?"

Anna lifted a shoulder. "I guess. But I think I'd rather enjoy the view." She sat in the chair between them and looked pointedly from one to the other.

Their responses were predictable—subtle puffing out of their chests accompanied by confident and slightly threatening looks at each other.

"So, what are you two in for?" she asked.

They explained their sports injuries and ensuing surgeries with an excessive amount of boasting, as if their ability to lie unconscious on an operating table was a source of pride.

"Did either of you meet my friend Makenna?" she asked.

"Was that the redhead who got stabbed in the leg?" the thicker one asked.

Anna nodded. "That's her."

"It oughta be a crime to damage a pair of legs that nice," he said. His friend guffawed in agreement.

"No kidding." Anna barely kept her eyes from rolling into her skull by casting a quick look in the direction of the door. She doubted any of the employees would recognize her from her previous visit, or even know that she'd been rejected today, but the receptionist definitely would. "Hey, you haven't seen her around, have you? I stopped by her room and she wasn't there."

"No, she checked out a couple of days ago," the lean one said. "But I did get her number before she left."

"Wow, bro! You got game!" his friend exclaimed.

The lean guy nodded smugly, and they bumped fists across the table.

This conversation wasn't quite heading the direction she had hoped. And she couldn't really ask for Makenna's phone number without making it obvious that she wasn't her friend. Her brain hummed through possibilities. There was one way that might work, but it was a long shot.

"Well, it was nice to meet you guys." She started to stand from the table, knowing that they weren't quite ready to see her go. "I hope you'll call me later," she said, looking pointedly at the lean one who had Makenna's number.

With a broad smirk, he replied, "Oh, I'll definitely call you, sweetie."

Anna gave him her most flirtatious fake smile—the one that made her feel like she was losing brain cells—and waited. And waited. Lean-jock simply stared back at her, an occasional subtle nod to his head.

Had Makenna needed to work so hard to give the guy her number? And if so, why had she bothered?

Finally, with a start, the guy said, "Wait. I don't have your number." He fished in the pocket of his basketball shorts and pulled out his phone.

Without letting her smile falter, she imagined how satisfying it would be to do a momentous eye-roll. Even though this guy's train was barely leaving the station, Anna's plan might actually work.

With expert manipulation, she navigated to his contacts list and entered her information—she put in an untraceable number that forwarded to the Banana Girls' cloud VOIP server. "I'm so glad I got to meet you two," she said in a sugary voice as she found Makenna's entry, texted the agent's number to herself, and immediately deleted the message.

Maybe the visit hadn't been a complete waste of time. She might still be able to talk to Makenna again. As she walked back across the activity room, Anna glanced out the window and saw a small group of employees gathered next to the Lexus. Not being accustomed to driving the luxury SUV, she had to do a double-take before realizing she was in serious trouble. The group all had their heads down staring at the ground in front of the Lexus. One man was on his belly, reaching under the front bumper.

In a flash, Anna realized what must have happened. Someone had caught sight of the micro-bot and followed it. Her one consolation was that the small device was programmed to self-destruct if it was caught, but that certainly wouldn't do anything good to Leo's Lexus if it was hanging from the undercarriage of the car when the AI triggered the command. Unfortunately, Leo's Lexus wasn't equipped with remote driving capabilities. That would have been an easy way out. What she wouldn't give to have Hot Banana in Miami with her.

Anna looked around for some distraction. The basketball court caught her attention, and her brain started to formulate a plan.

She walked back across the room to the two injured athletes, jabbing a thumb over her shoulder toward the court. "Hey, either of you guys up for a game of one-on-one? I can't guarantee it'll be a non-contact sport." Her tone dripped with suggestive implication to the point that she almost gagged. There was no way these guys would fall for it.

Their eyes both went wide for half a second before the lean one jumped up and hobbled away. "I'll grab the ball."

The thick one stood, too, waggling his eyebrows at her.

There was no way out of the crazy plan now. She smiled

suggestively at him. "That means you can escort me out." She threaded a hand through his arm. Truthfully, she wasn't sure how well he could walk on his own. But given how quickly his friend had moved—he was already on his way back across the room with a basketball—she figured they could help her make a quick escape.

When the lean one joined them, she gripped his free bicep with her other hand. Under any other circumstances—and perhaps with different personalities attached to the arms—she might have enjoyed the feeling of holding tightly to two strong men. But at the moment, her survival instinct was on heightened alert trying to formulate a way out of the rehab facility without being detained and discovered as a government operative. That would be sure to cause Stacia no end of headaches, and Anna had always prided herself on being low maintenance.

As they exited the activity room into the main hall, the men both turned toward the front reception area. Through the inset windows, Anna could see the receptionist and an older director-looking woman heading for the doors.

The doors shuddered and began to open automatically.

There was no place to hide in this hall. The receptionist was sure to recognize her as soon as they passed.

Anna pulled on the guys' arms, steering them toward a side hall. "Why don't we go this way? I think it might be faster." It definitely wasn't faster. The basketball court was in the opposite direction.

Fortunately for her, the guys didn't seem to care whether it was faster or not. They acted like they were in a parade with the prize horse, smiling and looking around at the open doors they passed. Anna, on the other hand, stared straight forward, listening intently for any indication that the receptionist and her boss had turned the corner to follow them.

When Anna and her escorts were about halfway down the side hall, she heard the footsteps in the main hall come to an abrupt stop. Unintelligible conversation came next followed by the footsteps resuming down the side hall in her direction. She didn't dare turn around or even cast a glance over her shoulder for fear of being recognized.

One option was to abandon her hobbling escorts right there and make a run for it. But that would leave her with no plan for getting to the Lexus undetected. She needed to hold the course, despite the footsteps growing closer.

Three steps from the exit door, Anna heard a perturbed voice say, "Uh, excuse me—"

Anna spoke over their polite pursuer as she and her escorts reached the door. "Normally I'd let one of you gentlemen get the door, but considering your situation . . ." She maneuvered to the side and pulled the door quickly open. With a surreptitious glance, she saw the receptionist and director were still twenty feet away but moving quickly.

"Hold on just a moment," the director called out.

Anna slid through the swinging door, deftly pulled up the RFID transmitter on her phone, set it to *Scramble*, and casually pointed it at the ID scanner as she passed. The phone blasted the scanner with dozens of RFID codes in quick succession. As Anna expected, this system was like most others on the market and immediately locked down to prevent hacking. That would buy her an extra minute or two as the director and receptionist realized they had to go back to the main exit.

Turning her focus to the parking lot and Leo's besieged Lexus, Anna evaluated the situation. There were only three employees left near the SUV. This plan might actually work.

When they were within ten feet of the car, she summoned her best flirtatious pout. "Wait a second. Which of you am I going to attack . . . I mean play against first?"

The muscle bros started volunteering, then arguing with each other.

"I know," Anna cut through the posturing, "let's ask somebody to help us decide. What about those guys?" She pointed toward the trio of workers.

Anna steered them toward the Lexus, positioning them directly on the other side of the gathered group from the vehicle. She slipped her hands from their arms as they simultaneously launched into their campaigns to win the vote of the three employees. Anna stood back and waited a few moments until they had both pointed to her as the reason they wanted to play basketball. Then once the attention of the employees was back on the argument, she slid sideways to the next car and quickly ducked behind it.

Crouching low, Anna scooted around the back of the car and darted to the rear of the Lexus. Knowing she wouldn't be able to open the driver's door unnoticed, even with the guys' distraction, she held the key fob close to the tailgate and pressed the latch. The door lifted a few feet, and she grabbed the handle. Holding tight to prevent it from going any farther, she crawled up into the space behind the back seat and pulled the door closed.

With patience honed through dozens of missions, Anna slowly and carefully lowered the rear seat and slid to the next row. She repeated the process with the middle seats. When she reached the front seats, she flattened herself against the center console and slithered forward. Huffing and grunting, Anna finally got herself right-side-up in the driver's seat. She didn't dare sit up straight despite the deeply tinted front windshield.

The distraction duo were still arguing with the rehab attendants—and each other—though Anna could tell the attendants were losing interest. Her habit of backing into parking spaces to allow for quick getaways hadn't done any good in this case because the five men blocked her only exit. She peeked at the side mirror to check how much sidewalk she had behind her. It was not much wider than the SUV. Driving in reverse along a narrow sidewalk wouldn't be her first choice for a sneaky escape. Maybe she could wait until the group lost interest and broke up.

Over the top of the dashboard, she caught a glimpse of the therapy center's front doors swinging open. The receptionist and her boss strode quickly out.

So much for waiting it out. Escape time was now or never.

She pushed the engine start button, threw the shift lever into reverse, and immediately mashed the accelerator. The tires squealed as the back wheels bit the curb and jumped onto the sidewalk. Anna swung the wheel hard to the side and barely missed clipping the sedan in the stall next to her.

The group of employees and residents in front of her were too shocked at the car's sudden movement—in reverse no less—to do anything more than gape and stare.

The Lexus' rear bumper glanced off the fence of the basketball court as Anna straightened the wheel. Hopefully that wouldn't leave too much of a mark on the court or the car.

She wondered if Leo's diplomatic immunity would extend to her. Hopefully so. But if she could get away in one piece, maybe she wouldn't have to find out.

While staying hunched over, Anna watched the backup camera's tiny video screen as she jerked back and forth on the wheel, trying to maneuver in the narrow sidewalk at the reverse gear's top speed. A narrow palm tree growing from a sidewalk planter blocked more than half the space. Fortunately, the fence of the tennis court ended at that same point. She hoped she hadn't misjudged the SUV's width.

Easing off ever so slightly on the gas, Anna expertly threaded the Lexus tail-first between the palm tree and the tall steel fence post. The passenger-side mirror scraped along the chain links and smacked the end post. The whole mirror bent toward the front of the car with the impact. Anna winced. They were meant to do that, right?

Once clear of the court fence, Anna swung the car around and jammed the shift lever into drive. From the sound of the spinning tires, she'd left a sizable pair of gashes in the facility's manicured lawn. Aiming the car for a small gap in traffic, Anna sped away without a backward glance.

Two blocks away, she slowly inched up to her full sitting height, and her breathing finally started returning to normal. That visit had gone differently when she'd pictured it beforehand.

Deciding not to press her luck, she headed straight back to the villa. Well, almost straight back to the villa. She made a few loops through a nearby neighborhood shopping center to make sure no one had followed her or identified the prince's car.

Chapter 13

After another full day under pseudo house-arrest, Leo begged Anna to intervene with Zane and Celine. Though they were initially skeptical of Anna's claim that the attacks had been directed at the agents rather than the prince, with the evidence Anna shared from her interviews with the former agents, Leo's two trusted chiefs eventually agreed to let him attend his friend's ship-launch party. The security risk was minimal. It would be held on a formidable yacht at a secluded berth in Port Miami—coded entry to the harbor marina and guards checking a guest list at the ramp to the yacht.

Even so, Zane agreed to the outing only on the condition that all the bodyguards and close security agents be present at the event—all hands on deck, so to speak. Anna and Jessie were pressed into service doing two security sweeps of the yacht beforehand. Only once the party had begun did Anna allow herself to relax somewhat, knowing that Zane had things well under control.

With the salty Atlantic breeze wafting across the upper deck of the multi-million-dollar luxury yacht, Anna stepped to the side as a waiter with a platter full of decadent cheeses bustled past. She tugged at the sleeve of her sweeping floral sundress. Before leaving Club Banana, she had packed for casual, business casual, and formal events, but she hadn't anticipated needing to blend in among Miami's who's-who of visiting European nobility and stardom—on a megayacht, no less. Given that it had all the amenities of a five-star hotel, it really felt more like a penthouse mansion on the water.

Prince Leo bounced from group to group through the upper deck of the boat, or more accurately, was being bounced around by the various members of the upper crust. Leo was the only member of royalty present—and the guest of honor—so it was only fitting that he barely had a moment to breathe.

If they hadn't already agreed that keeping their distance from each other during the party was the best course of action, Anna would have been tempted to swoop in and rescue the dashing prince from the talons of the aspiring princesses surrounding him. Even a flirtatious Party Prince didn't deserve that kind of torture.

Out of the corner of her eye, Anna caught sight of Andre moving casually toward her. She hadn't really changed her opinion of the bodyguard much since she first saw him enter the small Atlanta diner with the prince; she had pegged him as a consummate professional then, and it still held true. But she knew from their interactions that he was also a kind man, unwilling to resort to physical violence unless absolutely necessary. It made her respect him even more.

Zane and Celine's concern for the prince's safety had also forced a slight change in the bodyguards' habits; they were to stay even closer to him than normal. It was the only time she had ever seen Andre do anything casual, and the strain of acting relaxed emanated from him like a high-energy sunlamp.

He stood close enough to brush against her arm. "I've been asked to convey a request from Zane. Prince Leo will be taking the yacht tender out on a short trip prior to the official launch ceremony. It needs a security check before the trip."

Anna raised a brow but only turned slightly toward him. "Hasn't everything on the itinerary already had a security check?"

"I apologize, I should have said 'redundant security check.' You know how on-edge our security director is right now," Andre said.

Anna kept her eyes riveted on Leo as she leaned toward her fellow security agent. "What's a yacht tender?" she whispered.

The large bodyguard allowed a small smile. "As far as I understand, it's the boat they keep inside the yacht. They go out skiing on it or use it to ferry people to shore."

Anna glanced at Andre. "It's inside the yacht? A boat inside a boat?" She shook her head at the extravagance. "It seems like my lack of knowledge about a yacht tender ought to disqualify me from the assignment," she added with a laugh.

With a small grin still on his face, Andre shrugged. If you could call what he did with those enormous shoulders a shrug. "Don't shoot the messenger's messenger."

Anna blew out a soft breath.

"I'll keep an eye on the prince," Andre offered.

"Then he'll be in great hands." Anna patted his arm as she moved casually around him. "And probably safer if I'm not nearby," she muttered under her breath.

As she stepped toward the glass doors that separated the covered, open-air portion of the yacht's top deck from the enclosed portion, part of Anna really hoped to catch Leo's attention, not because she needed to communicate anything to him, but just for her vanity.

Apparently her wish was granted, because she hadn't taken two steps away from her post before his eyes snapped in her direction. Anna raised her brows at him before walking through the doors into the windowed salon. The last glimpse that she caught of his enigmatic smirk made her smile.

Despite her unfamiliarity with luxury boats that were the length of football fields, it only took a few minutes to find the tender garage. To call it a garage would have been a gross understatement. It was more like a speedboat showroom. Half a dozen high powered boats sat in their berths or hung from retrieval cranes. Plush sofas and chairs surrounded the boats as if guests on a superyacht had nothing better to do than come down and admire the smaller speedboats packed inside its hull.

The attendant on duty gave her a curious look as she approached, but once Anna explained who she was and why she was there, he politely pointed out the correct boat.

The attendant referred to it as the limo, and Anna could see why. The long boat had a small control deck at the very front of the boat and an enclosed cabin that took up the rest of its length. She peeked in through the windows as she approached the elegant boat. The cabin could seat ten people in limousine luxury.

"Can I set it down for you?" the attendant asked.

"No, that's alright," Anna said.

"Are you sure?" the attendant asked. "I don't have to put it in the water, I can just lower the lift. It'll be easier to get on." He eyed her sundress and clunky, thick-heeled sandals with skepticism.

Unwilling to concede that she couldn't do something as simple as scaling the side of a boat in her cute outfit, Anna turned away from the attendant, grabbed the bottom of her sundress with one hand and hiked it up above her knees. Clutching the front deck handrail with her other hand, she easily hoisted herself onboard.

Trying not to gloat at the attendant, Anna stepped across the front deck and made a show of inspecting the pilot's controls.

She recognized the throttle and steering wheel, but that was about it. Fortunately, she wasn't the one who had to work it. Did Leo know how to drive a yacht limo? Maybe the prince's friend had a professional limo pilot. Anna wondered if she would get to go along for the ride. Actually, a better question to ask was whether she would be *forced* to go along.

When Anna opened the door to the glass-enclosed cabin, the smell of leather and luxury greeted her. She stepped down into the long space and let the door swing closed behind her. Her Banana Girl assignments had put her in a variety of limos before, but this boat limo had them all beat. Two long leather benches ran the length of the cabin—one on each side facing each other. Behind the luxury seats was a long wall of thick, tinted windows. The only door was in the front of the cabin, and the back wall had two large video screens.

Running a hand along the smooth leather, Anna sat and tested out one of the benches.

Perfection.

She slipped off her sandals, laid back on the bench, and closed her eyes. Assuming one even wanted to be in a tiny boat on the water in the first place, this would be the way to do it. After a minute of guilty indulgence, Anna dragged herself back up to sitting. She needed to complete her inspection, though she wasn't quite sure what she was looking for.

She walked toward the rear of the cabin, looking at the wood floor and the paneling under the benches. Everything seemed to be in place until she got to the back wall. In the farthest corner of the cabin, below one of the video screens, a section of deck panel had been cracked. She got down on her hands and knees and reached for the broken piece of polished wood. The panel easily pulled away from the deck, exposing a massive hole in the boat. Leaning forward, Anna could look down through the hole and see the floor of the boat garage below her.

Even without an in-depth knowledge of boats, Anna felt pretty certain that hole shouldn't be there. She stood and walked toward the cabin door. It was a good thing someone had thought to do a boat inspection before Leo's ride; this boat wouldn't float for more than a few minutes once it was lowered into the water.

Anna grasped the doorknob and twisted. It didn't move. She knelt in front of the handle and jiggled it again. It wasn't actually locked, it was jammed. The handle wouldn't budge.

More exasperated than worried, Anna walked back to the middle of the cabin and knelt up on one of the benches, attempting to peer out through the windows. She couldn't see the attendant's station from her position, so she banged her fist against the glass to get his attention.

A sudden jolt threw her backward onto the floor. The distinct feeling of movement—plus the ceiling shifting sideways—told her that the boat was sliding along the lift gantry. Anna scrambled to her feet and pressed her face to the glass, hoping to catch a glimpse of the person operating the lift. She could see the gantry controls, but no one was there. It must be on automatic operation.

Looking out the opposite window, she saw that the gantry rails were fully extended out the side of the yacht over the water.

And the tender was headed that direction.

She leapt over to the door and tried the handle again.

Still jammed tight.

Taking a step back, she kicked the glass with the heel of her sandal.

Nothing.

Katie's flamethrower sandals were cute and definitely came in handy when something needed to be burned in a hurry, but they weren't much good when something needed to be broken.

She kicked again.

The glass was obviously reinforced to be bullet-proof. A sensible precaution considering the VIPs that it frequently carried.

After another try, she abandoned her attempts to break the window with sandals. She would bring up the issue of titanium-heeled footwear with Hannah when she got back to Club Banana. If she got back.

She stared through the jammed front door at the pilot's console. There was a storage cupboard marked Utility next to the steering column. It probably contained plenty of sharp, heavy items that would break glass. Maybe not reinforced glass, but it would be a start.

She looked around inside the cabin for something substantial to throw through the glass. All the items massive enough to break reinforced glass were bolted down. That was probably smart for a boat, but it didn't help her situation. The only thing she found was a gold-plated corkscrew.

As the tender passed through the garage door to the outside, light flooded the cabin. Squinting, she looked around at the other activity in Miami Harbor. If the limo tender was lowered into the water and started to sink, would any of the nearby boats notice? Even if they did, would anyone be able to get to her in time?

Holding the corkscrew like a dagger, she struck it against the glass. Nothing. Dragging the tip of the screw along the surface of the glass, she was able to make a small scratch, but it would take hours to cut her way through with that. She leaned forward and peered down at the water below.

She didn't have hours. She only had minutes. Maybe even seconds.

As the panic welled up in her gut, Anna felt her training kick in. She stopped and took a breath, forcing herself to evaluate the situation. Using valuable time trying to escape wasn't working. The more pressing issue at the moment was keeping the boat above water.

Anna rushed to the back of the cabin to assess the size of the hole in the hull. She looked around the cabin again, but this time for something big and squishy to plug the hole.

She pulled up on the nearest bench and reached into the under-seat storage for a pile of lifejackets. She bunched two in a tangled mess and held it over the hole. There were too many little crevices for that to keep the water out for long.

She lifted another bench and rooted around inside until she found a stack of beach towels. With a towel spread out on the cabin floor, she rolled the lifejackets into a lumpy bundle.

The towels would soak through too soon. She didn't have the time to consult a materials engineer. She grabbed the expensive corkscrew again and sliced through the leather of the nearest cushion. Tugging and ripping at the foam core, she liberated one of the luxury seats from the bench.

Back in the corner near the hole, she placed the lifejacket bundle into the center of the seat cover and wrapped the unwieldy mass into a roundish shape.

Kneeling next to the gash in the hull, Anna jammed the makeshift plug into the hole. She forced the wad through the deck panel until it was wedged between the outer hull and the wood flooring. Hopefully, that would keep water from gushing in just in case the limo tender did go into the bay.

Now that she had a solution for her immediate danger, it was time to figure out a way off the small boat. As much as it surprised her, she desperately wanted to be back on the big one again.

Though her independent personality usually prevented her from reaching out for help, desperate times called for desperate measures. She pulled her phone out and dialed Leo. "Don't laugh, but I'm stuck," she said as soon as he answered.

Of course the first thing he did was laugh. If her situation hadn't been so dire, she might have laughed with him.

"Where are you?" he asked.

"I'm down in the—"

Anna felt her stomach leap into her throat as the cabin ceiling rushed to meet her. With a brain-sloshing crack, her head hit the hard trim along one of the windows in the roof. As the boat splashed violently against the water, gravity reclaimed Anna and introduced her to the unforgiving metal edge of the now-uncovered leather bench.

She wasn't sure how much time passed as she clutched her lower ribs and writhed in pain on the wood deck of the cabin. The first sound she became aware of was a soft gurgling noise nearby. Next, she felt cool water against her shoulder. She turned over and squinted at the hole, groaning from the pain in her ribs and head.

Water leaked slowly into the cabin around the edges of the makeshift plug. She estimated about fifteen minutes before the cabin was filled, assuming the rate didn't change. That should be long enough for someone to see the small sinking boat and rescue her.

A banging sound on the front deck was accompanied by a slight rocking sensation. Someone must have jumped down onto the small boat. Anna tried to sit up. Her head swam and she suddenly saw stars.

The cabin door opened and Leo stepped through. "Ah, so you thought a nice, private rendezvous on the limo would be—"

"Leo, the door!" Anna reached out from across the cabin as if she could keep the door from swinging shut.

Bang.

Anna groaned, partly in pain, partly in frustration because Leo apparently couldn't read her mind.

Her groan brought the young prince rushing to her side. He wrapped an arm around her waist. "Are you hurt?" he asked, concern written on his face.

Anna let him lift her to sit on the opposite bench. "I've had bruises like this before. I'll live."

Leo looked down at the water lapping at his toes. "Anna, the boat has a leak. Let's get out of here."

Anna glared at him. "Why didn't I think of that?"

He tried to lift her from the bench, but she resisted.

"The latch is jammed," she said.

He frowned. "I just came through it."

"Only on the inside."

He walked back to the door and tried it anyway. After struggling with the handle for a few seconds, he turned back in resignation. Part of Anna was glad that he couldn't get it open either. As much as she wanted to be out of the sinking limo tender and on the yacht again—or better yet, solid ground—she definitely didn't want him to save them that easily. It would have been worse than when she would struggle with a jar lid only to have a guy easily pop it open after she had worked so hard to loosen it.

"Now what?" he asked.

Anna reached for her cellphone but couldn't find it. She looked around the cabin which was now an inch deep in sloshing water. She leaned down and fished it out of the corner.

"Just like that time at Splash Mountain," she said, shaking her head. "Katie even told me I needed the new waterproof version."

"Let me try mine." Leo reached into the small pocket of his deck shorts. He looked down, patting his shorts all over. "Where's my phone?"

Anna's shoulders slumped. This was going from bad to worse. "You jumped from the yacht onto the tender, didn't you?" she asked, even though she knew the answer.

Leo's eyes went wide. He stared out the cabin's glass door. "There it is." He pointed to the front deck, just beneath the steering controls. "I can't believe it fell out with such a short jump. It's the stupid mini-pockets of these deck shorts."

"Do not talk to me about mini-pockets. Do you have any idea how hard it is to fit lipstick, a phone, and even half a stick of gum into the pockets in women's clothing? And that's if the outfit even has pockets. I mean, we put a man on the moon, you'd think we could put sensible pockets into—" Anna stopped when she saw Leo grinning back at her. "What?"

"I like this passionate side of you," he said. "It's very attractive."

Anna held up her hand. "We don't have time for discussing passion or fashion." She stood and walked to Leo, holding a hand to the back of her head. "We've got about ten minutes until the cabin fills with water. How long before someone notices you're missing and finds us?"

Leo looked up at the megayacht towering over their tiny boat. "Zane or Andre should notice I'm gone soon, right?"

"Did you talk to anyone on the way down here? Does anyone know where you were heading?" she asked.

"I passed Andre and said I was going to find you."

"Didn't he offer to come with you?" Anna asked. It wasn't like Andre not to be thorough.

The prince rubbed the back of his neck, a chagrined look on his face. "I think I told him not to worry, that I had it all under control."

Anna rolled her eyes. "He probably thought you wanted to be alone with me."

"He's not wrong."

Anna blew out a long breath. "So no one will be joining us. We're completely on our own."

Leo nodded. "I would really love to hear you say that exact phrase again someday, just not in this particular circumstance."

She shot him a warning glance.

He held up his hands. "Sorry, just trying to make a little joke. Not that I wouldn't mind if the two of us—"

"Leo!" Anna heard the frustration in her voice and hoped the prince understood she wasn't mad, just anxious to get them both safely out. "Help me check all of the cabinets and drawers again. We need something sharp or heavy."

They tore through all of the storage cubbies in the cabin and found a dozen champagne flutes plus several bottles of bubbly.

"How about this?" Leo held out a small metal bottle opener.

Anna examined it. No sharp corners. Great for prying. Not great for breaking reinforced glass in order to escape a sinking boat. She shook her head and tossed it on the bench. "I already found a corkscrew, and it didn't work." She pointed at the discarded luxury accessory.

"We just need to get the boat to land. Can we drive from inside the cabin?" Leo asked.

Anna frowned and looked from him to the boat controls out on the small front deck. "With the controls out there and us locked in here, I can't see how . . ." Anna's brows drew together in concentration.

"What?" Leo asked eagerly.

Anna turned and glanced down the length of the cabin's wood deck. "The controls are up there, but the motor is back here. If the control system uses electronic signals instead of cabling, then we might be able to hot wire it. If we can find the wiring." She stared back out the front door at the steering system, trying to imagine where the wires would go on their way to the motor in the back. She grabbed the bottle opener and stepped to the back of the cabin where the hole continued to ominously bubble water out onto the deck panels. She reached down and hooked the metal opener under a piece of broken panel and pulled hard. The panel snapped free. She quickly double-checked the integrity of the plug. It was still in place.

With Leo's help, it only took a minute to tear off a long strip of the wood deck, exposing the support girding underneath. Through the lattice-work of metal, Anna spied a bundle of wiring. She reached in and yanked the wire harness, freeing several feet of slack that she pulled up above the deck panels.

"Now all I need are some wire clippers, a soldering gun, a digital signal generator, and my friend Katie to put it all together," she said with a fair amount of sarcasm. "Oh, and some gum."

"Like electrical adhesive gum?" Leo asked, staring eagerly at the wiring.

"No. Chewing gum," Anna said. "It helps me concentrate."

Leo stared at her for several seconds before bursting into laughter. "How do you do it?"

"What?" Anna frowned in his general direction as she considered whether the small pivoting arm of the fancy corkscrew could be used sort of like scissors. What she wouldn't give to have Hannah and Katie's prototype nail clipper and wire splicer. Unfortunately, that particular gadget was sitting uselessly in her bathroom bag back at the villa.

"You've been dropped into the ocean in a locked sardine can, and in the middle of planning an impossible rescue, you can make me laugh. You're amazing!"

Anna glanced up and saw the look of utter adoration on the prince's face. This was no time to talk about their feelings for each other. Hers were still a messy jumble anyway. She decided to brush it aside with more banter. "It's in the job description," she said with a shrug.

"Anna . . ." Leo's voice sounded husky and serious. Anna didn't dare look up. "I have every confidence that you'll be able to devise another miraculous rescue." He paused for a few seconds. "But just in case, I think you should know how I feel about you."

She reached for the discarded can opener. "You know, stressful life-or-death situations tend to heighten people's emotions. It's not a good time to talk about feelings."

Anna gripped the bundle of wires, separating each individually-colored line. With no scissors or any other tool to cut through the wiring, Anna was forced to use the edge of the can opener to gnaw back part of the plastic covering the metal cores.

"That may be true for some people," the prince said, "but this isn't just a heat-of-the-moment thing. Starting the day I met you, I've been falling head over heels for you."

Anna tried to ignore the explosion of giddy excitement rising in her stomach. Having a handsome prince confess his love for her was not incredibly helpful at the moment. But she couldn't help a small grin and a furtive glance his way.

He was every little girl's—and one particular Banana Girl's—dream come true.

She closed her eyes and tried to rattle a coherent thought free. Inclining her head toward the front of the boat, she said, "If I can get the engine started, I'll need you to tell me where we're going."

Leo gave her a dashing smile before moving to the cabin's front door. "See, I told you you're amazing."

Not that Leo could have seen the blush on her dark skin, but Anna was glad he was looking the other way regardless. Just breathing was becoming difficult while he was near her.

She examined the stripped wires, attempting to figure out which ones would be the ignition for the motor. "You've barely known me for a week," she said, despite her best intentions to ignore his declaration.

"It's been ten days," he countered. "And think about how much of that time we've spent together. Think of everything we've been through."

Taking a deep breath, Anna attempted to redirect her Leo-frazzled brain. The red wire would be the main power line. Could the blue one be the ignition ground? She touched the bare sections of the wire together.

Nothing.

What about the green wire?

Nope. Still nothing.

The yellow wire?

As Anna touched the wires together, the motor rumbled to life.

The green and blue were still the most likely candidates for the throttle control, so she held them close together near the red power wire.

She looked up at Leo. "Ready?" she asked.

"Ready." His gaze was glued ahead of the boat. "We have about forty meters clear before we have to turn."

After her impact with the bulkhead and Leo's proclamation of love, Anna's synapses weren't quite firing at full strength. "What's that in feet?"

Leo looked back at her. "What's the matter with Americans? Why can't they get caught up with the rest of the world on the metric system?"

Squeezing her eyes shut in frustration, Anna wailed, "Can we have this argument another time?"

Leo grinned. "And lots of other arguments I hope." He turned and looked forward again. "There's a jetty about forty *yards* ahead. We'll need to veer left."

Anna touched the blue wire to the power lead. That wasn't it. She glanced at the water, now sloshing over her calves as she knelt next to the cracked floor. Hopefully the green wire would be the right one because she wasn't sure there would be time to pull out and strip more of the wire harness.

She touched the green wire to the red, and the motor roared, throwing them both backward as the boat leapt forward. Leo slid along the polished, wet wood and slammed into her legs. She lost grip of the wires, and when they separated the engine dropped to idle again.

He pushed up on all fours, sputtering. "You Americans like speed, don't you?"

She shot him a dirty look. "I don't have a digital signal generator—or any chewing gum—so the engine's either on or off. That's all we've got."

As he splashed through water above his ankles back to the cabin door, Anna called after him, "Ten days isn't enough to know if you're really falling for someone."

Leo grabbed the nearest handrailing and called back to her, "Okay, go again with the throttle."

The boat jolted as the motor screamed to full throttle again. Anna twisted the throttle wire to the stripped section of red cable so it wouldn't accidentally separate again.

Leo watched out the front window. "Okay, we're clear. Turn left!" he yelled.

Anna grabbed the stripped signal wires that she assumed were for steering. She touched the orange one to the power wire. The boat tilted madly to the right. "Argh! Sorry!" Anna cried. She grabbed the other steering wire to correct her mistake.

"No! Wait!" Leo held out his hand while still staring out the window. "It's too narrow to turn around at this speed. We'll have to go farther down the channel and see if there's a place to turn around. Give it a little more right."

Anna obediently touched the orange to the power wire again, then she looked up at Leo to see his reaction.

"Good. We're in the harbor channel now. We just need to go straight." He glanced back at her with a broad smile. "And ten days is definitely enough to find out all of the important qualities a person has."

Looking out the short windows, Anna could see cargo containers stacked in neat rows with tall loading cranes standing nearby. "What could you possibly have found out about me in ten days?"

"A little left; we're drifting." Leo said. "You're beautiful, intelligent, confident. Those are very attractive qualities."

Anna tapped the purple wire to the red one. After a quick nod from Leo, she arranged the purple wire in her left hand and the orange wire in her right, clasping the red power wire—with the throttle wire still wrapped around it—as best she could between her other available fingers.

"Is there another outlet at the end of the channel?" Anna asked.

Leo frowned in concentration but didn't look back at her. "I can't tell from here. It just looks like skyscrapers. Maybe we can turn around if the channel opens up. A little right," he added.

Right wire.

Anna looked to the right and saw the top deck of a small ferry fly by. At full throttle, everything was a blur of colors and shapes. "I happen to know you're around beautiful, confident women all the time. That's not a good enough reason to fall for someone." She couldn't believe that she was trying to talk a handsome prince out of thinking he had fallen in love with her—particularly while flying at break-neck speed down a harbor channel. But that was better than the pain of her broken heart that would surely follow if he was wrong.

"Oh no," Leo said in a deadpan tone.

"What?"

"Cruise ships," he replied.

He left the ominous declaration hanging in the air as if that told her everything she needed to know. "What about them?" she demanded.

"Well, in addition to carrying passengers that are a general annoyance to have around when you're trying to find a nice place on vacation or see the sights of a certain city, we happen to have two particular cruise ships blocking our path."

"Leo, I don't care about your tourist pet peeves. Tell me which way to steer!"

"One is coming off the dock into the channel. The one behind it is going into the dock."

Anna looked left and saw the tall triangle mast of a cruise liner. "Can't we just stay clear of the dock and miss both of them?"

"Doubtful," Leo called over his shoulder. "The tugs already have the departing ship within ten meters of the causeway wall."

Anna scrunched her eyes closed. "Is that a lot? That doesn't sound like very much."

"It's not. We need to go left. Give it a medium left turn," Leo instructed.

With three brief touches of the left wire, the boat turned. They were getting better at this.

"The same amount of right to straighten out."

Right taps.

"Almost . . ." He leaned to the side. "A little left."

Left tap.

"It's not just your physical beauty—though that definitely got my attention at the beginning—you are incredibly fun to be around," Leo said.

"Like when I'm critiquing your driving or getting you trapped in a freezer or telling you your baking ideas are crazy?"

They were close enough to the docked cruise ships that Anna

could see the balconies of the upper decks and the bright red covers of the lifeboats hanging on the side of the vast ship.

"I enjoyed all of those . . . uh oh." Leo gaped at the view ahead.

"What?" Hurtling blindly through the narrow Miami Harbor channel was going to drive her crazy. If a certain lovesick prince didn't do it first.

"The second ship is closer to the dock than I thought," he said.

"How close?" she asked.

"That's it," he pointed ahead of them.

Anna craned her neck. She could see the upper mast of a cruise ship straight ahead of them. It must have been nearly touching the dock on their left.

"Can we still make it between the dock before it touches?"

"Maybe. Can you make us go faster?"

"Leo!"

"I'm just kidding. Give a little left then straighten out, we'll get as close to the dock wall as we can."

Anna touched the left wire then quickly the right. The last cruise ship loomed in the window, encompassing Anna's entire view as they sped by. She couldn't see any of the details of the white hull flying past. It just felt like the world was closing in on her.

"I'm pretty sure it's going to squish us!" Anna cried with rising panic.

"Not quite! Give me a small slide left again!"

Left tap. Right tap.

Anna looked anxiously at the towering hulk of a ship beside them. On the left she caught a glimpse of one of the extendible docking bridges. Hopefully the passengers were enjoying the last bit of entertainment on their cruise. She hoped the final spectacle wouldn't be a small limo tender smashing in a flaming fireball against the seawall.

Leo's jaw clenched, and he tightened his grip on the handrail.

Anna wanted to close her eyes to shut out the massive blur of a ship towering over them, but she didn't dare.

"We're through!" Leo yelled as Anna felt them brush over the wake at the back of the enormous ship.

She let out the breath she'd been holding. "Now what?"

"Well, you're also calm under pressure. I really do love that about you, especially in a situation like this."

"Leo!" If she weren't wedged in the ideal position against the bench and if her hands weren't already busy, she would have gotten up and wrung his neck.

"Sorry." Leo looked around. "The channel opened up. There's a bridge to the right, but there are boats everywhere." He looked left. "Another bridge to the left, but it's clear. Turn hard left."

Anna pressed the left wire to the power and braced herself as the boat turned hard to the left. The water sloshed up to her rib cage. "Is calm under pressure really a trait you're looking for in a girlfriend? Are you planning to frequently be getting into this much trouble?"

Leo tossed a playful smirk over his shoulder. When he looked back toward the front, his face morphed into a concerned frown. "I think I should have told you to go the other way. This bridge only has one opening."

"Should we stop and ask for directions?" Anna asked, heavy sarcasm in her voice.

Leo ignored her; or perhaps he didn't catch her tone. "No. It's bigger than the gap we just squeezed through, plus it's not closing in on us. It should be easy. Light left."

"You know," she began as she lightly touched the left wire, "if your idea of a nice date is to lock a girl in the cabin of a sinking boat, force her to hotwire it, then race wildly around Miami Harbor searching for deadly stunts to perform, we might not be that good of a match after all."

He turned back to her with a grin. "And here I thought I had you swooning for me."

"Spies don't swoon," she shot back.

"Wanna bet?" he said with a smoldering look.

"Watch where we're going, please." She motioned to the front of the boat with her head.

"Slide right."

Anna touched right then left.

"I also love that you're patient with me," Leo said. "Tiny touch left."

She touched the left wire for a split second. "Let's not test how far that particular trait can go," she said.

Watching something up ahead, Leo winced and leaned slowly to the right.

"Slide right?" Anna asked, ready to make another quick adjustment.

Leo held a palm out behind his back.

The shadow of the drawbridge quickly passed over the cabin.

"Now we're clear!" Leo announced.

"Great," Anna said.

"On a sadder note, my cell phone was not properly secured in a safety belt," he inclined his head toward the front deck where his phone had landed, "and did not survive our last turn."

Anna couldn't help a small smile and a shake of her head. Why did he have to be so charming when he was frustrating? "Let's find somewhere to land."

"Well, we're in the south channel now," he said. "If we can

negotiate passing under one more bridge, we'd be halfway back to the villa."

"Leo?" She waited until she had his full attention before looking very purposefully down at her middle. "I'm nearly underwater here. Let's find somewhere to crash now."

Leo glanced down at his own legs. The water was above his knees. "Right," he said. "Let's see . . ."

Anna looked out the windows, but couldn't see much except the tips of tall buildings. It was a welcome change to the claustrophobia of the cruise ship channel, but they were quickly running out of time.

"I don't see any beaches around here. Just docks, jetties, and seawalls—Whoa!" He looked left. "Superyacht! Hard right!"

The boat veered right at Anna's instinctive reaction. They were performing like a well-oiled machine now. She could only imagine what the driverless limo tender looked like from the perspective of the yacht they almost hit.

With a pulse left a few seconds later, she brought the boat back to their original course along the shoreline. "Shouldn't one of those high-rise condos have a beach?" she said, jerking her head to the right.

Leo shook his head. "Just barrier walls, which will kill us much faster than sinking."

Anna lifted the wires up to eye-level as the water reached her chest.

"Wait. I see an island with trees," Leo called out. "Maybe there's a beach. Medium left."

Anna steered the boat to the left and waited in anticipation of Leo's verdict. She found herself taking shorter breaths as the water lapped over her shoulders. She awkwardly stood and hunched over in the waist-high water, pulling the wires as far as they would go. Just inches above the water, the exposed portion of the cabling would be submerged in less than a minute. She wasn't sure if the control signals would still work once they touched the water.

"Leo! This needs to be it. I don't care if it's a rocky jetty. We need to hit something."

"No. It's perfect, Anna. Sandy, white beaches. We'll be safe in a minute. I need a soft left."

Anna touched the left wire to the power just as the water hit the exposed wiring. The left turn—and the motor—suddenly stopped. Fortunately, these were just signal wires which didn't have enough juice to electrocute them in the water, because, as far as Anna was concerned, dying by drowning versus dying by electrocution was a toss-up.

Hopefully their speed was enough, because they were coasting on momentum now.

"Hang on!" Leo yelled.

A long scraping—like fingernails on a chalkboard—reverberated up through the deck as the boat finally made contact with land. The water in the cabin rushed forward, pounding Leo against the front door as the boat screeched to a halt. A second later, the tidal wave returned in a deluge that knocked Anna off her feet.

Sloshing back and forth in their portable makeshift wave pool, Anna spluttered to the surface of the water. The cabin was suddenly silent except for the splashing the prince made wading toward her.

Together, they tugged the temporary plug free from the hole, and water began to drain out of the cabin onto the rocky beach.

She flopped down next to Leo on the squelchy leather bench, her flowery sundress completely soaked through. Leo looked spent, his wet shirt clinging to his well-defined chest and arms.

"So what shall we do on our own private little island? That

didn't sound like a white, sandy beach to me," she said, her brow raised.

Leo laughed. "Yes, sorry about the beach. It's not the picturesque spot I was hoping for. But I suppose we could roam around exploring it. Pick a place to build a romantic bungalow."

Just when Anna thought her heart rate might be returning to normal.

How was she ever going to disabuse him of the notion that he had fallen for her when her own heart refused to cooperate? The seconds of silence felt thick around her.

"Thank you—once again—for saving my life," Leo finally said. "I'm not sure how I'll ever be out of your debt."

Anna turned to look into those deep blue eyes. "That's what spy girls do," she said with an attempt at a casual shrug. Her breath hitched in her chest. His face was only a few inches away.

His gaze drifted down to her lips. "Do you think a limousine tender screaming full speed down Miami's cruise ship channel will be enough to get the attention of the harbor patrol?" He leaned slightly toward her.

Anna nodded slowly. "They'll probably be here to arrest us in a few minutes," she said.

"It's too bad we can't tell them there's no rush," he said, leaning even closer.

"Why would we do that?" she asked with feigned innocence as she explored the details of his face.

"I was going to prove that you have one more personality trait that I'm looking for."

"What's that?" She hoped he didn't notice the tremble in her voice.

"Chemistry," he said with a charming smirk.

His mouth moved slowly closer to hers, and her traitorous body leaned toward him. She closed her eyes and felt the tickle of his breath against her lips.

The sudden crunching of boots on the rocks and the abrupt tilting of the boat told them that the harbor patrol had arrived all too soon.

Leo winced at the sound of rapping knuckles on the cabin door, a look of disappointment and longing spreading across his handsome face.

Anna took a fortifying breath and leaned away from him. "It's probably for the best," she whispered.

"I disagree." A wry smile lifted the corners of his tempting lips. "But apparently you're going to take some convincing."

They had spent the remainder of the afternoon after the limo tender adventure explaining the whole story to the harbor patrol, who fortunately could see the evidence of tampering themselves. Then they spent part of the evening back at the villa rehashing everything with Zane and Celine. Despite Anna's continued insistence that the most recent attacks were directed at her, Zane made the decision to confine the prince to the villa again. She couldn't blame him; it certainly seemed like Leo had been in danger.

When she finally made it back to her room that evening, Anna sat contemplating the events of the day. Someone was clearly trying to kill her. There was no way the sabotaged boat was meant for Leo. He only ended up inside because she called to tell him she was trapped—and because he didn't listen when she told him to not let the door close.

The information she'd gleaned from visiting the former close agents was helpful, but if she could talk to Makenna and Kaitlynn again, she might gain some insight into who the perpetrator was.

Talk to Makenna.

In the commotion of her escape from the rehab facility,

she'd forgotten about texting Makenna's number to herself. She opened the secure Banana Girls' cloud connection on her phone and dialed Makenna's number.

After a quick reminder of who she was, Anna got straight to business. "I thought you might want to know that based on the latest evidence, we think the attack at the sandbar party was actually meant for you, not Prince Leo."

"Why would anyone attack me?" Makenna asked.

"That's what we're trying to figure out," Anna replied. "Can you tell me about your relationship with Prince Leo?"

There was a short pause on the line. "Well, I suppose I'd say we're friends, if that's what you mean."

"Were there any romantic feelings that developed?" Anna tried to stay professional, even while a part of her heart cringed.

Makenna let out a short laugh. "No."

Anna opened her mouth, ready to ask a follow-up question about when her relationship had started to shift in that direction, but she stopped, confused by Makenna's answer. "Wait. Did you say there wasn't a change in your feelings for the prince?"

"I mean, he's a great guy, and we definitely have lots of fun partying together. But, no, I've never had any romantic feelings for him. He's not really my type."

Anna wanted to ask what was wrong with the prince—or what was wrong with Makenna—that she didn't think he was her type. But all that came out was, "Huh."

After a pause, Makenna continued. "Did someone say I had feelings for Leo?"

"No," Anna quickly replied. "I just thought your situation would follow the same pattern I saw in some of the other agents." Anna wasn't quite sure where to go with the conversation. If there weren't any feelings on Makenna's part, then that poked holes in her entire theory. Unless there had been some indication of feelings on Leo's part. She hated what she had to ask next, but it needed to be done. "I wonder, did you ever see any indication from the prince that he might be interested in you? Romantically, I mean."

Makenna chuckled softly. "It's hard to tell with Leo sometimes, isn't it? He can be such a friendly guy. But I'm fairly confident it was just his regular, harmless flirtation."

Anna breathed a silent sigh of relief. "Okay, thanks, Makenna. I don't quite know how to make your experience fit in with what I've learned from the other agents. If you had said you had aspirations to be a princess that would have helped my case so much more." Anna kept her tone light, hoping that Makenna would know she was trying to make a joke.

"Actually, now that you mention it . . ." Makenna's voice trailed off and Anna's stomach dropped. "Kaitlynn and I were joking about that once."

"Oh yeah?" Anna forced herself to say.

"Yeah. We were talking about what great jobs we have. I mean, think about it—living in the lap of luxury, pampered at every turn, going to all the best parties and high-profile events. And all we have to do is know how to keep the prince safe."

"Then I pointed out to Kaitlynn that we would only get to keep our jobs as long as Leo stayed single. As soon as he got married, we'd be replaced by the new princess. Then Kaitlynn said something like, 'maybe I should quit and pursue him myself.' And I said, 'not if I beat you to it'."

A comment like that would definitely get the attention of a jealous would-be lover. "Where did this conversation happen?" Anna asked.

"It was after a beach party at Leo's friend's place a few weeks ago," Makenna said.

"You made a comment about pursuing the prince at a party with his friends around?"

"No. The party was over. Nobody was around." Makenna sounded defensive. "Besides, we were just joking about it."

Anna nodded absently as she tried to piece that bit of information into the mosaic of the case. Despite Makenna's insistence, Anna's instincts told her that someone must have overheard. "And you think Kaitlynn was joking, too, about wanting to pursue the prince?"

Makenna's casual tone returned. "Oh, definitely. She plays the party-girl part well, but she's still totally in love with this guy she dated in high school."

"Hmm." Anna glanced around her room, not really looking at anything in particular. "That's great information, Makenna. You've been a huge help."

After Anna finished the call, she stood up and paced the room. Two agents were fired and one quit after they all started getting close to the prince. Two more agents were injured on duty after a presumably-overheard conversation about pursuing him.

There was no doubt in her mind they were dealing with a jealous lover.

Now the only question was whether the perpetrator of the attacks was someone from Leo's social circle or from his inner circle.

Chapter 14

The next morning, Anna was behind schedule for her run. Just as she had finished tying her shoes, she received a cryptic text from Leo.

– Breakfast nook! ASAP!

Anna wasn't sure what Leo could need that would be ASAP—especially in the breakfast nook—but it was pretty good timing given that she needed to consult with him on what she'd learned from Makenna.

With a quick glance in the mirror to ensure she was presentable, she dashed out the door and up the stairs to the third-floor kitchen.

She still hadn't really had a chance to sort out her feelings about Leo yet, so hopefully he wasn't planning on confessing his love for her again. Heaven help her weak resolve to hold to Rule Number One if he wanted to prove they had chemistry.

As Anna entered the cozy kitchen, bright light from the rising sun reflected off the counter and hardwood floors, temporarily blinding her. She raised a hand to shield her face and glanced around the small space. She didn't see Leo anywhere.

Just as she turned to leave, she heard a loud whisper. "Psst!"

Anna spun around and squinted into the sunrise. Leo's head was sticking out from the hidden corner of the breakfast nook. He beckoned her forward.

Anna shook her head and smiled. What was he up to? She stepped more fully into the kitchen and stopped a few feet from the prince's hiding place. "Yes, Your Highness?" she said theatrically. A little use of his formal title to add distance couldn't hurt.

"Shhh!" he hissed. "And why are you 'Your Highness'-ing me?" He reached out and grabbed her hand, pulling her toward him. She could have resisted, but the look of adorable desperation on his face plus a dash of crumbling willpower made it hard to say no.

He scooted tighter into the hidden corner to make room for her. Then with a look of complete sincerity, he said, "I need you to bust me out of this joint."

Anna's eyes went wide, and she slapped a hand over her mouth to stifle a giggle threatening to escape.

"What?" Leo asked, looking puzzled. "Isn't that how you Americans would say it, bust me out?"

With a tilt of her head and a shrug, Anna gave the prince a patronizing smile. "Sort of."

The prince brushed aside her critique. "I've already contacted the pilot and crew, and they have the flight plans to Sint Maarten all arranged." Leo gave her a hesitant smile. "I promised my mother that I would visit Grootmoeder."

"What's grootmoeder?"

"My grootmoeder . . . my oma." Leo raised his brows expectantly.

Anna shook her head, still confused.

"My grandmother?"

"You're going to visit your grandmother?" she said with a smile. "That's sweet."

"Does that change your answer?" he asked expectantly.

"Maybe," she said.

Leo grinned proudly.

"And Sint Maarten?" Anna asked.

"It's an island in the Dutch Caribbean. When Grootvader passed away, Grootmoeder decided to enjoy her golden years somewhere warm."

"So you want me to help you sneak away to visit your grandmother?" Anna pretended to ponder the question's merit. "Okay," Anna replied.

Leo stared at her for a second, frowning. "Okay?"

"Sure," she said with a shrug.

"Not that I ever doubted my powers of persuasion, but I have to say I thought it would take much more than that to convince you to go along with my brilliant plan."

"No, I think it's a great idea. Otherwise, I was probably going to have to kidnap you," Anna said with a casual tone.

Leo's brows went up. "Kidnap me?"

As he scrutinized her expression, Anna found it difficult to keep a straight face. When she finally cracked a smile, Leo's shoulders visibly relaxed, and he leaned toward her. "I always knew you had a nefarious hidden agenda. What was your plan? To steal me away to some deserted island? Tie me to a coconut tree until I confess my undying adoration for you?"

Anna poked him in the chest. "Hey, I'm not the one who just suggested a secret escape to the Caribbean."

"I like your plan better."

She glared at him playfully. "Don't you want to hear my reason for kidnapping you first?"

He gave a regal wave. "Yes. Please proceed."

Forcing down a giggle, Anna took a deep breath. "I think I know *why* the attacks are happening, but I don't know who's behind them. If we can get you out of the villa without anyone knowing, that might help us figure it out."

"And that's why I have to be your island love slave?"

"Leo!"

The prince held up his hands in surrender. "Sorry, sorry. I couldn't resist. I'll try to be helpful." His brows furrowed in an expression of renewed concentration. "So we know the attacks were meant for you and the other agents. Why haven't any of the attacks come when you're away from me? I mean, you were driving around Miami most of the afternoon a few days ago. Wouldn't that have been the perfect opportunity for an attacker?"

Anna cocked her head to the side. "The attacker must think it will be easier to avoid getting caught if the attacks look like they're meant for you. If you think about it, that's not too far-fetched. No one would suspect a personal bodyguard of being the target if they get attacked while protecting their employer."

Leo nodded thoughtfully. "Hmm. And because none of the attacks have happened here at the villa, we can assume it must be someone from the general public."

"Not necessarily," Anna said. "If it's meant to throw off an investigation, the perpetrator might only orchestrate the attacks to happen when you're out in public."

"No, it has to be someone on the outside. No one on my staff would want to harm you. They all think you're amazing."

Anna could think of one particular fellow agent who wasn't fond of her at the moment, but she didn't want to say anything without more evidence.

"So then how does secretly leaving the villa help us figure out who's behind everything?" Leo asked.

"A sudden, unplanned trip somewhere—like a spontaneous

trip to a dance club or being kidnapped by an undercover agent"—Anna subtly indicated herself and Leo smiled—"wouldn't give the person any advanced notice to plan an attack. Then we slowly let out information about your whereabouts, and when the attack comes, we have a better idea where to focus the investigation based on who got the leaked information and when."

The prince scowled and slowly shook his head. "No. On second thought, I don't like this idea."

"Why not?" Anna asked. "Didn't you just suggest that I 'bust you out of this joint'? Aren't you getting exactly what you asked for?"

"No. There's a big difference. When I hatched the idea, it was the dashing prince escaping with his lady fair to a tropical island paradise. But you make it sound like a reckless plan where you're the bait to draw out a dangerous criminal."

"That's the real world, Leo. This is the job I was sent to do."

His frown slowly faded, but his brows were knit with concern. "I still don't like it, Anna. I want to keep you safe."

"Don't worry. We'll be safe," Anna said, touching him on the arm. "Unless of course, your grandmother is a lethal assassin."

Leo grinned. "She is known for her bone-breaking hugs."

"Then I can't wait to meet her," Anna said.

The prince's features lit up. "Great. Meet me down in the garage in five minutes."

"Five minutes? I can't pack for a trip and change clothes in five minutes."

"Why do you need to change? You look fantastic," Leo said with a quick glance at her workout attire.

Anna tried to ignore the rising heat that accompanied his compliment. "How about fifteen minutes?" She'd been sent on missions with short notice before, but she couldn't break the laws of physics.

"Perfect," he replied. "Oh, I almost forgot. Do you have a current passport?"

Anna raised a brow and pointed to herself. "World-renowned super-agent."

Leo laughed. "Yes, I know. I just wasn't sure if you used a legitimate passport. You might have dozens of fake passports, or you might not even use a passport at all."

"We sometimes need to enter a country by standard means," she said airily. Of course, that was embellishing things a bit.

The prince laughed again as they walked together out of the breakfast nook. "Get packed and meet me by the Lexus," he said. "We can have breakfast on the jet." He stopped and considered her. "Oma is going to love you."

Anna fought a smile all the way back to her room. As she packed, she made a call to Club Banana. Given that no one on Leo's villa staff would know where they'd gone for several hours, she figured it wouldn't be a bad idea to let the Banana Girls know where she was. Hannah answered.

"Hey Hannah, Prince Leo is taking me to Sint Maarten to visit his grandmother. I wanted to give you the heads up before it happened, so you wouldn't freak out."

"You're meeting his family?" Hannah asked in her dry tone. "What kind of assignment are you on anyway?"

Anna blew out a breath. Leave it to her friend to misinterpret everything. "We needed an excuse to get him away from the villa to draw out the attacker. It's official mission stuff."

"Oh, I have no doubt that you're working on the mission. I just find it interesting that he's taking you to meet his grandmother. Haven't you ever seen *An Affair to Remember*?"

"It's not like that, Han. You don't think there's something going on between us, do you?" Anna hated that she was such a bad liar when it came to her Banana Girls co-founder.

"Oh, I know there is. I'm just wondering how far you'll let it go."

"It's not like I'll suddenly go weak in the knees just because some dashing European prince looks at me with his smoldering blue eyes then invites me on a trip to the Caribbean." Anna laughed light-heartedly.

Hannah cocked her head and stared at Anna through the video screen. It was her skeptical, are-you-kidding-me look. Anna knew that look well.

"Don't look at me like that, Hannah. I know what I'm doing."

"I should hope so, with as much grief as you give the rest of us about Rule Number One."

"I'll be fine," Anna said, using her free hand to swat away Hannah's concern like a pesky fly. "Anyway, I have to finish packing. Tell the girls I said hi."

Anna disconnected the call and stuffed another outfit into her suitcase before zipping the small carry-on closed.

She stood, considering the suitcase on her bed—and what she and Leo were about to do. Rationally, the plan made sense. But more than that, she was tired of being the good girl when it came to guys and missions. A handsome prince had asked her to come on a visit to his grandmother's. Was it a crime that a small part of her wanted to enjoy it?

Her responsible side quickly kicked back in. She shook her head, attempting to dislodge thoughts of idyllic walks along Caribbean beaches. She needed to focus and stay strong.

Anna crept down the rear staircase that connected to the main floor right across from the garage access door. Sneaking quietly across the hall, she slipped through the door and into the wide garage.

Leo stood at the back of the Lexus, staring down at the bumper. Anna cringed. He probably hadn't seen the evidence of her run-in with the fence at the rehabilitation center yet.

"I had to make a quick getaway the other day," Anna said as she approached him.

He stared down at the bumper and held his hands out wide. "I can't believe you did this."

"Sorry," Anna said with a small wince.

"It's perfect!" he exclaimed.

"What?"

"I'll tell Hugo that you're taking the car to the shop for a quick repair. That'll give you the ideal excuse for leaving with the car. Plus, then I'll be seen here in the villa this morning. No one will realize I'm missing for a few more hours. By then, we'll be safely on the way to Sint Maarten."

Anna shook her head. "I can't believe you're happy I crashed your SUV."

"I'm not happy that you continually put yourself in danger," he said as he grabbed her hand, his expression suddenly serious. "You are far more important to me than a dumb—albeit very expensive—car." He winked at her. "But as long as you weren't hurt, I think it's perfect for our cover."

Anna nodded, a small smile touching her lips. Leo grinned and ran off to talk to the chauffeur. When he came back several minutes later, he opened the rear lift door and handed her the key fob. He stowed her suitcase next to his and then crawled in and threw a dark blanket over himself and the suitcases. He pulled back a corner of the blanket and peeked out. "I wouldn't complain if you stopped halfway to the airport and let me ride in the front."

"It's an SUV. You can just climb over the seats whenever you want."

"Good point," Leo said before pulling the blanket over his head again. "Tell me as soon as we're past the security gate."

Fortunately, Anna had no problem getting past the front

221

gate guards with her secret cargo. Her efforts to make friends with the behind-the-scenes employees had paid off again.

An hour and a half later, she was settling in across from Leo on the Luxembourg royal family jet taking a bite out of a raspberry-filled jelly doughnut fresh from a bakery. Jelly doughnuts had been another of Leo's American discoveries.

"Given your interest in only the highest-calorie American cuisine, it's amazing you don't weigh over five hundred pounds by now," Anna said as she tried to keep the raspberry filling from running down her chin.

With a broad smile, Leo chomped eagerly into the end of his own doughnut. The force sent a small stream of red jelly squirting out the back side onto the plate in front of him. Anna's sudden laugh blew the powdered sugar off the top of her doughnut into a large white cloud that drifted right into Leo's face.

Anna's eyes went wide. "I'm so sorry, Leo. Your filling came out and—"

Leo had doubled over with laughter, threatening to knock the rest of the breakfast off his tray. When Leo looked up at her, face lightly powdered with sugar, Anna cackled out loud.

Their laughter echoed around the cabin until Anna saw the curtain to the forward galley shift slightly. The flight attendant must be wondering what was going on. Fortunately, there was no one else on the flight besides the crew.

They both leaned back in their seats, continuing to wipe tears away, until the fit passed. Anna let out a deep sigh as she watched Leo wipe the sugar from his face and hair. He was incredibly handsome. Not to mention fun to be around.

She felt her stomach tighten in a knot. The mission would end, one way or another, in three days. And even if she succeeded, and he was safe, she would miss him when she had to leave.

Glancing around the empty cabin, Leo leaned forward across the narrow table. "You still haven't told me the rest of the details from your interviews."

Anna told him about her visits with Zoe, Lydia, and Sofia. She also told him about her attempt to see Makenna at the recovery center and how that had ended. By the end, Leo had his chin resting in his upturned palm while he gazed at her, awestruck.

"So what do you think?" she prompted.

"I think you're amazing, that's what I think."

Anna felt a tickling sensation bubbling up in her middle, but she did her best to push it back down. She refused to let herself swoon.

But honestly, what girl didn't want to have a real-life prince worship the ground she walked on?

"Seriously, Leo, what do you think about what they said?"

Leo leaned back in his chair and stared out the airplane window at the passing clouds. "It makes me sound like a shameless flirt bouncing from girl to girl only concerned about how new and beautiful they are."

Anna gave him a deadpan look, waiting for him to catch up to reality.

He stared back at her. "What? That's not what I'm truly like."

Was he really not aware of one of his defining characteristics? "Leo, you are always so friendly with people. It's what makes you fun to be around . . ." He still showed no sign of acknowledging the truth of what she said, so Anna pressed on. "Don't you think that when your friendliness is directed at young, beautiful women, it could sometimes be interpreted as flirtation or romantic interest?"

The frown on his face made it clear he didn't agree with her. "There's a big difference between being friendly and having romantic feelings for someone. Don't you think girls can tell the difference?"

With a tilt of her head, Anna gave the prince her best skeptical look. "Have you not been paying attention to how women react to your friendliness?"

"Fine," he huffed. "Maybe they interpret my friendliness as flirtation. But that should be the end of it. They must know that I would do more if I was truly serious about a relationship."

"Like long walks on the beach, or personal talks about her future, or seeking her out at parties?" Anna mentally ticked through the experiences each of the former agents had shared with her. She hated having to add her own to the list. "Or cooking private breakfasts together?"

The furrow in his brow deepened as he glanced out the window. A moment later he turned back and held up a hand. "Wait. That's what you and I do." He stared at her intently, obviously expecting some sort of explanation, but Anna didn't speak or look away. "Do you think I see you the same as the other agents?"

Anna bit her lip. If she was being honest with herself, she knew that his feelings for her were different, more than what he had felt for the others. She shook her head. "I suppose not. But, Leo, I've been trying so hard from the beginning not to let my heart get involved. And the thing that has worked the best is constantly telling myself that you are simply a flirtatious guy and nothing more."

"If you need convincing, I—"

She held up a finger. "Let me finish. I don't know what you've said in private to those other girls or if it was anything like what you've said to me." He tried to interrupt again but she talked over him. "But that doesn't really matter. I have to hold onto this right now because it's the only thing keeping my heart safe." Struggling to keep the emotion out of her voice, she blew out a breath at the end and looked down at her half-finished breakfast.

For several seconds, Leo didn't speak. When Anna ventured a glance, it was clear he had been waiting for her to look at him. "Is your only obstacle that you doubt my sincerity?" he asked softly.

"That's not the only thing, but it's the best defense I've got right now."

"Then let me assure you that my feelings for you are—"

"Leo," She reached across the table and took his hand, stopping his declaration short. "Maybe you shouldn't try to convince me. Maybe it would only make things more difficult in the end."

He stared at her for a long moment, indecision apparent in his expression. Finally he nodded and reluctantly allowed her to pull her hand away from his.

Awkward silence stretched for several minutes until the stewardess approached and offered to remove their breakfast plates. The threat of missing out on the remainder of the jelly doughnuts must have snapped Leo out of his funk, because he attacked the rest of his meal with his usual vigor.

"You'll love Sint Maarten," he said between mouthfuls. "It has the most beautiful beaches in the world."

The rest of the flight, he was equally friendly as before, yet slightly distant. Anna discovered that Leo liked double-cheese, deep-dish pizza and root beer floats, though not necessarily together.

As they descended toward the airport on Sint Maarten, Anna sent a specifically-worded message to Zane explaining that she was escorting Leo to visit his grandmother and that the secrecy—while hopefully making for an uneventful trip for the prince—was also necessary as part of the investigation. In the message, she asked Zane to have Celine inform the Grand Ducal

Family—and no one else—of the prince's whereabouts. To be thorough, she and Leo had decided to rule out his family involvement first.

"Sent," she said as she looked up at Leo.

He nodded in acknowledgment.

"Now we'll see how long it takes for something to happen," she added.

His lips formed a tight line. Anna wasn't sure if he was unhappy about their earlier discussion or the trap they were trying to lay.

A limousine collected them at the airport and drove them to a modest mansion perched on the side of a hill facing a small bay. Anna stayed close by Leo's side as they approached the door.

"Grootmoeder will like you, trust me."

"I'm only a temporary security guard, remember? She doesn't have to like me, she just has to not kill you in front of me."

Leo chuckled. "No promises."

The door opened and a thin woman a little shorter than Anna stepped out. "Léopold!"

"Oma!"

Leo's grandmother pulled him into a firm embrace, kissing his cheeks several times. His grandmother held him back at arm's length and looked him up and down. Leo tossed a playful grimace over his shoulder at Anna.

"You've been indulging in American food again, haven't you?" She said with an impish grin.

"You know it's my weakness, Oma."

Leo's grandmother looked at Anna. "And who is this lovely young lady?"

"Oma, this is Anna Rivers."

Anna wasn't sure if she was supposed to curtsey or bow or kiss the woman's hand.

"Anna, this is my grandmother, Elisabeth Gevers."

Leo's grandmother pulled Anna toward her and kissed her on the cheeks as well. "Welcome to my home, Anna. Please come in, both of you."

They followed Leo's grandmother inside and through a large living room. She didn't stop there, but proceeded with them to a broad covered terrace behind the home. A warm breeze whispered through the shrub and palm trees as Anna walked to the edge of the terrace. The home's perch on the hill provided a perfect view of the beautiful bay below them. Anna stood gazing out at the crystal blue waters and white sandy beaches.

The prince was suddenly at her side. "Didn't I say you'd love Sint Maarten?"

"Mm-hmm. It's lovely." Anna turned back to the terrace and saw Leo's grandmother sitting at a nearby table, studying them with a knowing look.

Hoping to avoid giving her the wrong idea, Anna took a step away from Leo and moved toward the table. Her effort did nothing to change the twinkle in his grandmother's eyes. After considering her for a few moments, Leo's grandmother turned to the approaching attendant and asked him to bring lemonade and treats.

Leo settled in next to his grandmother, and she patted his hand.

"Tell me everything that is going on with your life," she said.

Leo told her about several of the official functions he had attended in the past few months as well as some parties he had enjoyed. She made grandmotherly observations and peppered him with astute questions throughout. Anna noticed that he conveniently left out any mention of attacks or sabotage. That was probably for the best. No need to worry a grandmother unnecessarily.

Leo told his grandmother about how his siblings and parents were doing. She was excited about the news that his little niece, Olivia, had learned to walk and delighted by the disagreements he and his siblings were having in planning their annual summer trip to Cabasson.

His grandmother also asked Anna about her family and listened with equal attentiveness.

When there was a lull in the conversation, his grandmother looked at her empty glass. "Oh, I'm all out of lemonade. Léopold, be a dear and go get some more, would you?"

"Anything for you, Oma," he said with a smile. As he walked away, he caught Anna's eye and gave her a wink.

Once he was out of earshot, Oma turned very deliberately to face Anna. She waited a moment then spoke. "I hope your investigation is going well." Her tone was casual, but there was a quick alertness in her eyes.

Anna nearly fell out of her chair. "You know about that?"

Leo's grandmother gave her a patient smile. "You think I wouldn't know if there was an attack on my grandson? My daughter, Léopold's mother, told me that the American government would have a specialist investigate the attacks. I assume that is you."

Anna nodded, still entirely taken aback by the older woman's keen observational skills and direct manner.

"Have you discovered who's behind the attacks? I hear you don't have much time left."

Again, Anna was surprised at his grandmother's knowledge of the situation. "Unfortunately, not yet," Anna replied. "But you'll be happy to know that I don't think the attacks have actually been meant for Leo."

His grandmother's eyebrows shot up. "Who then?"

"The evidence suggests that they've been directed at his close security agents. Though I think it was meant to look like they were attacks on Leo."

She considered Anna. "So any agent near Léopold, including you, would be in danger?"

Anna nodded slowly. "It would seem so."

The woman's gaze narrowed at her for several seconds before shifting out over the terrace balcony. After a few moments in silence, she spoke again, "I have never really agreed with his family's plan to have these beautiful young women stay close to him as protection. It keeps up a good appearance, yes. But where does that leave my grandson? How will he ever have a close relationship with a woman if the only ones near him are paid to be attentive?"

Anna was tempted to tell Leo's grandmother that he had apparently found a way to develop relationships despite the obvious obstacle, but she decided against it. She saw an opportunity to get his grandmother's honest opinion about the other agents. "Which of his close security agents have you met?"

"None of them," she answered flatly.

"He hasn't ever brought anyone to Sint Maarten to meet you?"

His grandmother opened her mouth to reply, but she was interrupted by Leo's return with more lemonade. He poured his grandmother a glass, then did the same for Anna.

"So, were you talking about me while I was gone?" he casually asked.

"No," Anna said.

"Yes," his grandmother answered at the same time.

Leo laughed and patted his grandmother's hand.

Anna was desperate to avoid the subject of what they had been talking about, so she asked Leo's grandmother, "What's it like to live on Sint Maarten? Do you enjoy it?"

"Oh, it's wonderful. Warm weather nearly year round, though I could do without the hurricanes. And so many lovely people to meet in town, though some of the tourists could improve their manners." She smiled at Anna and Leo. Suddenly she clapped her hands together. "I know what you should do. Léopold, you need to take Anna down to Great Bay to show her the beach and the shops. You could take her to your favorite cafe on the boardwalk . . . assuming you still have a taste for Caribbean food."

"Is there any food that Leo doesn't like?" Anna asked with a grin.

"Beets," Leo answered immediately.

Anna and his grandmother laughed.

"It's settled then," his grandmother said with a smile. "You'll take Anna to the beach for lunch while I have my afternoon rest. And when you return, I'll make sure my cook is preparing the largest spread of beets he can find."

"Oma," Leo chided.

"I'm only joking, little dear." His grandmother's eyes sparkled with mischief. "But maybe if I had the cook secretly put some in the—"

"We're going now, Oma," Leo said, standing and taking Anna's hand. "Enjoy your rest."

His grandmother smiled and waved them away. "And you enjoy your lunch."

Leo borrowed the keys to his grandmother's small electric car. It wasn't as fast as the Ferrari or Hot Banana, but it worked well for Sint Maarten. He drove down and around the hill revealing the breathtakingly beautiful view of a large bay with sparkling turquoise water.

The only available spots to park were several blocks from the beach, so they walked the remainder of the distance to his favorite cafe. After ordering their food, Anna sat back and soaked in the moment. She was sitting at a table on a boardwalk cafe with a handsome prince, listening to the sounds and the music of island life, inhaling the sweet scents of the beach and the ocean. Life really didn't get much better than this.

"I've been thinking about what we were talking about earlier," Leo began.

Anna warily nodded for him to continue.

"Despite the other agents' erroneous portrayal of me as a flirtatious Party Prince—"

"I thought you were proud of that moniker."

Leo ignored her comment. "—I think there is a connection between the three girls."

"And what's that?"

"None of my close security agents—with the exception of Jessie—have been with me very long," he said, sweeping his gaze casually across the ocean vista.

Anna gaped at him. That was what he had decided they had in common?

"And I don't have much hope that a certain agent currently in that role will do much better." He glared at her as if the looming mission deadline was her fault.

Anna pinched her lips together to keep a loud, very rude laugh from escaping. "You remember when I asked whether you were looking into espionage training as a fallback job, in case the prince thing didn't work out?"

Leo nodded, grinning.

"Well, don't bother. You really stink at the investigation part."

"What do you mean?! Was my conclusion invalid?" he asked.

"No. Just incredibly obvious while not being very helpful. Anyone could figure out that your female security agents aren't staying on long. The real work is figuring out why it's happening."

Leo folded his arms with a huff. "Well, what's your conclusion then?"

"The common thread is that as soon as you started showing particular interest in them, they suddenly had something happen that affected their job."

The waiter arrived at that moment with their food, so Anna was forced to wait until they had a bit more privacy to find out what he thought of her conclusion. She could tell by his scowl that he didn't agree with something she'd said.

"Why do you say that I showed interest in them?" he finally asked. "I don't think I ever showed any more or less interest in any of them."

Anna placed both her hands on the table and took a deep, calming breath. She leaned forward and glared at the frustrating prince. "Leo, I know you're not that blind. You have to see how your relationship changed with each of them."

"No, I don't." He folded his arms like a petulant child.

"A few weeks before Sofia quit, you started taking long walks along the beach together." Anna didn't want it to come out like an accusation, but she was fighting a hurricane of jealousy in her gut, and losing.

Leo threw up his hands. "Her mother had just passed away. I was trying to comfort her."

"I'm not saying that's bad, but your relationship changed."

The prince rolled his eyes in acknowledgement but said nothing.

"And what about Zoe? She says you were always striking up conversations with her about her future," Anna said.

Leo ran a hand through his hair. "Zoe is an intelligent woman who has incredible potential. She just can't see it. She doesn't have any goals or aspirations. I thought I could help her find some direction in her life." He shrugged.

His defiant expression had shifted. His body language made it look like he was open to the idea that Anna might be right.

She reached across the table and patted his hand, hoping he accepted the proffered olive branch. "And I think that's wonderful of you. It shows what a caring person you are."

He gave a tight-lipped smile at her compliment. "So who does that leave? Lydia?"

Anna nodded. "She said you two got very close and that your relationship was heading in a great direction." Her eyebrows lifted, waiting for him to explain.

"That one was all on Lydia's part. She was the one making the moves on me. I didn't do anything but be friendly," he said.

"Your regular brand of friendly, I assume?"

"Yes, if you must know." His tone was defensive. "Because until recently, I didn't know it was a problem."

Anna let out a deep sigh. "That's your charismatic personality. You draw people to you. But you might need to be careful in directing all that charisma toward women."

A guilty look spread across his face. "To be honest, I actually did know that Lydia thought I was interested in her, but she didn't take the hint when I tried to ease back and shift my attention elsewhere."

Anna frowned, tapping a finger to her chin as she gazed out at a passing cruise ship. "Hmm. That's interesting. She didn't mention that. You don't think she could still be upset about you snubbing her, do you? Could she be taking it out on the other agents who get too close to you?"

With an expression of resignation, Leo said, "If her behavior at the end was any indication, I'm not sure she realized I was trying to put space between us." He shrugged. "But you talked to her more recently. Did she seem like jealousy had driven her to attempt murder?"

Anna let out a short laugh. "No. She seemed proud of where your relationship had been." She thought back to the smug look of confidence on Lydia's aggravatingly pretty face. "I was the one who was jealous."

A broad grin slowly spread across Leo's face and his eyebrows waggled at her.

"Did I say that out loud?" she whispered.

He nodded, deep blue eyes dancing with laughter.

She clapped a hand to her mouth as she felt heat creeping up her neck and cheeks. She couldn't believe she had just admitted her feelings for the prince. The same feelings that she had, only that morning, denied having at all. Forcing herself to breathe regularly, she cast around for something to distract him. "It really is beautiful here," she said as she watched beachgoers dive into the gentle surf. "I'm surprised you don't visit more often."

He continued to grin at her, his gaze nearly boring into her soul. "Yes, some of the sights are absolutely breathtaking. I find I can't take my eyes off them." He stared intently at her, clearly not talking about the beauty of the nearby beach and ocean.

Anna did her best to convince herself that he was just being playful and flirtatious, but the argument sounded hollow even in her own head.

Pulling out her phone, she began typing a message to Zane. "I think it's time to let Zane inform the next group in your circle."

Leo shrugged and nodded at the same time. Anna decided to proceed. At this point, she really just needed a distraction.

She finished the quick message telling Zane to go ahead and let the rest of the security team know where the prince was. She stood from the table and walked out to the edge of the covered veranda. "Should we continue the tour?" She didn't look back to see his reaction, but after a few moments, she heard the scrapping of his chair.

He stepped out onto the boardwalk next to her and tilted his head toward the beach. As they walked together along the sand, Leo showed her various shops, restaurants, and other points of interest. Clearly, he had visited his grandmother often.

If he was disappointed in her desire to avoid discussing her accidental disclosure, he didn't show it. In fact, there seemed to be a lightness in his step. Meanwhile, her mind and heart were a swirling mess. Could she allow herself to hope that he really was falling for her, that it was more than simply a passing fancy for the new woman in his life?

She tried to be rational about the situation, but every time she did that, her brain started making lists of his good qualities. He was kind and considerate. He was handsome, charming, and witty. She absolutely loved being around him. And best of all, he loved his family and was quite obviously devoted to his grandmother. Any one of those things would have drawn her to him, but all combined into one, he was like a gravitational force that she would never be able to resist. Not as long as she was this close to him.

During their stroll, he frequently let his arm brush against hers. She did her best to keep her distance without making it look like she was keeping her distance. She kept her arms folded or her hands in her pockets for pretty much the entire afternoon. He didn't seem to mind, or notice really. He would playfully bump against her shoulder or let his gaze linger on her face.

She wanted him, but she knew she couldn't have him.

It was the worst kind of torture Anna could imagine.

––––––––––––––––

Around dinner, they drove back up to his grandmother's home on the side of the hill. She was waiting for them in the living room, lounging on a sofa reading a book.

"How was the tour of town?" she asked.

Leo smiled broadly and turned to Anna, apparently deferring the question to her.

"It was nice," Anna said. She glanced briefly at Leo and then back to the decor of the beautifully furnished room. He still felt too close to her, so she took a small step away from him.

Leo's grandmother looked at him, then at Anna, then back. Her eyebrows lifted. "Hmm," she said to no one in particular. Standing from the couch, she beckoned them to join her on the terrace again. Her kitchen staff had laid out the dinner meal for them. Leo seated his grandmother, then hurried around and helped Anna to her seat.

"Thank you, Leo," Anna said quietly.

True to her word, his grandmother had somehow arranged to have beets on the menu, but it was just a small dish of cooked beets next to Leo's place setting.

Settling into his own seat, he smiled at his grandmother when he saw it. "Are you trying to poison me, Oma?"

"Just trying to improve you as a well-rounded gentleman," she shot back. She turned to Anna and added. "He could use a little improving, don't you think?"

Anna didn't look at her; she simply gazed at Leo across the table considering him, his confident bearing, that perfect smile, and those eyes that she could get absolutely lost in. He stared back at her. Not the bright, cheery, expression he usually wore. Or even the flirtatious look he often gave her. His look in that moment was intense. It was pure smolder. And there really wasn't any other word to describe him.

He was perfect.

What would life be like with an actual prince charming?

What kind of fairytale ending would she have? Could she leave behind everything from her own world to be a part of his? How could she be sure if that was even the right thing to do?

Realizing that his grandmother was probably waiting for an answer to her question, Anna pulled herself back to reality. Those dreams were fantasy. Staring down at her plate, she picked up a fork and stabbed at the salad. "No, he's fine," she said.

His grandmother smiled and her conversation turned to more pleasant topics about the island and its beauties. Anna barely heard—much less participated in—any of it. Her head swirled with dreams of a paradise island that could never be—romantic swims in aqua-blue water, walks along the beach with wet sand squishing between her toes, and late nights gazing at moonlit waves while encircled in the arms of a dashing prince.

She risked a quick glance up at Leo. Her heart ached for what was so close but could never be. She wasn't even sure how enduring his feelings were for her, to say nothing of whether such a fantasy could even work out between a prince and a girl like her.

As they finished their meal, Leo's grandmother turned to him and said, "Dear, why don't you take Anna for a walk down to the ruins? I'm sure she would enjoy it."

Anna knew she would enjoy it. That was basically the entire problem.

Leo gave his grandmother a knowing smile and rose. "Would you like to come on a walk with me?"

For a split second, she considered refusing him. It would certainly be better on her heart. She smiled sweetly up at him. "I suppose. If it's in the job description . . ." A fake smile and their normal banter were her best defense at the moment. She stood and moved to join him.

"It's not," he said in complete seriousness. "You can only come if you really want to."

Anna gazed into those amazing eyes, so full of longing and frustration and torment. She let out a sigh to match. "I would love to take a walk with you," she said softly.

His expression lightened. They stood staring at each other for a long moment.

She knew, deep inside, that she wouldn't be able to take much more of this torture.

"Léopold, why don't you go get a water bottle to take on your walk. I'm sure Anna would appreciate it. And she can keep me company while you're gone."

Leo winked at Anna and dutifully trotted off on an errand that Anna suspected was entirely made up for her benefit. She turned toward Leo's grandmother, waiting for whatever it was she had in store for her.

His grandmother eyed her for a moment before speaking. "I need to give you a better answer to your question earlier. You see, since I retired here to Sint Maarten, I don't travel much. I chat with my daughter and my other children on video conference, and many of my family come to visit me here. But I only meet the people in their lives that they choose to bring. So, no, I've never met any of Léopold's female security agents. In fact, I've only ever met one of the girls in Leo's life, a young woman named Amy, his girlfriend in college." The older woman paused, a small smile playing across her lips. "Does that help you understand how Leo feels about those he chooses to bring to Sint Maarten?"

The full meaning of his grandmother's explanation smashed over her like a wave on the beach. "You mean . . . he hasn't brought anyone to the island to meet you since Amy?"

Leo's grandmother gave her a very meaningful look, as if to

convey the importance of what she was about to say. "Only you."

Even as Leo approached, his grandmother's words hung in the air. Any lingering doubts that hadn't been eradicated by his grandmother's assertion were completely swept away by the besotted look she saw on Leo's face when he rejoined her, water bottle in hand.

"Can't have a romantic, sunset walk without a water bottle, apparently," he said in a conspiratorial whisper.

Anna smiled at Leo's grandmother as she turned and slipped her hand into the crook of Leo's arm. His surprise lasted only a fleeting moment, and he quickly placed his hand tightly over hers.

Together they walked out the terrace gate, around the house, and onto the small road. The setting sun sparkled on the ocean like a thousand diamonds on a bed of a million sapphires. As the road that descended to the beach grew steeper, Leo took Anna's hand in his, steadying their steps.

After a few minutes, they reached the main road that looped around the island and crossed it onto a tiny peninsula jutting out into the sea. It sort of resembled a mini Florida. Though the need to steady each other during their descent had passed, Anna refused to release the prince's hand.

She knew the magic of the island was partly to blame, but when would they ever be together like this again?

And how could an experience be so exquisite and so painful at the same time?

Leo led her through the ruins of Fort Amsterdam to a rocky outcropping on the farthest tip of the peninsula. As the evening breeze intensified around them, Anna leaned closer to the prince, enjoying the warmth of his nearness. After a moment, he wrapped his arms around her shoulders, pulling her to him. Anna rested her head against his shoulder.

That countdown timer in the back of her head started up again, but it wasn't Rule Number One she risked breaking this time. That had already been shattered to a million pieces.

It was her heart she was worried about.

She only waited a few seconds, maybe a dozen or so, beyond when her mental timer reached zero.

Slowly and painfully, she placed her hands on his chest and pushed him away. Leo looked down at her, his expression vulnerable and questioning.

"We can't do this, Leo," she whispered. "You know we can't."

He lifted his chin a fraction, setting it at a stubborn angle. "Who says we can't? I'm a prince, aren't I?" He took her hands in his, refusing to let her put distance between them.

"You are," she agreed. "That's pretty much the problem."

He stared at her with those mesmerizing blue eyes now dancing with the reflected gold of the dying sunlight. As the truth settled in, his bravado completely deflated.

"So that's it then?" he asked softly. "I find the girl of my dreams, and I'm supposed to watch her walk out of my life without a fight?" He slowly released her hands by the fingertips, letting them drop back to her sides.

Anna let out a long, mournful groan as she stared back at him.

A real-life prince stood in front of her, and he had just declared his willingness to fight for her. How was Anna supposed to resist that?

It would be so easy to simply fall into his arms and let him sweep her away to whatever—wherever—it didn't even matter. And she was so tired of trying to be strong and do the sensible thing.

As she took a tentative step back toward him, the sound of approaching voices and tromping boots reached them. They glanced back toward the ruins and saw half a dozen uniformed police officers hustling over the rise in their direction. The officers formed a semi-circle in front of them, basically cutting off any escape up the peninsula. Leo pulled Anna close to his side as they watched the gathered members of the local police force. A few held flashlights. None had their weapons drawn, but their body language told Anna that this wasn't a complimentary visit.

One of the officers approached. "Are you Prince Léopold?" he asked Leo in an island accent.

Leo frowned. "Yes. I'm Prince Léopold."

The officer turned to Anna. "And I assume you are Anna Rivers."

She nodded warily.

"We received a report this afternoon that you," the officer looked at Leo again, "were abducted by this woman." He nodded at Anna. "We have spent most of the evening trying to locate you. My orders are to arrest Miss Rivers on charges of kidnapping."

Anna looked up at Leo, his arm still protectively around her shoulders. When he glanced down at her, they shared a meaningful look. This wasn't exactly the attack they had expected, but it was clearly an orchestrated aggression toward her.

Leo held his free hand out to the side in an exaggerated shrug. "Well, Lieutenant, as you can see, I haven't been abducted by this woman. Beguiled, maybe, but not abducted."

Leave it to Leo to figure out a way to use a little humor to lighten the situation. In the row behind the lieutenant, several of the officers exchanged quick smiles.

The lieutenant relaxed somewhat but still appeared to be unsure.

"If you don't mind my asking," Leo began, "who called in the report?"

"She would not give her name," the officer in charge replied. "But I believe it was a concerned member of your staff."

She.

Anna and Leo shared another quick look. They still didn't know the identity of the attacker, but it certainly narrowed things down. The timing of the police's arrival meant it had to be someone at the villa. In fact, assuming Zane had followed the instructions in her messages, it was mostly likely someone on the security team. The fact that it was a woman certainly seemed to fit into Anna's pre-existing suspicions.

The lieutenant stepped forward. "May I speak with Your Highness privately?"

Leo glanced at Anna. "You aren't going to drag me away and arrest her once you have us separated, are you?"

The lieutenant smiled and shook his head. "No, sir." As if to assure the prince of his intentions, he barked a quick order over his shoulder and the line of police officers took several quick steps backward.

With a quick squeeze on Anna's arm, Leo released her and stepped a few paces away to visit with the lieutenant. Anna felt suddenly vulnerable and alone, not in the physical sense—she had already sized up the police force and determined she had better than even odds of taking them down on her own. The turmoil inside, left her feeling exposed emotionally. Her brain and her heart fought deadlocked in a battle of reality versus fantasy. The lightest proverbial breeze could have pushed her one way or the other.

Knowing that focusing on the mission could bring some clarity, she strained to hear what the lieutenant was saying to Leo. She thought she overheard the words "American" and "spy." Of course, none of that was news to Leo, who continued to nod his head and gesture in Anna's direction.

As they made their way back to Anna, she picked up more of

what the lieutenant was saying. ". . . I'm sure you can understand that with an American . . . operative, we needed to take certain precautions."

"I understand perfectly, Lieutenant. That was very wise," Leo said.

"I apologize for the misunderstanding, Miss Rivers." The lieutenant executed a short bow in her direction and another toward the prince. "I hope you both enjoy the rest of your stay on our lovely island." He promptly turned and ushered his force back up the peninsula and out of sight.

"What did he say?" Anna couldn't help asking.

"Quite shocking news, actually," Leo replied with an exaggerated look of surprise. "He said you were a CIA operative who could kill me in my sleep with two squares of toilet paper and a sticky note."

Anna arched an eyebrow at him. "Did he really say that?" she asked.

"Only the first part," Leo said.

"Funny," Anna said drily, "only the second part was true."

That only made the prince laugh more. He grabbed Anna and enveloped her in his strong arms. "What am I going to do with you, Miss Spy Girl?"

Anna pushed gently back on his chest. "Walk me back up the hill to say goodnight to your dear grandmother."

Leo nodded, a smile on his lips.

"And then fly me back to Miami," Anna added.

The prince's smile faded. He scrutinized her face, but Anna held her impassive—yet polite—mask in place.

There would certainly be future opportunities to debate their relationship and discuss their feelings for each other, but the interaction with the police force of Sint Maarten had brought some clarity and helped Anna reaffirm her previous decision.

It would never work out between them. She was an American girl from a small town in Alabama. He was a European prince of international significance.

Now that her brain understood, the only thing left to do was convince her heart.

Chapter 15

I t wasn't technically the next morning when Anna woke up because she hadn't gotten into her bed until about five o'clock that same morning as the sun was barely starting to turn the sky from black to dark blue. On the flight back from Sint Maarten, Anna and Leo had discussed the case as it currently stood. Though not all of the attacks had been as violent as the last few, they all had occurred shortly after the female agent had become—or threatened to become—romantically involved with the prince. That definitely pointed to one common motivation for the attacks:

Jealousy.

Fortunately, the trap they had set in Sint Maarten had very quickly yielded another attack, of sorts. Fortunate because neither the mission deadline nor Anna's heart would have allowed them to spend days on the island waiting for something to happen. The timing of the police's arrival ruled out Leo's family and put the suspicion squarely on his security team.

That really left only one suspect—the one remaining female member of the team.

Jessie.

There was also the very glaring reality that, despite having been the first female close security agent hired, Jessie hadn't suffered the fate of the rest. Anna needed to find out why.

Which meant Anna's first order of business that morning was to track down Jessie.

After changing into a casual outfit for lounging around the villa, she headed out in search of her fellow agent. As she moved across the second-floor balcony overlooking the vaulted living room, Anna stopped. Where would Jessie be at this time of day?

Glancing back and forth down the second-floor corridor, Anna caught a glimpse of someone ducking into an alcove halfway down the hall. She wasn't sure, but it looked like one of the prince's bodyguards. Based on the flash of blondish hair, probably Frederic. In an effort to get a better idea of who it might have been, Anna started down the grand staircase and, halfway down, she turned around, heading back up to the second floor. At the top of the stairs, she turned toward her room and nearly ran directly into Frederic. He stepped aside, muttering a brief greeting, and continued down the stairs.

He hadn't even flinched when he saw her. That was professional-level trailing. Anna frowned as she walked past the door to her room and down the back staircase. Maybe she was seeing things that weren't there. Maybe Frederic was just walking along the hallway. Besides, she really needed to focus on finding and interrogating Jessie, not worrying about being watched inside the villa.

She walked along the first floor, past the kitchens and dining rooms. As she walked through the living room, she glanced through the tall, floor-to-ceiling windows and saw Frederic out on the deck. With his back to her, he held his cellphone up as if taking a picture of the scene—which would have been a strange enough thing for the bodyguard to do in the middle of a regular day—but the screen was black. Not a very efficient way to take a picture.

Something was very off about that. As she passed through the living room, Frederic angled his phone in sync with her movement. He was watching her in the reflection on the dark screen.

Why would one of her fellow security agents be tracking her?

Anna shook her head. She could deal with that later. She needed to find Jessie.

She took the smaller staircase at the end of the far wing and climbed back to the second floor. Perhaps Jessie was still doing her morning workout in the weight room. Anna peeked in through the glass doors. Sure enough, Jessie was alone inside. Hoping not to distract her in the middle of a set, Anna slipped in through the doors and approached, waiting for her to finish.

Jessie glanced her way, but didn't stop her routine until she had completed an additional twenty reps of arm curls—Anna had counted. She had an inkling that Jessie might be showing off.

"Do you need me for something?" Jessie asked, wiping her forehead with a towel. Her tone wasn't rude, but it wasn't exactly warm either.

"You're the only close agent that I haven't talked to about the attacks." Anna said.

Jessie shrugged as she reconfigured the weight machine for squats. Arms and legs on the same day? Now Anna *knew* Jessie was just showing off.

"How long have you worked for the prince?" Anna asked.

"About two years," Jessie said without looking at her.

"And you're also from Luxembourg, isn't that right?" Anna asked.

Jessie's chin rose a fraction. It was clearly a source of pride for the woman. "Yes. And the honor of serving a member of the Grand Ducal Family is a privilege that most citizens never receive."

"Having worked for the prince for so long, and the fact that both of you are from Luxembourg, you two must be pretty close. Pretty good friends, I mean." Anna's observation was meant to sting only if Jessie hoped for more than a friendship with the prince.

Jessie's expression clouded momentarily, but she quickly recovered. "Yes. I'd say we have a camaraderie because of our shared homeland." Jessie waved her hand as if brushing away the explanation.

Anna had hoped for something more incriminating. Time for the gloves to come off. "But from my interviews, it doesn't sound like you get to spend as much time with Leo—that you don't get as much attention from him—as some of the other agents have."

Jessie glared at Anna for a long time before speaking. "That might be true, but who is still here serving Prince Léopold? I am. I've outlasted them all." A triumphant sneer spread across her face.

Anna sensed she had the girl on the ropes. Time to go for the sucker punch. "Hmm. I have been curious about how you've been able to stay on so long when other agents have come and gone. What is it that makes you so special?"

"I'll tell you what makes me special," she huffed. "I don't let anything distract me from my job of keeping the prince safe." She looked pointedly at Anna as she said it.

"What do you mean?" Anna hated how silly she sounded when she was forced to play dumb. She didn't know how Katie could stomach acting that way all the time.

Jessie tilted her head to the side, a deadpan expression on

her face. Anna felt even more ridiculous, given how easily Jessie saw through her act.

Jessie's face regained some of its original composure. "When you first came here, I thought you were different from the others. I wanted to give you a chance. But now I can see you're just the same as the rest—daily breakfasts together, lounging around by the pool, taking a private ride in the limo tender, flying to Sint Maarten for the day to meet his grandmother—all you care about is Prince Léopold's attention and your own enjoyment!"

Anna opened her mouth to point out that the limo experience had not been as romantic as it might have seemed, but she decided to let Jessie continue.

Jessie hadn't waited for a response. "I've done my job—the real job we've been hired to do—for years. Longer than anyone. But do I get any special thanks for it? No. Do I get noticed or singled out like the others? No!"

"I'm sure the prince appreciates your dedicated—"

"Don't!" Jessie shot up from the weight bench, glaring daggers at Anna. "I certainly don't want pity from someone like *you*." She spat the last word. "But you'll see. You won't last any longer than those ditzy airheads. You'll end up just like the rest of them." She turned and stormed from the room.

As the door slammed behind Jessie, Anna let out a long, low whistle.

She definitely got what she'd wanted: one extremely jealous coworker.

Anna sat down on a yoga ball, going over what Jessie had said. Could she be the one responsible for the attacks on Leo and his close security agents? It sounded like she had the motive, and very likely, the opportunity.

Movement through the window caught Anna's eye. Was Frederic still spying on her? She stood and moved quickly to the door. Out in the hall, she saw Frederic heading toward the auxiliary staircase. He must have known she'd seen him and started walking away.

"Frederic!" she called out.

He was already halfway down the stairs, and he didn't stop or turn around. Maybe he hadn't heard her. Anna hurried to catch him. She couldn't be looking over her shoulder for the rest of her stay; apparently, she and Frederic had issues that needed to be addressed.

On the main floor, she called out to him again. He stopped right in front of Zane's office. She walked up, eyeing his reaction.

"What's the deal, Frederic?" she asked. "Why are you following me around?"

Frederic's eyebrows went up a fraction of an inch, but otherwise his expression was one of complete innocence. He opened his mouth to respond.

But before Frederic could say anything, she heard Zane's voice from inside his office. "Anna, would you join me for a moment?" he said.

Frederic smiled and shrugged before walking away.

Anna stepped into Zane's office and stood in front of his desk, her arms folded. She expected a good explanation, and she hoped he could tell. "What's going on, Zane?"

"The biggest problem right now is that I don't know what to do with you." Zane waved a hand toward one of the chairs in front of his desk.

Anna put her hands on her hips but didn't take a seat. "Let's talk about that later. Why was Frederic following me?"

The security chief leaned back in his chair, placing his hands behind his head, and chuckled lightly. "I asked him to keep an eye on you. I didn't realize he was going to follow you around the villa. He is very dedicated to his job."

Anna scowled at him. "Why would you need him to keep an eye on me?"

"That brings us back to my first problem—what to do with you." Again he indicated the seats. Anna begrudgingly sat, staring directly at him. He took a deep breath and continued, "Because you're not employed by the prince or the Grand Ducal Family, I do not technically have any authority over your actions. And because Prince Léopold actually wants you to stay, I can't have you thrown out of the villa. But as the prince's chief of security, responsibility for his safety ultimately rests with me, and I can't simply let things continue as they have."

"And what does that have to do with me?" Anna didn't like his insinuation.

Zane opened his hands wide, clearly trying to pacify Anna. "I'm not saying that we did not have issues before you came. That's why you were assigned to help us. But I'm sure you can see that the number of incidents has increased since you arrived."

"Are you implying that the attacks have been my fault?" Anna wasn't usually the irrational Banana Girl, but she could feel her impatience rising.

"At the ship launching, for example, if you had stayed disciplined and remained at your post, you wouldn't have found yourself trapped in a limo cabin in a free-fall into Port Miami's shipping channel."

Anna gaped at him. "What? I went to inspect the tender on your orders!"

Zane frowned. "Why would I have assigned the inspection to you? Do you know anything about boats?"

A half laugh escaped Anna's lips. "That's what I told Andre." At least she felt somewhat justified in her original objection.

Zane rubbed his chin, frowning in thought. "Why would Andre send you down to the limo tender unless . . ." He scowled and shook his head. "No, I can't believe he would have done anything to harm the prince. He's been a loyal member of my team for years." He turned back to Anna. "Andre's out on another assignment right now, otherwise we could ask him about it. Do you remember what he said when he gave you the instructions?"

"Not exactly," Anna said, scrunching her eyes closed, trying to think back to the conversation. "I do remember him mentioning something about not shooting the messenger's messenger. I thought that was a weird thing to say. You're telling me that you didn't send him to have me inspect the limo tender?"

Zane shook his head. "I did not. He must have simply been passing the information along. It is rather common in such a small, close-knit team. I will talk to him about it before the gala this evening."

Anna frowned. "What gala?"

With a deep sigh, Zane leaned back into his chair. "I suppose you would have found out eventually. The Bolivian ambassador is holding a celebrity charity gala this evening at one of the hotels on the Blue Lagoon."

"And you're okay with Leo going?" she asked with wide eyes.

"Not particularly. For obvious reasons, it had been removed from the prince's schedule. But after his sudden disappearance yesterday, not to mention last night's debacle with the Sint Maarten police"—He gave Anna a deliberate and meaningful look. She hadn't been able to bring herself to feel sorry for her choice to sneak Leo to Sint Maarten yet—"the Grand Ducal Family believes that it is important for Prince Léopold to make a public appearance. Partially to dispel the rumors that he is sick or dead or some other such nonsense, and partially to show that we press forward with courage in the face of adversity." He sounded as if he were quoting a line of pompous propaganda.

Anna took a deep breath. "Well, I had planned to wait to tell you this until I had some proof, but I believe Jessie may be the one behind the attacks."

An expression of mild shock crossed Zane's face. "Jessie? How could it be Jessie?"

"Like I said, I don't have any proof. But she's been the only close security agent to not lose her job, quit, or be attacked while working for the prince. Also, I just spoke to her, and she has some latent hostility for me. Plus, she clearly had the opportunity to carry out the attacks, and possibly the sabotages of the past weeks and before. I think you'd be smart to keep her away from Leo tonight."

"But you said the attacks were never meant for the prince."

Anna lifted a shoulder in acknowledgment. "Even so, I don't trust her. I have no intention of letting her closer to the prince than I am."

Zane's brow furrowed in contemplation. "If you are correct about Jessie, then having you near the prince would also be dangerous. I think recent events prove that." He raised a brow at her.

With the evidence obviously against her, Anna didn't offer any protest.

Zane stood and paced the small space behind his desk. He stopped. "I might have an idea," he said, turning slowly toward her. "If you will agree to keep your distance from the prince at the gala, I will give Jessie instructions to do the same."

Obviously, Leo's safety was the highest priority. And she absolutely wanted Jessie kept away from him. Plus, as an added bonus, Anna could use this arrangement to prepare herself for saying goodbye to the prince forever. "I can agree to that," she finally said.

After informing Anna that he would arrange the details of

their mutually exclusive assignments, Zane excused her from his office.

Halfway back to her room, Anna realized there might be one other benefit to Zane's proposal. She had already thrown down the gauntlet with Jessie. The woman obviously recognized—and resented—Leo's preference for Anna. Hopefully she could also see Anna's growing interest in him. If Zane forced the two agents into a stalemate of keeping equally distanced from the prince, maybe Anna could use that tug-of-war to tip the unstable woman off balance. Perhaps even tricking her into revealing her role in the attacks.

A little bending of her agreement with Zane might be required.

Assuming her heart could take it.

Chapter 16

Even wearing her favorite gown to a fancy gala, Anna knew she would be miserable. It was funny, she realized, how in two short weeks she had gone from happily observing Leo from a distance to resenting the mandate that she stay away from him. She shook her head at the irony and made one final twirl in front of the mirror, the shimmery, royal blue dress rising effortlessly from the ground. At least she would look like a princess while she was miserable.

Wearing his tuxedo, Leo stood waiting for her in the front entryway at the base of the grand staircase. The tailored tux fit him incredibly well across the shoulders—and other places she was trying not to notice.

"You look beautiful," he said, taking her hand. "Tell me again why I can't keep you next to me all evening?"

Anna squeezed his hand and gave him a sympathetic look. "You know why," she said in her best pleading voice. If he pressed too hard on this, she would cave like a house of cards.

Leo placed her hand on his arm as he escorted her across the spacious entryway. "Zane gave me his reasons. But I get the feeling he thinks just having you around is trouble, so I'm not sure I trust his judgment on the matter." He turned and grinned at her. "Having you close has been the best thing that has ever happened to me, and not only because you keep saving my life." He grinned at her.

Anna nearly melted at the compliment. And it was nice to have someone to defend her skills as a ninja—not that she usually needed help defending herself. "Get this." She stopped them at the front door and glanced around before lowering her voice. "Zane even implied that it was my fault I got trapped in the limo boat and dropped out of the side of the yacht."

"Wait, the tender was dropped?" Leo asked.

She nodded.

"Like free-fall?"

"With me inside," she added with a wry smile.

Leo stopped short. "I didn't know that. Is that why you were so groggy when I found you?"

"I wasn't groggy!"

"You yelled, 'Flea-O the Thor!' when I stepped into the cabin."

Anna's eyes went wide, and her cheeks flushed. Leo laughed out loud, and after a few moments Anna joined in.

As their laughter died down, Leo's gaze focused on her, his mouth tipped in a small grin. "I'm going to miss you tonight."

She glanced down, trying to avoid those intense eyes. But seeing how nicely the tuxedo fit him didn't help things either. "I wish there was a way I could be with you." She meant the comment for more than just the evening's event.

He leaned closer, eyes flitting to her lips. Anna placed her free hand on his chest and pushed feebly.

"Leo," she pleaded.

After a tortuous moment of feeling his breath against her cheek and inhaling the warm scent of his skin—a moment that felt like an eternity—the prince finally leaned back. He placed a hand on the front door, took a long breath, then pushed it open. Together, they walked down the steps toward the waiting motorcade.

"You know," Anna leaned in and whispered to Leo, "if the night goes by without Jessie trying to get rid of me, we might need to do something to set her off. Do you have any powerful weapons in that flirtation arsenal of yours?"

With a smirk, Leo said, "I could unleash the wooing Armageddon, if necessary."

"Don't do anything rash just yet. We want to see what she'll do first." Anna pulled the prince to a stop and looked up into that charismatic face she had grown to care for so much. "Whatever happens, Leo, please be careful. We don't think the attacks are meant for you, but let's not take any chances. You could simply avoid Jessie the whole night, if you want."

Leo nodded. "Thank you, Anna. For everything." They parted, Anna for the second of four black sedans waiting in the driveway, Leo for the stretch limo.

The drive to the hotel was uneventful—and particularly boring—without Leo to talk to.

The sedans diverted to the underground parking garage and stopped in front of the service entrance. Anna and the rest of the prince's security detachment queued up at the metal detectors. Jessie ended up directly in front of Anna as they went through the screening process. After Anna passed through the detector arch, Jessie slowed her pace, forcing Anna to either slow down or move around her. Anna's senses went on high alert. She hadn't expected an encounter with her fellow agent so soon, but it didn't look like she had a choice.

As Anna walked past, Jessie glanced her way, her gaze shooting daggers. "Stay away from him," she said shortly.

Anna raised her eyebrows and made a waving motion with her hand to encourage Jessie to continue. "A demand like that is usually followed by a threat of some sort. Like, 'stay away from him' or else . . ."

Jessie glared back at her. "Just stay away from him. That's all." Jessie stormed off along the corridor toward her assigned post.

Anna rolled her eyes. Of all the adversaries she'd faced, Jessie had the least flair.

Anna arrived at the main entrance in time to see the prince emerge from his limousine. He was escorted promptly into the main ballroom. Like any good security agent—or ninja—Anna hung back in the shadows. Tracking the prince's movements, she made her way to her own post.

From her spot in the back corner of the ballroom, Anna watched the gathering guests. She caught sight of Jessie standing in her assigned spot near the side door leading to the kitchens. Jessie narrowed her eyes and glared back at Anna.

So that's how it would be.

Anna moved along the outside wall to get a better view of the prince—purely for security purposes. He bowed low over the hand of the young Baroness de Pélichy. The young teenage girl blushed an adorable shade of scarlet.

As the evening progressed, a long stream of dignitaries and celebrities greeted the prince and made small talk with him. He was so comfortable with all of them.

After finishing a dance with one of Bolivia's soap opera starlets, Leo plodded back through the crowd to his table. Anna caught his eye and winked. He smiled and raised his brows, nodding toward an empty seat next to his.

She would certainly have loved to sit with him all evening, hoarding his smiles and laughs for herself. But she couldn't. She had a job to do.

Anna shook her head slightly. Leo's shoulders slumped theatrically, but he put on a brave smile.

Realizing she hadn't checked Jessie's position in several minutes, Anna glanced over to the opposite corner of the ballroom.

No Jessie.

Mild panic jolted Anna's stomach. She leaned forward on her tiptoes, frantically scanning the crowd until she caught sight of Jessie inching her way along the side wall toward Leo's table.

That was completely unacceptable.

Plus, it went against their deal.

Anna glared at her nemesis and casually strolled along her edge of the room toward the prince's corner. Jessie countered by stepping away from the wall, putting herself three feet closer to Leo's table, staring back at Anna with a gloating smirk. Anna's eyes bulged at the woman's audacity.

At that moment, the Panamanian consul invited Leo to meet a friend of hers, and Leo followed her across the crowded ballroom. Jessie and Anna scowled at each other. Neither had won this round.

Jessie walked through the scattered tables to take up position next to the entrance. Rather than continue this childish game, Anna turned toward the staircase leading up to the balcony. From there, she could keep an eye on the prince and hopefully trick Jessie into doing something stupid.

As Anna came around the columns at the top of the stairs and gazed over the ornate balcony railing into the ballroom below, she just caught sight of Leo walking out of the ballroom into the front hallway. Jessie followed close behind, glancing up at Anna with a triumphant sneer.

With a frustrated growl, Anna flew back down the stairs and out into the hall at the most dignified speed possible. Glancing up and down the corridor, Anna peered over the heads of the gala attendees coming and going through the entrance of the main ballroom. She caught a glimpse of Jessie turning the next corner and ran after her.

As she rounded the corner, a door several feet down the hall slammed shut. Anna sprinted to the door. Pulling it open as gently as possible, she quietly slipped into the empty conference room. Empty except for Leo and Jessie.

Anna still felt confident in her belief that Jessie wouldn't hurt Leo, but she wasn't willing to risk it.

". . . mind waiting for me back in the ballroom, I'll be there shortly." Leo stood in the middle of the room, slowly backing away from Jessie. An expression of concern bordering on mild panic flashed across his face.

"Remain calm, Your Highness. I'm trying to keep you safe," Jessie said as she moved slowly toward him.

Anna lunged forward, catching Jessie with a powerful kick in the back of the legs. Jessie cried out as she crumpled to the floor, then quickly rolled to the side and jumped back to her feet.

"I told you to stay away from him!" she snarled at Anna.

Anna took several steps to the side, placing herself between the crazy woman and Leo. Jessie charged forward and swung for Anna's head. Anna ducked, catching a grazing blow against her shoulder. Immediately, Jessie aimed a kick at Anna's midsection.

Anna reacted fast enough to prevent the sharp edge of Jessie's heel from making contact, but not fast enough to deflect the force of Jessie's kick. Anna sailed backward, crashing into a stack of chairs.

Coughing with the loss of breath, Anna scrambled back to her feet as Jessie ran forward and put her body between Anna and Leo. "Stay away!" she yelled, holding her arms out as if to cover Leo.

Leo fought past Jessie's arms, placing himself between Anna

and Jessie, and turned to face Jessie. He held both hands out toward her. "Jessie, if you're trying to get to me by hurting people, it won't work."

"Leo, please move out of the way," Anna calmly instructed as she approached them.

"No," the prince said over his shoulder to Anna. "She doesn't want to hurt me. You're the one in danger."

Anna grabbed Leo's shoulder and tried to nudge him aside. "But I'm the one who's supposed to be protecting you." She grunted with the effort of moving Leo's muscular frame.

Jessie darted forward and pushed Anna's hand off of his shoulder. "No, *I'm* the one protecting the prince—from you! He's in danger anytime you're around."

Leo grappled with Jessie's hand, attempting to shoehorn himself between the women again. "No. You're trying to kill her," Leo said.

Anna grabbed Jessie's other free hand while Leo fought to push Anna away.

They grunted and wrestled, each trying to insert themself between the other two.

"I'm not trying to kill *her*." Jessie jerked her head toward Anna. "*She's* trying to kill *you*!"

"I'm not trying to kill him," Anna spat. "I'm trying to protect him!"

"Nice protecting!" Jessie yelled. "Every time he goes outside with you, he nearly gets killed!"

"Wait." Leo stared, dumbfounded, at Jessie. "You're not trying to kill Anna?"

Jessie continued glaring at Anna while she spoke to the prince. "If she keeps putting you in danger, I'll strongly consider hurting her." Some of the fire went out of her eyes. "But, no, I wouldn't want her dead."

Anna felt as surprised as Leo looked. She stopped struggling against Leo and released Jessie's hand.

Jessie stared at the prince. "What did you mean that she was the one in danger? Weren't all of the attacks meant for you?"

Leo shook his head.

Jessie looked from Leo to Anna, perhaps wanting more explanation.

"We doubled-checked the ballistics. All three bullets were shot at me. They were nowhere near the prince," Anna explained.

"Are you sure?" Jessie pressed.

Leo chuckled at the note of skepticism in her voice. "I didn't believe it at first either."

"What about the speedboat ride?" Jessie asked.

"The boat was already starting to sink before Leo got there. He was just unlucky to get locked in with me," Anna said.

"And the walk-in freezer? And the Ferrari?" Jessie added.

"The Ferrari sabotage was meant for Kaitlynn—or possibly me—and the walk-in freezer was definitely meant for me," Anna said.

"It was pure coincidence that I was even near those incidents," Leo added.

Anna considered Jessie with new eyes. "So, you don't hold any romantic aspirations for the prince?"

Jessie's eyes went wide and her head dipped slightly. "Certainly not. I would never presume to be of the same social standing as the prince." Jessie turned back to Leo. "Your Highness, I only want you to be safe and happy. That's all I've ever wanted."

The prince stepped toward Jessie. "I've always appreciated your devotion to our country and my family."

Jessie looked up at him with what could only be described as utter adoration in her eyes. "If I can continue to be of any service to you and the Grand Ducal Family, it would be my honor."

Leo's gaze flitted to Anna before returning to Jessie. He placed a hand on Jessie's shoulder. "Your caliber of loyalty and dedication will always be welcome to our country and my family."

Jessie nodded before turning to Anna. "I hope you can understand why I thought you were a danger to the prince. I truly don't wish you any harm."

Anna smiled. "I feel the same."

When Jessie looked back at the prince, Anna shifted out of her view and caught his eye. She tilted her head back toward the ballroom while looking intently at the back of Jessie's head, hoping he understood her suggestion.

After a moment of confusion, the prince's face lit up. "Ah. Jessie, would you be so kind as to join me in the ballroom for some refreshment."

"I'm technically supposed to keep my distance from you tonight," Jessie said with a sideways glance at Anna.

Anna stepped back into the conversation. "Now that we understand what's going on, I think we can ignore that arrangement."

Jessie turned back to Leo with a shy smile on her face. He offered her his arm.

The complete lack of any feelings of jealousy as Leo and Jessie left the conference room together surprised Anna. Perhaps it came as a result of her newfound confidence in Leo's feelings for her. She shook her head in an effort to remind herself that she needed to be ready to watch the prince walk out of her life for good.

On her way back to the ballroom, Anna did a quick sweep of the main entryway and the kitchen then made her way back to her perch in the balcony, content knowing that Leo wasn't in any danger from Jessie. In fact, if anyone so much as sneezed in his direction, she was sure Jessie would take them out. Anna watched as they ate hors d'oeuvres and visited with other guests.

Anna fought the green-eyed monster for a brief moment when the prince escorted Jessie to the floor for a dance. Anna did her best to force those feelings back down, trying to focus her mind on the mission. The relief at discovering that Jessie hadn't been responsible for the attacks—and it seemed increasingly likely that she wasn't—was slowly replaced by a feeling of apprehension.

With a start, Anna realized that she only had one more day to figure out who the attacker was. Worse, she was back at square one in terms of suspects. Who else would be jealous enough of Leo's attention to have orchestrated such assaults?

Leo's repeated glances up in her direction distracted Anna from her efforts—and her feelings of jealousy. Jessie must have noticed Leo's attention, because she also glanced up at Anna. When they finished the dance, Jessie pulled Leo into a light embrace, whispering something in his ear. He smiled at her and nodded. When they parted, Jessie walked to the far corner and took up her station. Anna watched her for a while, wondering why she hadn't stayed with the prince. Surely she had been enjoying herself. And it would have been the most natural thing for Leo to have a guest at his side for the evening. A few seconds later Jessie stared intentionally up at Anna. Instead of a malicious glare, this time it was a look of gratitude and contentment. She even gave Anna a very genuine, if somewhat conspiratorial, smile.

When a hand suddenly touched her shoulder, Anna jolted and spun around, ready to swing an elbow into the throat of her assailant. Instead, she found herself staring at the prince's handsome, bemused face.

"Can't you just be a little bit startled like everyone else? Why does it always have to be an attack?" He pulled her hand onto his arm and led her away from the balcony banister.

Anna glanced at him in confusion. "Where are we going? I'm supposed to stay away from you tonight, remember?"

Leo let out a short laugh. "I thought we agreed to ignore that plan."

He swept her out onto the dance floor, pulling her close to him with practiced skill. She cast around for something to focus on besides his deep blue eyes, not to mention those lips that she'd been trying not to think about for the past two weeks. Her mission wasn't to fall in love with this handsome prince. In fact, it was strictly against Rule Number One, though she couldn't remember the specific wording of that particular rule at the moment.

"I'm glad you're willing to dance with me," he said.

"I could have refused, but I'm sure you would have made up some nonsense about it being in the job description," Anna said with a smirk.

"I'm pretty sure dancing with me actually is in the job description."

She raised a brow. "So you say."

He grinned at her, then suddenly became quiet, his gaze still intense. She tried to look away but found she didn't want to anymore.

"Did I tell you how breathtaking you look tonight?" Leo asked in a low voice.

Anna gazed up at him. "Please don't do this, Leo. As much as I wish we could be together, we both know it can't work."

His face fell a bit and he stared off into the distance. "In moments when I'm thinking clearly, my brain tells me the same thing." His eyes found hers again. "But when I'm near you, the

265

only thing I can think of is wanting to hold you and never let go."

Through sheer willpower, Anna forced her legs not to buckle.

"There has to be a way that a beautiful woman like you would be willing to give a guy like me a chance." He finished with a boyish grin.

If she didn't put some space between them soon, she'd be melting into his arms before the dance was over. She forced herself to straighten and lean away from his irresistible magnetism. "Well, it would be hard for a girl like me, who always dreamed of spending her life in a small town with a simple, hardworking guy to have to settle for traveling the world . . . with a prince. Do you realize what kind of sacrifice that would be?"

Leo's lips turn up at the corners. "I do believe you are teasing me."

"It seems only fair considering what you've put me through."

He gazed at her face, pulling her a fraction closer. "Anna?"

"Yes?" she managed.

"I am seriously considering asking you to do something that most definitely is not in the job description." His eyes were drawn to her lips.

Her heart beat out an erratic rhythm. She looked up into his eyes, feeling all of the air being sucked from her lungs. "Leo, we can't," she whispered. "In the end, you'll just have to let me go."

He blinked, then a broad smile spread across his face. "Let you go . . ." he repeated slowly. "Isn't that the phrase you Americans use when someone is dismissed from employment? Now that you mention it, dismissing you would be a great idea . . . except I never hired you in the first place. I suppose I could hire you, and then fire you."

Anna smiled at his sense of humor.

He was everything that was warm and charming.

And unattainable.

She looked away, distracting herself by watching the other dancers.

How could she get involved with him only to later be forced to break his heart?

And her own.

But was she protecting him, or herself? She might be throwing away the possibility of something amazing simply because she was afraid.

Their dancing slowed until they barely moved.

She might be afraid, but she was a Banana Girl, and Banana Girls never let fear stop them.

As she turned back to Leo's waiting gaze, the rest of the room faded away.

Anna knew what she wanted, and fear of what couldn't be in the future was not going to stop her from having it.

She smiled and closed her eyes as she felt him lean ever closer.

His breath was on her lips, just a whisper away.

Suddenly, Anna felt a buzz against her hip. Her eyes flew open.

Leo had pulled her close enough against this body that she felt his phone notification a second before the trumpeting of his text alert sounded.

Reluctantly, Anna slid out of his arms just enough to take a calming breath.

Perhaps a crowded gala ballroom wasn't quite the right time or place.

His phone buzzed again, and he pulled it from his pocket to silence the ringer. He glanced down at the message and frowned. "Zane says our ambassador is waiting for me in the conference room."

They both glanced toward the main entry. Andre stood next to the door, acting casual, but he gave a meaningful nod when he caught Leo's eye.

Leo looked back at Anna with an apology on his face. "I should probably go. He's been bugging me about this meeting all evening."

Anna nodded, not trusting her voice at the moment. Her hand lingered for a few more seconds on his arm, finally dropping as he walked away. He exited toward the conference wing with Andre following close on his heels. The prince's absence left her feeling cold and more than a little exposed, alone in the middle of the dance floor. She struck off in the opposite direction, hoping to find something that would pass for an excuse to focus on her job again.

A niggling in the back of her brain told her she definitely did need to focus on her job again, specifically the part about the mission ending the next day and still not knowing who the attacker was. But who else could it be? Who could have been so close to the prince and so jealous at the same time?

Her mission deadline had come, and she hadn't found the attacker. She might have been willing to concede defeat if it weren't for the nagging feeling that she was missing something. That, and Banana Girls not being good at giving up.

At the entrance to the large dining hall, she stopped next to Frederic, pretending to talk to him about the status of security.

His brow went up ever so slightly as he considered her. "Having a good time?"

She tried to ignore the insinuation and the rising heat in her cheeks. "Prince Leo is holding an impromptu meeting with the ambassador. I doubt he'll need close security for that. I can take this position for a while if you need a break."

"I could use a chance to move around a bit," he said as he rolled his shoulders. He started to move away before turning back to her. "Wait, did you mean our ambassador to America? Or the American ambassador to Luxembourg?"

"Wouldn't the American ambassador to Luxembourg be in . . . Luxembourg?" she said with a quirk of her brow.

"Well, it can't be our ambassador to America. He isn't here this evening," Frederic said bluntly.

"What do you mean?"

"He would have found me already," the bodyguard insisted.

That niggling in the back of Anna's brain was throwing a tantrum now.

Frederic continued. "Several months ago, I made the mistake of laughing at one of Ambassador Stronck's jokes. He hasn't left me alone since." He glanced around as if assuring himself that no one was listening in. "It wasn't even that funny. None of his jokes are."

Anna gave him a half-hearted smile that quickly faded. If Leo wasn't meeting with the ambassador, who was he with? At least he was with Zane and Andre. He wouldn't be in danger with his security chief and bodyguard around.

With a flash of emotion, Anna remembered the feeling of defensiveness when Zane had implied it was her fault she plunged into Port Miami in a limo tender. But then Leo had been surprised when she mentioned the free-fall. How could Zane have known about it and not Leo? She wasn't exactly sure what she had shared with whom, but she knew that Leo had been with her the entire rest of that day as they gave official statements to the harbor patrol then later explained everything again to Zane and Celine. Zane couldn't have known anything about the incident that she hadn't shared right in front of Leo.

The only way for Zane to know what had happened to the limo tender was if he—

"I have to find Leo." Anna blurted.

"No break for me, I guess," Frederic said with a smirk.

Anna grabbed Frederic's arm. "Contact the security posted at the exits. We need to know if Zane or Leo has left the hotel."

Frederic's expression turned instantly serious. "I can just check with Andre. Didn't he leave with the prince?" Frederic touched his earpiece and frowned. "My comm link is dead."

Anna's insides went cold. Communications down. Leo missing. This was a disaster in the making.

"Lock down the building. I'll look for Leo and Andre." She turned and rushed across the ballroom, hoping the bodyguard would know his part in an emergency like this.

She flew out into the hallway, scanning the rows of doors on each side. Which room would they have gone into? Would they even have gone into a conference room at all? She needed to find Andre. He was with Leo when they left the ballroom. He would know where they went.

A man in a concierge uniform stood behind a nearby desk. She rushed at him. "Have you seen Prince Leo? I'm part of his security team." Anna knew she looked wild-eyed, but she didn't care.

Despite his obvious surprise, the concierge pointed toward the stairs. "Um, yes. He went with his bodyguard up to the mezzanine level."

The concierge had barely finished his sentence before Anna was halfway up the grand staircase. On the mezzanine landing, she stopped and glanced around.

Celine came around a corner and halted abruptly, taking in Anna's frantic appearance. "Miss Rivers, what's the matter?"

"Where's Prince Leo?" Anna asked.

"I think I saw him headed to the hotel bar with Andre," Celine's tone conveyed a concern for Anna's current mental state.

Anna shook her head. "No, the concierge saw them coming up the stairs a few minutes ago. The Prince had a meeting with the ambassador in one of the conference rooms."

Celine stared at her for a moment before speaking softly, almost as if trying not to spook a wild animal. "Anna, the ambassador isn't here tonight. He isn't even on the guest list."

Anna rounded on Celine. "I saw the text on Leo's phone. He left with Andre to meet with the ambassador!"

Celine held her hands up in a gesture of calm. "Okay. It will be alright. Let's find them."

Anna huffed and stormed away. She didn't have time for patronizing, especially not from Celine. But she didn't argue when Celine followed her.

As a result of her posting on this level earlier in the evening, she had already checked the rooms nearby. There were four large conference rooms adjoining the mezzanine. She ran to the nearest door and threw it open. A long table sat in perfect anticipation of its next meeting, but other than that the room was empty.

She pulled open the door to the next conference room.

Empty.

Anna's stomach sank. How would she ever find them?

The third conference room was just as empty as the others except that the door hit something as it opened. Anna pulled the door back and saw Andre slumped behind it, unconscious.

Anna knelt next to Andre and shook his hulking form. He groaned and rolled to the side. At least he was alive. "Andre! What happened? Where's Prince Leo?"

His face instantly transformed from groggy to concerned. Wincing, he sat up. "I don't know. We walked into the conference room to meet the ambassador, but he wasn't here. That's the last thing I remember." He gingerly touched the back of his head. "Someone got me from behind."

"How did you know the meeting was in this conference room?" Anna asked.

Andre shrugged. "Zane was waiting at the door to usher us in."

Zane. It couldn't be an accident that Zane had orchestrated the meeting and been the one standing by when they arrived.

"Was anyone in the room when you walked in?" Anna asked.

Andre squinted then shook his head. "No. It was completely empty," he said as he struggled to his feet.

The clues pointing toward Zane continued to increase. But how could she have been so wrong about the motive for the attacks? Zane obviously didn't attack and sabotage the close security agents out of jealousy. What possible reason could Zane have to try and get rid of them?

Her phone buzzed and she glanced down at the message. It was from Leo.

The message was short and to the point.

– *It's Z.*

It was Zane.

And if Leo knew, that meant Zane had already tipped his hand, and the prince was in serious danger. Her head spun with confusion and adrenaline.

How could she have left Leo alone? How could she have let her guard down so easily?

"I have to find Leo," Anna said as she reached for the door, abandoning Andre leaning against the wall. She wished she could stay to help him, but there wasn't time. "Celine, get Andre some medical attention, then come help me look for Leo."

Celine nodded, but Andre attempted to stand. "I'm not going to sit here useless," the bodyguard said as his eyes swam in and out of focus.

Anna understood the sentiment. She nodded at Celine. "You two work together, then."

Bolting from the conference room, Anna headed back toward the front staircase. Halfway there she met Jessie.

"Anna, what's happening? Our security comms are dead, and Frederic told me that the prince is missing."

Anna grabbed Jessie by the arm and pulled her along. "Someone jumped Andre as he and Leo were entering a conference room. I think the prince is with Zane."

"That's good. At least he—"

"Zane isn't helping Leo; he's the one who jumped them."

Jessie's eyes went wide. To her credit as a professional, she simply nodded and kept pace with Anna.

Anna stopped at the top of the stairs, attempting to collect her thoughts. Jessie watched her, waiting for instructions.

She took a deep breath. What would Zane do with Leo? The most likely motive would be abduction for ransom. But how would he get the prince out of the hotel? They could have made it out before the lockdown, it was difficult to say how much of a head start they would have had. But they wouldn't have gone on foot.

"Jessie, go secure the garage. Make sure all the entourage vehicles are there. Then use the hotel employees to communicate with Frederic and Andre when he's back in action. I'm sure the hotel security has some sort of two-way radio system. I'm going to check the roof for helicopters."

Jessie tore down the grand staircase as Anna moved to the nearest bank of elevators.

She entered the empty elevator compartment and checked the panel for options. The elevator went all the way to the helicopter pad, but blindly stepping out onto the roof was too much of a risk, so she jabbed the button for the last regular floor. She'd use the stairs to access the roof.

As the doors slid closed, Celine darted into the elevator car. "I'm coming with you."

"You should stay with Andre," Anna said.

"If Léopold is in trouble, I need to be there," Celine insisted firmly.

Anna nodded absently at the prince's chief of staff. With her eyes focused on the steadily increasing numbers of the floor readout, Anna reached down and pulled her gun from the holster on her thigh.

The door opened on the top floor to a deserted hallway. Anna held her gun down against her leg, watching for danger ahead. She glanced over her shoulder at Celine. The woman would only be a liability if things got violent. "Celine, I need you to stay here until I can secure the area."

Celine nodded and shrank back against the walls of the elevator.

Anna stepped out of the elevator and moved around the corner to the stairwell. She pushed hard against the door then winced as it swung faster than she anticipated and clanged against the wall. The sound echoed off the cement walls of the deep stairwell. She stepped into the harshly lit space and glanced down the stairs before carefully making her way to the roof access. She stopped and listened. The muffled sound of helicopter rotors bled through the door. She knew it was crazy to rush out onto the helipad alone. But could she risk waiting for backup to arrive? What if the helicopter took off with Leo inside?

As Anna nudged the door open, the humid Miami night air blew into the stairwell. She didn't see anyone on the roof, only the tail end of a mid-sized helicopter, its rotor blades idling. It was fortunate that the stairwell had dumped her out on the roof behind the helicopter. She quickly slipped out the door and behind the stairwell structure to hide.

Peeking around the corner, she inspected the waiting helicopter. The glare of the city's lights on the helicopter windows made it difficult to know if anyone was inside. She moved in a wide arc behind the tail of the helicopter, ducking when she saw that there was definitely someone sitting in the pilot's seat. Crouching low, she approached the left side of the aircraft. She touched the warm metal skin as she crept carefully forward.

When Anna was just a few feet from the cabin's rear window, she paused and stole a quick peek inside. Zane sat at the controls, looking steadily out the window toward the elevator doors.

What could he be waiting for? Surely he wasn't sticking around hoping to fight off a rescue attempt.

As Anna pulled back from the window, hoping she hadn't been seen, she caught a glimpse of someone perched in the rear seat, behind the copilot. She couldn't be sure, but she thought it was Leo. Really, it could have been anyone; but Anna wanted it to be Leo.

Keeping her gun at the ready, Anna crouched and moved forward half a step. With her free hand, she reached up and tested the handle to the cabin's rear door.

"Stop!" yelled a voice from behind her.

Anna's body tensed, her hand still on the door lever. Ever so slowly, she moved her gun up to her torso, attempting to shield it from view with her body.

"I saw your gun, Anna. You pulled it out right in front of me in the elevator when you thought I was a helpless, cowering little girl."

Celine?

How was she involved in this?

As the realization hit her, Anna closed her eyes and let out a defeated sigh.

Zane and Celine's secret relationship. That explained it.

If Zane was attempting to abduct Leo, and he was romantically involved with Celine, it wasn't too far-fetched to think she would be helping him.

People do crazy things when they think they're in love.

"I want you to put the gun on the ground or I'll be forced to put a hole in the back of your head." Celine's voice was full of contempt.

Anna slowly placed her weapon next to the helicopter's skid. Then she stood with her hands up and turned around. Celine stood ten feet away, pointing a gun at her.

Anna tried not to let her jaw hit the floor. Even seeing it with her own eyes, it was hard to believe. How could Celine be standing on the hotel roof threatening Anna with a gun? Anna's brain refused to process it.

"We were planning to simply fly away, but now that you've seen us, you'll need to join us for the flight." Celine waved the gun toward the door. "Part of it, anyway."

Anna pulled open the rear door. Leo looked up, his face full of relief that quickly changed to confusion. He glanced toward Zane sitting in the front seat, clearly concerned that Anna would be seen if she wasn't careful. Little did Leo know that Anna had already not been careful enough. A trained Banana Girl outsmarted by the prince's overpaid secretary.

Leo's look of confusion quickly vanished as he realized she hadn't been successful in her rescue attempt. She wasn't sure what gave it away, but it might have been her hands raised in surrender.

"Get in!" Celine yelled.

Leo jolted at the order from his soon-to-be former chief of staff. As additional realization dawned on him, it showed on his face. He held up his bound hands, obviously communicating an apology that he couldn't do anything to help her. Anna shook her head to dismiss his apology. She wouldn't have wanted him to try anything anyway, at least not until he got some real training in his backup career.

Anna climbed in next to him. "Are you okay?" she whispered.

Leo nodded a silent reply.

"What's she doing here?" Zane asked with a nod toward Anna.

"It's complicated," Celine replied as she opened the door and handed the gun to Zane. "If she tries anything, shoot her."

Zane nodded grimly and pointed the gun at Anna. Celine pulled out a length of rope and tied Anna's hands behind her back—more tightly than Anna would have expected from someone she assumed was accustomed to working behind a desk. With the rest of the rope, she tied Anna's legs together just as tightly.

Celine secured the rear door and settled into the seat next to Zane. "Take off," she said.

Zane nodded and spurred the engine to life with the twist of the throttle. The rooftop pad quickly fell away as the helicopter lifted off into the night sky and swung out over the glittering city.

Anna met Leo's gaze.

"I'm so sorry," she mouthed to him.

He nodded. "Me, too."

Unlike Anna's hands, Leo's had been tied in his lap. He struggled and pulled against the ropes.

Anna shook her head. "No, Leo, don't," she whispered, hoping her eyes conveyed the seriousness of her warning.

He let out a breath and nodded his understanding.

It wasn't time to try anything foolhardy. Not hundreds of feet above the city. Anna needed to figure out what was going on. Clearly, Zane and Celine had never meant for Anna to come along, so that meant her presence would probably come to a very abrupt end.

Maybe if she could get the pair talking, she could figure a way out.

Anna gave Leo a very deliberate nod toward the front seat. She mimed talking with her mouth.

Leo seemed to get the message. He straightened his back and took a deep breath. "You'll never get away with this!" he declared. "When my family finds out, you'll be punished for your betrayal!" He glanced at Anna, apparently seeking her stamp of approval.

Though she admired Leo's bravery, and his regal bearing had been known to melt her heart from time to time, this was no time for blustery proclamations. Anna rolled her eyes and whispered, "Ransom" as she nodded toward the pair again.

Leo's eyebrows shot up, and he nodded a quick agreement. He cleared his throat. His tone was much more unassuming this time. "Of course, you'll want me to contact my family about a ransom. I can promise you'll be paid handsomely."

This time when he looked back at Anna, she nodded in agreement.

"They'll pay all right. But it's nothing personal, *Your Highness*." Zane spoke the title with disdain. "I happen to know your family has plenty of gold in the coffers to help fund a lifetime pension for two hardworking, underappreciated staffers who've spent the last seven years babysitting their spoiled brat."

In the seat directly in front of Anna, Celine flinched ever so slightly. A few seconds later, she cast an apologetic look at the prince.

That didn't make any sense. Why would Celine carry out a violent abduction that she felt guilty about? There was more going on than met the eye.

Anna glanced at the compass on the console in front of Zane's knees. The icon was pegged almost exactly east. Looking out the window, Anna watched the line of bright lights—where the city met the ocean—receding behind them. If they were heading directly east from Miami, Zane and Celine were either planning a stop at an airport somewhere in the Bahamas— which would be difficult with a world-famous prince in tow—or they were planning to hide out on one of the thousands of tiny islands dotting the water below them.

As the helicopter rushed along through the dark sky, Anna tried to figure out the power dynamic between Zane and Celine. She had initially thought Zane was the one in charge, but given the way Celine was bossing Zane around, there was no doubt in Anna's mind that Celine was the one calling the shots. But why would she act so sorry toward the prince? Why would she care about Leo's opinion of her?

Anna needed to find out more. "Leo's family will pay well to keep the prince safe. You'd even have enough to buy your own little island down there." She leaned over and looked out the window.

Zan laughed. "And what would we do with that? Live out our days like shipwrecked lovers?" He laughed again.

Watching closely for a reaction, Anna saw Celine cringe. Maybe Zane had hit a little too close to the mark with that comment. But if that's what Celine wanted, why wasn't Zane on the same page?

Zane continued. "We only need an island as a place to hide the prince until we get paid the ransom."

"You're quite the brilliant mastermind, Zane, coming up with this plan to kidnap me." Leo joined in, following Anna's lead. Though it didn't seem like Leo had yet clued into the fact that Celine was running the show.

"I'm not the brilliant one. It's Celine." He glanced adoringly at her. "When she told me about the plan, I knew this was our chance to finally be together."

This was the same lovesick Zane Anna had overheard in Celine's office. The one who sounded willing to do anything for her. Things were starting to make sense.

"And the attacks?" Leo asked.

Zane chuckled. "Perhaps you should be thanking us for kidnapping you, Your Highness. After you're ransomed, your family will keep you in Luxembourg where you'll finally be safe from whoever is trying to kill you. You might even say that we're doing you and your family a favor. All we ask is a small compensation in return. Enough to put us in the lap of luxury, right darling?" Zane glanced at Celine with a look of adoration.

"You talk too much, *darling*," Celine said with a false smile.

When Zane turned forward again, Celine immediately glanced back at Prince Leo, a bashful coyness in her expression.

If Anna's hands hadn't been tied behind her back, she would have palmed her forehead.

Celine wasn't in love with Zane—it was as clear as day—she was in love with the prince.

Anna's original suspicions about jealousy had been right all along. And she would be willing to bet her favorite outfit that Celine had been the one to orchestrate the attacks, too.

It suddenly made sense how Celine had arranged everything—Kaitlynn's stint as valet, Anna's trip to the freezer, Anna standing in as chauffeur. Celine had probably been the one to arrange for the previous agents to be accused of drug use and theft. She might have even been the one under the boat with the harpoon meant for Makenna. Celine hadn't asked Anna to inspect the limo tender, but she might have passed the instructions through Andre.

Two thoughts occurred to Anna almost simultaneously: Leo would definitely be safe, and she would definitely not be. The first thought set Anna's mind at ease; the second sent her heart racing double-time.

After about half an hour, Zane brought the helicopter down on the sandy beach of a tiny, isolated island. Several groves of tall trees stood clustered in the center of the island with scrub brush scattered throughout the sand. The helicopter's landing lights illuminated a small bungalow nestled within one of the nearby groves. It looked like the perfect place to take a private vacation—or hide a hostage. Next to the bungalow stood more than a dozen pallets of boxes. Those must be the food and supplies. But why so much?

Celine jumped out and moved around the helicopter.

Turning toward the prince, Anna spoke quickly. "Leo, promise me you'll do whatever Celine says, okay? Just go along with it, and you'll be safe."

Leo's brow furrowed as he considered Anna's request. Despite her efforts, he must have caught the finality in Anna's tone. He shook his head. "No. No! What are you going to do with Anna?" he yelled at Zane.

Celine opened Leo's door and attempted to pull him out.

"No!" The prince lashed out, kicking Celine in her middle.

Zane turned around in his chair and leveled his gun at the prince.

"Leo, please!" Anna cried.

Leo stopped struggling, his gaze fixed on Anna as he allowed himself to be dragged away from the helicopter.

After dropping Leo on a sandy bluff halfway to the bungalow, Celine returned to the helicopter and started fishing around in the rear utility compartment.

"What about her?" Zane called above the noise coming in through the open door.

Celine pulled out a large lithium battery that looked like the type that Hannah used on her quadcopters, only twice the size.

Anna's eyes went wide as Celine slid a short-circuited plug onto the battery connector. In a matter of minutes, a battery that size would heat up and possibly burst into flames.

As Celine tucked the soon-to-be explosive battery under the pilot's seat, she eyed Anna for several long seconds, almost gloating. "Get rid of her." Celine spoke to Zane but reached down and grabbed the end of the rope tying Anna's feet. "Fly back over the water and push her out." Celine quickly loosened the rope but left it wound around Anna's ankles. She gave Anna a long, triumphant look before slamming the door and traipsing back across the beach to Leo.

Zane lifted the helicopter into the air again. He was clearly willing to do anything Celine asked—he always had been. Apparently the feeling wasn't mutual on Celine's part. In about two minutes, the cabin would start filling with smoke and fumes. Even if the battery didn't catch fire, flying the helicopter was about to get much more difficult.

And why would Celine loosen the rope on Anna's ankles? Anna could easily free her feet now, but with her wrists still tied tight, her only real option would be kicking Zane in the head. If she succeeded in incapacitating him, he'd crash the helicopter, and they would both be dead.

The woman had just doubly sabotaged Zane's flight, and he had no idea.

It was almost as if Celine wanted them to crash.

But that would leave her stranded on an unknown island with Prince Leo.

With a huge stockpile of food and supplies.

All alone.

The light in Anna's mind suddenly went on.

Anna looked down at her loosely bound feet and began silently working the coils off. "Listen to me, Zane. Celine isn't going to ransom the prince. She's trying to get herself stuck on the island with him."

"The prince is worth millions. We won't be stuck on a tiny island. We'll travel the world in style."

"You're not listening to me. Celine doesn't want to be with you. She wants to be with Leo. She just put a battery bomb under your seat."

"Nice try, but your secret-agent distractions won't work on me, Miss Rivers."

Anna strained against the last coil around her ankles. If she could get her feet free, maybe she could fish the battery out from under the seat before it caught on fire. Smoke had already begun seeping out from under the front seat.

Zane craned his neck to get a look behind him. "Hey, what are you doing back there?!" He must have noticed the smoke as well.

"I'm trying to save us," she said, stretching her free foot under the seat. "Celine wants to sabotage you so she can be with Leo."

"Stop that!" Zane pushed her backward onto the bench.

"Zane, she untied my feet so that I could overpower you!"

"No more games! This is over." Zane twisted in his seat and opened the rear door.

As he tilted the helicopter in an attempt to dump her out, Anna was forced to brace her feet against the harness mounts. With her hands still bound, she couldn't really grab onto anything, so she pressed herself hard against the back seat.

"Zane, you don't have to do this," Anna yelled. "I know you're trying to help Celine, but she doesn't really love you!"

"You're lying! We're going to run away together. We'll finally be free." He dipped the craft steeper and steeper, swinging the tail back and forth, trying to dislodge Anna.

Anna fumbled around behind her back until she found one of the seat harnesses, gripping it between her bound hands as the helicopter threatened to dump her into the empty waters below. She shifted one foot to the back of Zane's pilot seat as he flew them deeper into a corkscrew spiral. In quick bursts—as much as gravity permitted—she thrashed Zane's head and shoulders with her free leg.

Zane pulled the helicopter level and released the controls. "This is stupid," he said, drawing a handgun from his belt and pointing it at Anna.

With a powerful kick, she knocked the handgun from his grasp just as he pulled the trigger. The bullet shattered the safety glass behind her, and the gun clattered to the floor on the copilot's side of the cabin. Anna jumped over the copilot's chair, blocking Zane from reaching the gun with a shin to his ear. As Zane lunged for it a second time, his body slammed the control stick down, killing the helicopter's lift. The sudden drop in altitude left them floating for a split second.

"Zane! You'll kill us both!" Anna screamed, kicking at him with both feet.

She twisted sideways in the seat, going for the copilot controls. She finally succeeded in restoring some power to the rotors. The helicopter's engine whined in complaint, but the aircraft slowed in its descent. The cabin air stank of burning plastic and electrolyte.

As Zane reached across her and pushed the copilot door open, Anna kneed him in the chest. Fighting was nearly impossible with her hands still tied behind her back.

He grunted against her onslaught and grabbed her by the legs, heaving and pushing her toward the open door. Anna twisted and squirmed, desperate to stay inside the cabin. When his grip slipped, she delivered a savage knee to his nose.

In a dazed stupor, Zane slipped forward out of his seat. Anna kicked him hard in the face, slamming his head backward against the control panel. His now-limp form fell onto the control stick. With all of his dead weight against the stick, the helicopter's nose tilted down and the craft lurched forward. Still hanging tightly to the copilot chair, Anna rolled into an upright position and hooked her leg on the linked control stick on her side, pulling it backward as far as she could in an attempt to keep them airborne. With the other leg, she shoved hard against his body, but she couldn't dislodge his hulking frame from the controls.

Abandoning her efforts to move Zane, she pulled back on the stick with both knees. The craft leveled out, sort of.

A sudden hissing sound—accompanied by a yellow glow—came from the back of the cabin. A jet of flame shooting from under Zane's chair licked the leather of the luxury back seats.

Glancing at the instrument panel in front of her, she realized they were still falling, though not as fast as before. It was a toss-up whether the water or the fire would kill them first.

The helicopter continued spinning as it fell. Part of Zane must have been on the steering pedals, too, but Anna couldn't do much about that. She fought with both legs to get either the control stick or pedals to return to regular flight position. Clearly helicopters weren't meant to be flown with legs only.

It was no use.

They were going to crash.

Coughing through the wafting smoke, Anna worked furiously at the ropes binding her wrists. Her imminent destruction propelled her to feats of contortion that she wouldn't have thought possible. She finally got one hand free—quickly using it to pull up hard on the throttle—a second before the spinning altimeter hit zero.

The helicopter smashed into the black ocean, slamming Anna forward against the hard metal control panel. Several loud bangs followed as the helicopter's rotors struck the water and tore off.

Water rushed in through the two open doors and the burning back seats were snuffed out.

Death by fire had lost.

Hopefully she could still beat the odds against death by water.

Anna scrambled over the controls and pulled Zane off the floor of the cabin. More water poured in as she opened the pilot door. With one arm, Anna grabbed Zane across the chest. She reached down and yanked a life jacket from under the seat before rolling into the warm ocean, still clutching Zane. She kicked hard, pushing away from the sinking craft. The flooded engine belched steam as it succumbed to the waves.

After a short struggle, Anna got the life jacket over Zane's head and fished the straps around his chest to secure it. She activated the built-in emergency flasher. Hopefully he would survive, but there wasn't much more she could do for him.

Anna swam several feet away from Zane and rolled to float on her back. A sea of stars swirled above her. Getting her bearings, she traced the Big Dipper to the North Star. Zane had been flying back toward the mainland, looking for open water to dump her in. She pivoted east and took a few deep breaths, preparing to strike out in hopes of finding Leo's island.

A soft, yellow light peeked above the horizon directly in front of her. The half-moon silhouetted a small grove of trees as it rose behind them.

There was an island nearby.

Knowing she could never live with herself if she left Zane to float out to sea, she turned back and followed his flashing emergency beacon. Reaching his still-unconscious form, Anna grabbed the life jacket's harness and started pulling him along. After what seemed like an eternity, her feet finally brushed sand. She stood and dragged Zane onto the beach, dropping him above high tide level. After checking that he was still alive, Anna made her way across the tiny cay to the east-facing side. Standing upright, she could see so much more of the surrounding ocean than when she was bobbing up and down in the water.

Watching the shimmery reflection of the rising moon, Anna noticed several irregularities in the line of the horizon that must be more islands. She moved along the sand toward them. When she ran out of land, she stopped, preparing herself for another swim.

Glancing down at her beautiful sapphire gown hanging in tatters, Anna shrugged. The dress was beyond saving now. She grabbed the fabric of the lower skirt and tore it away at mid-thigh. She removed her empty gun holster as well and tossed it onto the beach. That should make swimming much easier.

Anna waded into the water until she could no longer touch the bottom and started swimming. She wondered what Celine was doing with Leo. Was he cooperating? Anna hoped he wasn't trying to play the spy-hero. If he could just stay alive until she found him, Anna knew she'd figure out a way to rescue him.

After about ten minutes, she could make out the details of another island in the moonlight. A minute later, she tested the depth and hit sand again. She trudged out of the water onto the sandy beach and made her way to the shore on the opposite side. After a quick glance toward the horizon, she waded into the water once more, and struck out for the next island in the chain.

Anna repeated the process at least half a dozen times—she lost count after three. As she staggered up onto another long, sandy beach, she absently wondered who owned this particular island and why they didn't keep a fully gassed speedboat tethered to a pier—with the keys in the ignition. Some people just had no sense of how to use their wealth properly.

The sound of voices carrying on the wind cut her thoughts short. She crouched low and hurried forward. Soon she reached the back of the small grove of trees with the old hut she'd seen from the helicopter. The open windows of the island cottage glowed with a dim light. Anna snuck up to a large palm tree within earshot.

"You need to eat something, my prince." Celine's sickly, sweet voice nearly made Anna gag.

"Please untie me, Celine," the prince begged. His voice sounded ragged and tired. "You know you can't keep me here. You need to let me go."

"I can't untie you yet, sweetie. You need to earn my trust first. Then, when you've proven that you love me, I can untie you."

Anna crept closer to the back of the bungalow, grateful her deep blue dress and dark skin made her difficult to see. She peeked in through the window. The flickering candle light illuminated a small living area. Leo sat in a large lounge chair, hands and legs still bound, while Celine crouched nearby with a tray of food. He wasn't in any immediate danger—except maybe from the food. Anna doubted the prince had ever eaten survival rations before. Content to wait for an opportunity, Anna slumped down against the wall of the hut.

After several more minutes of begging, Celine finally switched tactics. "Is it the food? I'll get other food." Footsteps moved out of the room into another part of the bungalow. Anna ventured another glance through the window. Leo was alone. She moved to the patio door and slowly slid it open. Leo looked up as Anna moved toward him.

His face changed from absolute shock to relief. "You are the most beautiful thing I've ever seen," he whispered. "And not just because you look like a goddess emerging from the sea."

Anna smiled at his ability to flirt with her in a circumstance like this.

"What was that, sweetie?" Celine called from the other room.

The prince flinched. "Uh, nothing. Never mind, darling."

Anna cocked her head and gave him a wide-eyed glare. Celine wasn't stupid enough to not notice the sudden change in the prince's feelings for her.

"I mean, I order you to release me," the prince amended.

Anna rolled her eyes and immediately attacked the ropes at his feet. If she could just get his legs free, maybe—

A tray clattered to the ground behind her, and Anna whirled around.

Celine looked murderous. "You!" she spat. Grabbing a large butcher knife from the counter behind the doorway, she started toward Anna. "How are you still alive?"

Anna looked around the room for something to use as a weapon. Nothing but wicker furniture, too bulky to fight with. She fought the instinct to stand between Celine and Leo. Being near him would only put him in more danger. She slid sideways behind a nearby end table.

"Aren't you wondering how your lover, Zane, fared against me?"

"That big oaf isn't my lover. He was a willing fool, that's all."

"How'd you convince him to get rid of your competition?" Anna asked as she glanced down at the table that stood between them.

Celine's chin lifted a fraction. "I didn't need that moron's help to eliminate those bimbos. Don't you think I'm capable of taking care of that sort of thing alone?"

As Celine moved across the room, Anna continued around the table. "So you fired or attacked anyone who got too close to

Leo. Did you think that would make him finally see you?" Anna was testing Celine for her weaknesses.

"Don't you get it? I'm the one who should be with Léopold. I'm the only one who's been standing by his side all these years. Women have come in and out of his life, but I'm the one who's been constant." She looked longing at Leo. "I'm the one who's loved him his whole life." She turned back toward Anna and brandished the knife at her again. "But girls like you keep coming around stealing his attention from me. He would love me if it weren't for you!"

Anna held her hands up in a calming gesture. "Celine, you can't force someone to—"

"Yes, I can!" she bellowed. "If I can get him away from everyone for long enough, he'll see how much he loves me. We can live happily ever after, just like in the fairy tales."

With one last glance around the small living space, Anna gave up on the idea of fighting Celine so close to Leo. She inched backward toward the patio door, dragging the end table. Celine pressed forward, knife in hand.

"Please, don't hurt her!" Leo called out.

"She can't come between us!" Celine shouted.

Anna flung the fragile table at Celine then ran out the back door and dashed around the side of the bungalow toward the clearing in front. She hid behind a clump of trunks in a spot where she could still see both corners of the hut. Weak light from the still rising half-moon filtered through the trees and dappled the ground. When Celine's dark shape came around the corner, long knife gleaming, Anna ducked behind the trees.

Celine staggered out into the clearing and rushed to the closest bush, slashing through the leaves and branches with the knife. Finding nothing, Celine turned back toward the clearing. "Come out, Anna," she said in a sing-song voice. "You can't hide forever. It's a very small island."

The lovelorn woman weaved back and forth across the clearing, searching the trees and bushes, coming closer and closer to Anna's hiding spot. Celine halted in front of Anna's clump of trees and listened. Anna held her breath, sure that Celine would hear her heart trying to beat its way out.

As she turned away, Anna sprang from the foliage and grasped the base of Celine's knife-wielding hand. But before she could strip the knife away, Celine slammed Anna in the gut with her knee. Anna staggered back and tripped over a rocky outcropping in the sand. Celine advanced on Anna, knife raised. Anna grabbed a handful of sand and flung it in Celine's eyes.

Celine screamed and stumbled backward, coughing and sputtering. "I hate you! I hate every last one of you!" She rubbed her eyes and glared at Anna. Brandishing the knife, she stepped toward Anna again. "You waltz into the prince's life, flaunting your allure, and think you matter to him. Well, you don't! He doesn't care about any of you!"

"Celine, you don't have to do this. Put down the knife and let's talk this out."

"There's nothing to talk about!" Celine rushed at her, swinging the knife.

Years of training took over. Spinning around Celine's attack, Anna slammed a fist into the back of Celine's hand. The knife flew high across the clearing and into the dark brush. Celine growled and swung at Anna, landing a brutal blow to the side of her head.

How could this woman—who Anna had figured was just the prince's glorified assistant—be so skilled at hand-to-hand combat? She wasn't an expert, by any means, but what she lacked in finesse, she made up for in ferocity.

Anna punched back, knocking Celine off balance, then lunged after her, ready to strike a quick follow-up blow. She kicked low for Celine's knee, but the woman dodged. Before

Anna could regain her balance, Celine kicked her hard in the side of the ribs. Anna blocked a second blow, but the force sent her reeling, and she fell again.

Celine stood over her. "Once I've destroyed you, I'll tie you to a tree and make you watch Léopold fall in love with me."

"Not a chance," Anna retorted, swinging a kick to buckle Celine's knees.

Celine crumpled to the sand, and Anna rolled away. Celine scrambled back to her feet, her eyes shooting daggers. Anna crouched and waited until Celine approached. When Celine swung a fist at Anna's head, she ducked and savagely drove her knee into Celine's gut. Celine flew backward onto the sand again, gasping for air.

"Leo?" Anna called toward the bungalow, all the while keeping her eyes on Celine's writhing form. "If you ever wanted to play spy-hero, now would be a great time."

"I'm tied to a chair," he called back.

"That's okay, bring the chair," Anna replied.

Celine was back on her feet again, but visibly weaker. She snarled at Anna and lunged forward. Anna parried her flailing fists and brought an elbow down hard against the base of Celine's neck, dropping her to the ground.

Prince Leo hopped awkwardly out onto the front deck, his legs and arms still tied to the chair. "My ninja skills are ready." He flailed both hands in a passable karate pose considering his predicament.

Anna smiled. His sense of humor was still intact. "Actually, I didn't really need you. I only need your rope."

He gave a mirthless laugh. "I get that a lot."

With a chuckle, Anna inched her way closer to him, not willing to risk turning her back on Celine. "I guess I shouldn't say that I don't really need you, but we can talk about that later."

Leo's goofy grin faltered as he missed the front porch's first step. Struggling with the weight of the chair, he stumbled and toppled over sideways, landing on his back like an upended turtle.

Anna gasped and rushed to him. "Are you okay?"

"Nothing injured but my pride."

Doing her best to stifle a giggle—and keeping a watchful eye on Celine—Anna reached for the rope binding Leo's hands to the chair. She spared him a quick wink as she worked on loosening the knot.

"Does this mean I failed the spy school entrance exam?" Leo said as he stared at the palm trees overhead.

"If we get off this island in one piece, you can consider yourself an honorary spy-in-training," Anna said. "The induction ceremony will be—"

"Watch out!" Leo yelled.

Celine charged full speed at Anna. With a quick side step, Anna dodged the tackle. Celine's motions were becoming more and more erratic.

Anna ducked Celine's next swing and grabbed her wrist, twisting it quickly backward. At the same time, Anna wrapped her other arm around Celine's neck, immediately cutting off the blood flow to the woman's brain. Ten seconds later, Celine was unconscious in the sand.

Anna returned to the prince and pulled off the rope binding his ankles just as he finally freed his wrists. He held up his arms, waiting to be helped out of the tipped chair. With a small smirk, Anna took the lengths of rope she'd removed from his legs and returned to Celine's inert form.

"No help for the newly-minted spy-hero? What if I throw a passionate embrace into the deal?" Leo said, struggling to untie the rope across his chest.

"Spy-heroes don't need help up, but I'll definitely be

collecting on a well-deserved and long-awaited passionate embrace." Anna secured Celine's ankles then her wrists. She had just cinched down the final knot when Celine began to regain consciousness.

"I hate you, Anna Rivers," Celine spat.

Anna stood, the longest length of rope still in her hand. "We should probably tie her to a tree or something. Do we want her out of earshot?"

The prince grinned mischievously. "That depends. How much noise are we planning to make?"

Anna just shook her head at him, but she couldn't help the broad smile. "I'll put her far enough away that we can't hear her screams. That would be distracting."

Leo held up a finger. "Actually, I have a solution for that." He walked stiffly back into the hut and returned with a roll of duct tape. "She gave me a few rounds of this when I refused to declare my undying devotion. So if you don't mind, I'd like to do the honors."

"I guess I'm glad you didn't go along with *everything* she asked you to do," Anna said with a grin.

Anna stepped back as the prince approached their struggling captive and applied a generous piece of tape to Celine's mouth. The tape cut her off in the middle of, "I've always loved—" Anna supposed they would never really know what Celine had always loved. Maybe piña coladas.

Together, they tied their prisoner to a tree within easy distance—and sight—of the bungalow. Walking back to the small house, Prince Leo took Anna's hand through his arm, as if escorting her to the dance floor.

Inside the bungalow, he stopped and turned toward her. Anna's heart raced as Leo touched her arms. His fingers brushed lightly against the large bump on her cheekbone. Cupping her face in his warm, strong hands, he gazed at her.

His dark blue eyes—dazzling in the flickering candlelight of the bungalow—spoke volumes of his gratitude. He leaned forward, his breath whispering across her skin.

She had always known it was foolish to get involved on a mission—especially to swoon for a handsome prince. But given the same chance to fall for Leo, Anna would gladly break Rule Number One all over again. Besides, it was really more of a guideline than a rule.

In the end it didn't matter what had brought them together. They were together now, and she was completely gone for him. They could figure out the rest later.

The intensity of Leo's gaze had Anna's stomach doing somersaults. Her eyes flitted to his lips. She smiled and leaned toward him.

As Leo's lips pressed softly against hers, Anna wrapped her arms around his strong back and pulled him closer.

She had longed for and avoided this moment for so long, she could hardly believe it was happening.

His kisses, tentative at first, turned more urgent as the floodgates opened.

After several minutes of blissful recklessness, Leo pulled back from the kiss. "You know," he began as he ran his hands lovingly through her hair. "This definitely wasn't in the job description. You'd be well within your rights to refuse."

"Then, it's lucky for you I never officially took the job." She placed a kiss on his chin, then the corner of his lips.

"I would've had to fire you anyway," he said, smiling his charming, princely smile.

Anna's eyebrow quirked up. "Oh, really?"

He nodded in apparent earnestness, still eying her lips. "You're always getting me into trouble."

Anna closed her eyes and leaned in for another kiss. "You're welcome," she mumbled into his lips. She felt him smile back.

The prince's kisses moved down her cheek to her neck. "I'm glad there are no harbor patrol boats to come and interrupt us this time," he said. "But eventually we'll need to figure out how to get off this island."

Given Celine's obsession with the prince, Anna doubted very much that she would have risked living on a small island with no way to get help if something went wrong—or when her delusional plan of making him fall in love with her eventually worked. Anna was sure they would find a satellite phone somewhere in the supply crates.

They'd just need to do some searching for it.

Later.

Chapter 17

"**I** still can't believe you were stranded with a handsome prince on a deserted island." Katie sighed. "Didn't you just want to stay there forever?"

Anna finished putting her earrings in as she walked into the living room of Club Banana. She looked out the windows of the high-rise penthouse and saw only the twinkling lights of the Atlanta skyline. She smiled at Katie and heaved a deep sigh for her benefit. In reality, Anna wasn't being overly theatrical; as glad as she was to be back home, she missed the ocean views already.

"And what about living with a prince?" Susan awkwardly stepped into a deep curtsey. "Weren't you pampered at every turn? Breakfast with him every day. Did he kiss your hand all the time?" She held out her hand at a pretentious angle.

"C'mon girls, it was just part of the job. You know. The assignment's over and you move on." Anna walked over and checked herself in the full-length mirror. She had intentionally not worn anything over-the-top formal so as not to arouse suspicions—at least not until it was too late.

"Won't you miss it, though?" Katie asked. "The lifestyle?

And . . . the prince?" She and Mari shared a giggle.

Anna fought the smile that threatened to spread over her face. She didn't dare tell them the truth, but a little teaser couldn't hurt. "I won't have to miss it too much."

The door chime rang and the Banana Girls stared at each other in dismay.

"Did someone bypass security?" Mari asked.

"I already approved it," Hannah said in a bored voice.

Susan grabbed the nearest tablet to check the camera. She did a double-take then gaped at Anna. "He's here?!"

Katie sat up. "Who's here?"

Susan turned the tablet to Katie. "The prince," she said.

Katie squealed.

Hannah scowled at them from her corner chair. "Chill out, girls. Please."

Anna's heart beat a little faster as she approached the door. Their farewell at the airport had not been as private as their time on the island. This would be her first chance to be alone with him since they were rescued.

She opened the door and the charming prince stood there in front of her. In all his . . . charmingness.

"Hi," he said with a smirk. "I'm glad you were available tonight. No national security problems to solve?"

"Leo!" she whispered through a smile while glancing over her shoulder. "You're not supposed to know our secrets."

The prince leaned in and gave Anna a long kiss right there in the doorway. Katie and Susan's sighs were easily audible, as was Hannah's grumbling.

Prince Leo held out his arm. "Come. Let me charm you with fancy cars and expensive food."

Anna gazed into his beguiling eyes. She would have to surface again someday, but for now she was content to drown herself in their depths.

"Don't wait up," she called over her shoulder.

"Have a great time," Katie said with exaggerated eyebrows lifted.

"Don't forget we have a chemistry exam tomorrow," Mari called out.

Anna glanced at Leo, wondering what he knew about chemistry. A moment later, she saw a mischievous smirk creep onto his handsome face.

"No need to worry," he said to the girls while staring back at Anna. "Chemistry is definitely not a problem."

Origin Story & Next Book

That's the end, but I wanted to make sure you didn't miss this.

The Banana Girls action continues with *Spies Never Lose*, where Hannah teams up with an arrogant federal agent to crack an illegal international adoption case.

If you've already read *Spies Never Quit* (Banana Girls: book 1) but you somehow didn't grab *Spies Never Share*, the Banana Girls' origin story novella—including Anna and Hannah's first mission and the first guy they fought over—you can sign up for it here: www.myleschristensen.com/banana2.

And if I could ask one big favor—it would really help my book succeed if you would leave a review on Amazon and Goodreads. Thank you so very much!

Acknowledgments

Thanks to the readers of my first book who gave me the confidence that I could write another and they would read it.

I appreciate the early feedback that I got from my beta readers: BingeingonBooks, Maddy216, and SarahMaew. Thanks for the words of encouragement and re-direction.

Thanks to Courtney at Courtney Larkin Editing. It was the actions as beats interrupting dialog that got me this time. And commas. Still.

I appreciate my youngest sons allowing me to read the final proof copy out loud to them (again). Nice catch on the wrong name, Matthew. Sorry it was more mushy stuff than the first one.

As always, my biggest thanks goes to my sweet wife who puts up with my endless rambling about plot ideas and writing roadblocks. You were such a huge help on this one, sweetheart.

Myles Christensen writes cozy thriller/suspense with sweet romance under the pen name M. Taylor Christensen.

He loves to write exciting adventures because he loves to read exciting adventures. The hopeless romantic in him will usually sprinkle a teensy bit of romance into his stories. While writing, he listens to music that matches—and sometimes inspires—the storyline.

His mild-mannered alter ego is a product development engineer, university professor, and game inventor. He lives in Utah with his wife and children.

Made in the USA
Coppell, TX
19 December 2021

69437512R00174